THE EARL OF MERCIA'S FATHER

THE EARLS OF MERCIA
BOOK ONE

MJ PORTER

MJ PUBLISHING

Copyright notice
Porter, M J
The Earl of Mercia's Father

Copyright ©2019, Porter, M.J
All characters and events in this publication, other than those clearly in the public domain, are fictitious and any resemblance to actual persons, living or dead, is purely coincidental.

ALL RIGHTS RESERVED. No part of this publication may be reproduced, stored in a retrieval system or transmitted in any form or by any means without the prior written permission of the author, nor be otherwise circulated in any form of binding or cover other than that in which it is published and without a similar condition being imposed on the subsequent buyer.

Cover design by 100Covers
Chapter Headings by WritersEmporiumCo

ISBN: 9781072915973 (ebook)
ISBN: 9781072915973 (Amazon Trade paperback)
ISBN: 9781914332463 (hardback/large print)
ISBN: 9781917374606 (Ingram paperback)

 Formatted with Vellum

For my Dad

You bought me books on castles, told stories of old Mercian kings buried at the top of my garden and stood by as I changed my mind about studying History at GCSE, A Level and even Degree level. This one's for you!

CONTENTS

PROLOGUE
AD991

The terrible sound of battle faded almost to nothingness as he stood, seemingly motionless but moving, his actions preordained by the long years of training. His shield in one hand, his spear in the other and his blade still sheathed. He fought side-by-side with those of his warband he'd deemed fit and able enough to escort him. Ealdorman Bryhtnoth, his distant relative, had raised the fyrd to tackle the scourge of Olaf's ravaging ship army along the Eastern coastline.

Not that any of that mattered now. The strong words of Bryhtnoth to the Viking raiders that morning had caused all the men to cheer him, espousing their exclusive support for this venture. Now they were as feathers dispersed by the wind, fleeting and quickly forgotten. And yet they reverberated in his head, the older voice rich and intense with age, condescension dripping, with a now misplaced confidence.

'Do you hear, Vikings, what this nation says? They will give you only spears as a tribute, the poison-tipped javelin and ancient swords. These weapons will profit you nothing in battle.'

Cries from the men behind him brought him back to the here and now and made him turn and stare. All the time, he held his shield in place, overlapping with his great friend and commended man, Wulfstan. Bile filled his throat as he watched some of the weakest running from the enemy now that their ealdorman lay dead at the hands of the Raiders. He could only hope they weren't men from his own household troop, men sworn to him through the commendatory oath.

A thought, a moment, sadness and conviction swirled in his mind. Stay and die as his ealdorman had, or run and flee as these others were.

His vision of the battle site faded, replaced by an image of what he would leave behind if he died. His son grown to a young man now but vulnerable all the same. As yet untried in the way of the King's witan, Leofwine had so much promise if only he had the right guide.

But what if he ran? Could he live with the knowledge that men better than him had lost their lives against this Northern bastard Olaf and his ship-army?

And then, no more time for thought.

A whistle of sound, a hail of spears above his head, and he knew the enemy warriors were turning their attention to the shield wall arrayed against them on dry land, a few steps from the narrow neck of the causeway. He must make his decision.

A hand on his arm and a look of disquiet from Wulfstan.

'My lord?' his friend queried, understanding in those few short words.

'I must,' a simple reply, thick with conviction.

'Then so must I.'

'No, you must not.'

An agonised howl of dismay arose from Wulfstan's mouth while all the time he held his place in the press and sweat of the men. A stalwart to the end.

'I'm no coward,' through gritted teeth, spittle dropping into his greying beard. Old men, the both of them.

'No, and nor am I, but my son will have need of you.'

'Ask another,' a terse reply, head forward and down, concentrating on the attack before him, every muscle tuned to the advancing force, waiting to attack and strike, to fight to the death. An honour not to be denied him.

'There are others you can trust to slip away, most with far more to live for than I,' bitterness and contempt in Wulfstan's words. Would the man ever stop hating himself?

'And yet none carry your wisdom. You've counselled me more than you can ever know. I've turned to you in my moments of indecision, and your steadiness has calmed me and led me where I should go. You can advise him and ensure he leads a better life. Ensure he has a better death as well.'

'My lord?' ambiguous in the press of bodies. A quirk of a smile as Ælfwine wondered whether Wulfstan was thanking his Lord for his kind words or still querying the request.

'You must agree, or I'll command you.'

A wail of real rage as Wulfstan lowered his shield and thrust aside one of the enemy spear points. The arm of the man who'd raised it against the finest warrior Ælfwine had ever known trailed to the floor in a haze of flashing steel followed by flying crimson. And then Wulfstan was back in the shield wall beside his lord.

'I'll do as you command,' soft words, barely heard above

the screams and cries of the men, the clash of the iron weapons on seasoned wood.

'Then go now, with my thanks and speak to my son the words you once spoke to me.'

The two men spoke as though beside the hearth, ale mugs in hand and not embroiled in a bitter battle of life and death.

'Any personal words for your son?' Wulfstan probed Ælfwine's unease, but this was to be their last conversation, so Ælfwine allowed it.

'Too many to voice now. Relay our words shared over ale and meat. Spare him nothing and let him know that I loved him and was proud of him.'

'But not too proud to return to him?' Wulfstan asked bitterly, perhaps meaning to turn Ælfwine's words against him all along. Ælfwine's arm reverberated with the force of an attacker against his wooden shield.

'If death must come, it needs to be worthy, and this is proper, dying for my lord and for my country.'

'And yet you deny it to me?'

'No, I save it for you for another day when you can serve my son and die well for him.'

Temporarily Ælfwine could see nothing, his eyes blinded by the defeat he anticipated and the knowledge that he'd not see his son again, not in this lifetime. The boy he'd protected since his mother's death. The boy he'd sacrificed his own political career for in order to ensure he had a childhood. A boy who must now become a man, whether he willed it or not. His boy.

'Go, now!' Ælfwine cried, his voice finding strength while his body felt weak.

'As you command,' a terse reply, nothing more, and then

a gaping hole in the shield wall where Wulfstan had once stood. Another determined warrior quickly filled the gap, a smile of pleasure on his face for the death he knew was coming and for the honour of dying beside his commended Lord. But Ælfwine felt only the loss of his ally, friend, and counsellor. The gap might well be filled, but the ache of sorrow remained. What had he done?

And then full engagement and no more time for thought.

The enemy, numbers matched so evenly, forcing their way against them all. Sweat sheened Ælfwine's face, and determination tightened his hold on his exquisite weapons. He'd slay as many of these men as he could in retribution for what they'd done to his Lord and what they planned to do to his king's people and their wealth.

A rippling crescendo of thick glee reached his ears, and Ælfwine found himself facing a heavily built man with laughter lines evident on his face even beneath the helm and blood that coated him. Around him, Ælfwine felt the shield wall begin to break up, and he stepped forward to face the warrior who led the band of upstart Raiders. His spear long since discarded, Ælfwine grasped his sword in one hand, shield in the other and turned to face Olaf Tryggvason, the Northern bastard who would steal his life this day.

A smile graced Ælfwine's face, his grief forgotten for now. He'd have a good death, or he'd slay the murdering Raider. Either would bring him renown enough to help his son in his future endeavours.

He stepped toward the Northerner, sword in hand, knowing his fate was all his own now.

THE ANGLO-SAXON CHRONICLE ENTRY FOR AD991

This year was Ipswich plundered; and very soon afterwards was Ealdorman Bryhtnoth slain at Maldon.

1

AD991

NEAR DEERHURST, MERCIA

Sweat beaded his face, and Leofwine distractedly wiped it away with the back of his gloved hand. The movement was ineffectual, serving more to smear dust from the summer crops across his face than clear it.

He bit back his frustration and forced himself to concentrate above the discomfort caused by the heat of the late summer sun. He had to practice. His father hadn't let him go with him when the household troops had been called to action. No his father had deemed his fighting skills a little rusty from his time away, in attendance upon the king.

Leofwine couldn't deny his father's judgement, but it grated on his already slightly wounded self-image. His time with the king had been enjoyable, but Æthelred had not shared his desire to train and be physically fit. When his father returned, Leofwine was adamant that he'd have improved enough to join the household troop when the king next commanded his ealdormen to protect the country from the attacks of the Northerners.

Tempering his emotions, Leofwine eyed his opponent

with interest from above his heavy wooden shield. Oscetel was younger than him by at least five years, and he lacked Leofwine's wider frame and bulging muscles. Still, he was an interesting opponent, and Leofwine was not convinced he'd beat the lanky, blue-eyed youth easily.

A sharp stabbing action from his short sword, and Leofwine hovered behind his shield again as Oscetel eyed him with an equal amount of curiosity. They were childhood friends, but that worked to make them bitter rivals when the other men of the household troop, those few of them who'd been left behind on guard duty, were watching and shouting wagers on who'd win.

A thunk on his shield and Leofwine knew that Oscetel was trying to tempt him to make a rash move. Firmly, he stayed focused on the tactics he'd decided to employ. If it meant standing in the noonday sun until Oscetel tired and made a foolish move, then he'd do so.

One of his father's favourite lessons, reinforced endlessly by Wulfstan, was that it wasn't always necessary to attack to win. An enraged enemy would tire quickly and make ill-conceived moves. A man with a calm mind, able to think clearly, was more likely to be the victor unless he was very unlucky.

The yard they trained in sat before his father's well-kept house. Those of the servants and slaves who weren't distracted by the duel were busy with the business of harvesting the crops, and the occasional honk of one of the ducks reminded Leofwine that there were any number of hazards that could fell his careful plan. A duck underfoot or one of the small children of the servants or household troop could at any moment undo his efforts, handing the victory to Oscetel.

With the stream of sweat in his eyes and the taste of it in his parched mouth, Leofwine decided that he needed to act. Be a little rash, a little unexpected. That was another of his father's favourite lessons. It was always good to unnerve your enemy by acting out of character.

Without another sound, Leofwine dropped his heavy shield to the ground, where it thudded loudly, its wooden rims reverberating from the blow. While Oscetel dropped his guard to see what had happened, Leofwine stepped forward and effectively stabbed him through the chest. Or rather, Leofwine could have done. Instead, he made his intentions clear, and a groan of dismay erupted from Oscetel's mouth. Those who'd been watching cheered a little and clapped their hands before wandering away, some happy, some dismayed at losing their wagers.

'Sorry, my friend,' Leofwine said as he bent to pick up his discarded shield, inspecting the rim as he spoke. If it needed sanding, he would have to see to it sooner rather than later.

'It was a good move, and certainly one I wasn't expecting, so no need to apologise. I'll watch for that in future.' Oscetel's tone was rueful but not begrudging. They were often to be found discussing tactics, and the more they considered, the better, they hoped, it made them as warriors.

'It was a mean trick, but Oscetel, I was too damn hot.'

His friend smacked him on his sweaty back, a grimace for the wet fabric, laughing at the honesty.

'No injury was done, and I think you have the right to it. I'm parched.'

Tiredly, the heat making them drag their feet, they walked inside his father's home. It was pleasantly cool inside the wooden interior as one of the equally hot servants rushed to bring them both a drink and refill their cups when they immediately drained them.

Leofwine sank onto the wooden bench closest to the door and tugged on his gloves so that he could remove them before taking off his heavily padded byrnie. Besides him, Oscetel did the same, and then the two boys lay down on the long, narrow wooden bench so that their heads were almost touching. Leofwine felt his eyes closing in the heat, and he fought to stay awake.

'It's hot today,' Leofwine muttered.

'Too right. Far too hot to be training.'

'I know, but my father said….'

'We're all aware of what he said Leofwine, and he was wrong. Your time away hasn't dampened your skills. In fact, if anything, they've improved by leaps and bounds.'

Leofwine could feel his already hot face glowing a little brighter with the unlooked-for praise. Before he could deny or accept the words, Oscetel carried on speaking.

'Did you ever think that maybe, just maybe, your father just didn't want you in battle with him?'

Leofwine sat upright abruptly, his hands to either side of him on the smooth, cool bench.

'What do you mean?'

Oscetel sat upright too and gazed at Leofwine, his young face earnest, 'Well, you know. It's not always the best idea to go into battle and take your one and only heir with you. Who'd have this place if the worst happened?' Oscetel gestured to the lofty house they sat within as he spoke. Leofwine considered his friend's words, as he too considered his father's home. It was a beautiful building, the seasoned Mercian oak lending it an inviting glow, no matter the season.

'Here, I'd not thought of that.'

'Then maybe you're not quite as bright as you think you are,' his friend countered, rising to his feet and stretching his arms above his head.

'I can't cool down. I'm going for a quick dip in the river. You coming?' Oscetel asked as a parting shot.

'I'm just going to get another drink, and I'll meet you there,' Leofwine responded slowly.

Why had he never considered his friend's words as the truth of his father's motive? Perhaps he'd been a little too self-involved, a bit too desperate to prove himself worthy of his father. Standing, he absentmindedly slugged another drink of refreshing water.

Perhaps it would have been nice if his father had explained it to him. He'd ask him when he got back. Resolved, Leofwine walked towards the open doorway, only to stop abruptly.

In the doorway stood a figure he'd not been expecting to see. Wulfstan. Excitedly he looked behind him and back into the main room, wondering how he could have missed seeing or hearing his father and the return of the rest of the household troop.

Only then did the expression on Wulfstan's face register. The seriousness, Leofwine was used to seeing on his father's closest confidant; the grief he was not. Wulfstan appeared devoid of all colour, white as a corpse.

Leofwine felt his knees buckle beneath him, and he stepped sideways to grab for the bench he'd only just stood up from.

Wulfstan rushed forward and offered him an arm of support as he sat just in time to prevent himself from falling over. By all that was holy, not his father!

Once he was seated, Wulfstan stepped back and bowed respectfully to him. When Leofwine failed to speak, his mouth opening and closing without sound, desperately trying to avoid saying the final words, Wulfstan nodded his head again and roughly began to speak his words of commendation to his new Lord.

'By the Lord, and these holy relics, I pledge to be loyal and true to Leofwine, and love all that he loves, and hate all that he hates, in accordance with God's rights and my noble obligations; and never, willingly and intentionally, in word or deed, do anything that is hateful to him; on condition that he keep me as was our agreement when I subjected myself to him and took his service.'

Belatedly, Leofwine noted the holy relic in Wulfstan's hand, the piece of ancient cloth from the church at Deerhurst, widely recognised as from a cloak King Oswald had once worn before his death. Its colours were long faded, and now it seemed little more than a piece of used hemp sacking, and yet all still revered it.

Looking from his father's man to that relic, the terrible truth finally penetrated Leofwine's consciousness. His father was dead at the hands of the Raiders, and he'd never be able to ask him anything again.

2

AD995

SOMEWHERE NEAR SHETLAND

The sky stretched grey as far as the eye could see. It didn't threaten rain, merely signifying that the sun would not shine that day. No chance.

Where the overcast sky ended, the flat sea began, both merging into an unbroken expanse that stretched across the horizon.

Only when Leofwine turned to face his fellow shipmates was there even a flash of colour to contrast with the seemingly endless iron view; the red of smiling lips, a flash of bright clothing and the blond of shining heads bowed low to their work.

With the dull day, there was no wind to power the mighty russet beast beneath them. It plunged through the quiet sea to the call of the sixty oars dipping in and out of the never-ending sweep. Perched as the men were on their war chests of varying hues of winter brown and seasonal yellow, they strained with each stroke of the mighty oars they commanded.

Only he was exempt from the heavy labour; he and Olaf

and mighty Bjorn, the foul-tempered and burly helmsman, who occasionally cast him barely veiled looks of contempt for his inaction.

The quiet of the day didn't yet herald a storm. It would come, but in a few days more, when winter finally struck its first note and by then, they'd have reached their destination and be wrapped up snug and warm against the coming hostile weather. Or so Bjorn had promised him on the only occasion they'd spoken.

A shout at the front of the ship caught Leofwine's attention. Olaf Tryggvason. He was in remarkably good spirits. His excellent cheer was catching, infecting all the men as they strained and relaxed their hold on the oars. They extended far out to either side of Olaf's great longship, flickering in and out of sight over the tempered sea.

Leofwine found himself smiling along with the man as he yet again ran his hands through his own war chest, heaped high with dulled coins and shining treasures. The money held a fascination that Leofwine could understand without any bitterness. Yes, his own money had contributed to the large geld of sixteen thousand pounds, and he should probably feel some remorse that it was no longer in his possession, or even his king's, but he could laugh along with Olaf. There was plenty more where that came from!

Not that Olaf knew that. If he did then, the Northern bastard would only turn his tail and head back to England, like he'd done last time. A taste for treasure would drive back onto England's shores. Greed, and the seeming ease of the attack, making it irresistible.

If nothing else, Leofwine's own newly given importance was to convince Olaf of England's poverty in the wake of his recent attacks and to ensure that he made it safely back to

Norway. Once there, Olaf could do as he pleased, provided it involved him staying there for a long time.

The fabulous riches Olaf now possessed far outweighed anything he'd ever acquired in his long and varied travels. The weight of silver and gold, nearly double that paid only three years before, was the most that Olaf was ever likely to acquire, provided he was convinced of England's poverty and future attacks averted.

Olaf never seemed to tire of running his hands through his new wealth. Even on the heavy day, the treasure contained within flashed a burnished gold and shimmering silver, flashing across his face, on a sunny day Leofwine didn't doubt that opening the lid would be blinding.

Olaf was a well-built man, his age a little difficult to tell, but Leofwine was sure he couldn't be far short of forty. His blond hair was beginning to grow thin upon the crown of his head, and his beard was flecked here and there with silver threads. His eyes were dark cobalt flanked by creases and wrinkles that intensified whenever he laughed, which he often did.

As Leofwine continued to watch him, his deep blue eyes opened wide in shock, and from deep within his war chest, he pulled forth an enormous golden cross decorated with four blood rubies that seemed to pulse even on such a leaden and overcast day.

Leofwine schooled his expression; this was a treasure he knew and valued above all the others, and the one thing he did truly resent being in the grabbing hands of Olaf. Olaf had no comprehension of its personal meaning to Leofwine, and Leofwine knew he must do his best to keep it that way. He had a role to play, and it didn't involve petty hatred over what should be viewed as just another object in the vast hoard, albeit a precious one for Leofwine.

Still, Leofwine watched Olaf intently, wondering what he would do now other than admiring the priceless jewel in his hand, a gift from his sponsor at his recent baptism and a gift given by Leofwine to his king for the very purpose. A man more cynical than Leofwine would have seen it as a further payment to buy Olaf's good behaviour, to buy him off and send him back to Norway.

Leofwine hoped that Olaf would appreciate the potent symbolism of the cross and embrace his new God above the many heathen Gods he'd previously worshipped.

Leofwine's eyes narrowed as he watched the other man trace the gilded decoration on the four arms of the cross with his large, sea-roughened hands and then gently stroke the four inlaid rubies with the fingers on his right hand. His war armbands clattered against the glowing cross as his hands moved, the golden hue of the cross flashing briefly across the silver armbands that Olaf proudly displayed, a symbol of his wealth and, more importantly, his prowess in battle.

Before it had come into Olaf's greedy hands, the cross had been the centrepiece of Leofwine's own church; a relic from his now dead father who'd taken his affluence and concentrated it in a cross as a testimony to his unfailing faith and sign of his own conspicuous wealth.

Leofwine tried not to think bitter thoughts because he didn't want to reflect those feelings on his countenance; he knew that there were some on the crew who didn't trust him and who would look for any sign of discontent to rise against him and, at the worse, slit his throat without a second thought.

Leofwine needed to keep neutral and to stay on Olaf's

good side to ensure his own safety amongst men he'd like to call his friends, but amongst whom he was a stranger and perhaps worse; the envoy of a weak king manipulated into paying out huge sums of coins and gold.

Leofwine admired the work ethic while at the same time being wary of the loyalty the shipmen showed to their Jarl. It appeared as though it could be a fickle friend amongst these men. They were always looking for the next war leader who could lead them to victory and plunder.

Some of these men had, until recently, sailed with a different warrior leader, a king no less. Yet they'd abandoned him as soon as Olaf had enticed them with the hopes and dreams of more wealth.

Abruptly, Leofwine rapidly re-evaluated his opinion of the northern warrior as Olaf took the cross, raised it before his face and kissed it, reverently. Olaf's eyes closed for some few moments before he again spoke and raised the cross above his head as he'd seen Leofwine's holy men do. Then Olaf was talking in his clear, gravelly voice, which carried whether the seas were rough or calm.

'My lord, I make this pledge to you here and now. Your bounty has been great, and I vow that this cross will adorn a similar church to that which it came from, only in my homeland and similarly raised in your glory to commemorate my kingship.'

Respectful silence greeted Olaf's words. The man the shipmen followed had led them on their most successful raid ever. While they still thrived on the purloined geld, they'd do anything for their leader, whether they agreed with his newfound faith or not. Leofwine watched a few reach for their own pagan sigils, strung around their necks, as though offering an apology.

Yet, as soon as Olaf had finished speaking, the warriors erupted into cheers, not once ever leaving their seats or loosening their hold or losing their rhythm on their oars. Leofwine was amazed. He had a shared distant ancestry with some of these men, but he'd never appreciated that some might also share his beliefs.

Perhaps there was more to his journey than Leofwine had at first thought. Maybe the men who had brokered this peace, his king and his bishops, had understood the needs of Olaf more than Leofwine had until now.

Leofwine smiled to himself. It was beginning to look as though his task was more significant than just shepherding the wolf out of the flock. His king had been in conferences with his confidantes for days following the initial truce agreement. They'd all dealt with Olaf before, albeit unsuccessfully. The king must have been aware of Olaf's desires.

In Olaf's long years of raiding and trading, it had probably always been his goal to have his own land, and a sure way to legitimise it as his own was to lay the foundations for the first church there. Then Olaf would gain the sanction of the Church in Rome, and they'd work with him to protect that land and status quo.

With his own kingdom, Olaf could satisfy his individual needs and those of his shipmen. Æthelred had just given Olaf not only the means to conquer the land by using the huge geld he'd been bribed with to leave England, but with the conversion to Christianity, Æthelred had also given him ways to justify it.

Leofwine finally understood why his own ship was encumbered with five stray missionaries. It was not as he'd thought because his own king feared the mission doomed from the word go. Leofwine now assumed they had their instructions to stay in Norway and help the new king spread the word of God.

As the men slowly calmed and silence returned to the ship, save for the sharp slap of the oars on the smooth, glassy surface, Leofwine met Olaf's eyes, which seemed to burn with fervour. The look filled him with hope and foreboding. Leofwine's life was in the hands of this man. How far could he trust him to keep his crew in check and to ensure his own survival?

While Leofwine was a vigorous and sturdy fighter, his talents had not yet been called into play as his homelands were so far away from the regular raiding grounds of the coast. They were also virtually landlocked, meaning that the enemy had to either carry their ships for long distances over difficult terrain to find the rivers which fed his land, or they had to adopt the horses of the people they quelled on their advance and contend with the more demanding feeding regime of the animals.

Neither option had allowed Leofwine to face an attacking force of the Northern men in the few years since his father's death.

Still, Leofwine knew he could fight and fight well with his sword and war axe, but he didn't want to face the odds of over sixty-to-one as they currently stood. His own name had been little muttered at Court, and he knew that he was an unknown quality to Olaf.

Olaf was not unknown to him. He was aware that Olaf had been paid a considerable geld only three years before and that, somehow, it had not been enough for him. There was bitterness with that knowledge. His father had died in the famous battle of Maldon, attempting to defeat Olaf and his crew, and it had all been in vain, for Olaf had come back, joining forces with other war leaders and successfully causing massive problems for Æthelred and his councillors.

The Raiders speed and determination to attack in as many areas as possible had made it impossible for the local ealdormen and thegns to offer any effective resistance.

Olaf and his men moved as swiftly as ghosts, and their actions were ever unpredictable. With their lightweight ships holding up to eighty men at a time, even one ship was a lethal fighting force that could overcome any of the small coastal villages within mere moments. There was no time to call for help, and often all that was left were the smoking ruins of the thatched buildings and the odd old stringy animal, not worth the attention of the raiders.

And the dead. Of course, not to forget the poor slain souls who died fighting for the little they had.

Looking all around him, anywhere but at his own golden cross still in Olaf's hands, Leofwine's gaze caught sight of his own longship, a few lengths behind him. She shone a deep golden hue, like shimmering bronze, even in the gloom, and Leofwine smiled with pleasure. She was a gift from the king, or rather a gift to the king that had then been bequeathed to him on his promotion to the ealdordom and to help him fulfil his king's orders of seeing Olaf safely away from the too tempting shores of England.

The vast sail hung limply in the still day; its red and golden colours still that of Æthelweard, Ealdorman of the Western Provinces, the original owner of the ship. The turn-around time had been too quick and sudden to allow him to have his own sails made.

Leofwine felt possessive of her now, pleased with his ship, and although he had initially intended to gift the ship back at the end of his journey, he now doubted that he'd be able to. He could already envisage the savage beauty crowned by his own ship head of choice, perhaps a mighty dragon taken from the stories he'd been told as a boy, and in his mind's eyes, he could see it installed with his own sail.

Leofwine was sure his wife would have some ideas regarding colour and style. He ignored his common sense, which repeatedly asked him what need he had for a ship equipped to carry over eighty men. His home territory was without a coast on all sides. He loved his ship, and he would keep her. He would rename her. Again, he would ask his wife. She was more deeply steeped in the myths and legends of their lands. She would see that he didn't inadvertently embarrass himself, his family and his king with his choice.

For a brief moment, the late summer sun penetrated the thick, grey clouds, and a single ray shone fully on his pride and joy. She was a beautiful golden beast, all polished russet down the side where the slightly greyer oars rose and dipped in time to the rhythm mirrored on the ship he travelled in.

Her beauty was more pronounced because of the pent-up terror she contained, a full force of sixty fighting men in one innocent-looking, innocuous ship. He wondered if that was what the monks of Lindisfarne had thought so long ago when the Raiders had first appeared in their own ship. Just a single ship. What harm could it do them?

Leofwine's eye caught that of his closest advisor, Wulfs-tan, and he raised his hand in salute across the waves. Wulf-stan returned the gesture, but his eyes were wary even across the distance.

He was a massive wolf of a man who carried his slowly advancing years around him like a cloak. Leofwine was in awe of him. He dealt so fairly with men and always had alternatives and suggestions to make on all of Leofwine's actions. Leofwine had come to rely on his judgment in the three years since he'd become his own commended man.

Wulfstan was uncomfortable now, and although he'd initially ignored the perfectly formed arguments for not accepting his current task, Leofwine was beginning to share in Wulfstan's feeling of uneasiness. There was nothing Leofwine could narrow down to being the cause of his emotions. It just hovered there, on the periphery of his consciousness. Was treachery being planned against them? Was this Olaf's plan to see him dead, or worse, was this his king's plan to rid himself of an ally he was unsure about?

Wulfstan stood to the front of the English ship, a resplendent figure in wolf pelts and sealskin cloak, to keep his furs dry from the splashing waves if there had been any. His hair was long and turned to silver, and his long beard and moustache changed to white. He looked strangely mystical, and Leofwine's mind drifted, as it often did, to Wulfstan's past.

Leofwine knew little about Wulfstan's early days as a warrior and remembered only hints from the time they'd first met, him no more than a babe. While Wulfstan had been his father's closest friend and ally, a loyalty transferred to him on his father's untimely death; Leofwine sometimes looked to Wulfstan as a son to father, and in those times, he appreciated his steady presence and unassuming ways. Wulfstan didn't exploit his Lord's need of him, seeming to be happy to serve and never be the master.

Wulfstan was reticent about his time with Leofwine's father, and Leofwine had long ago learnt not to ask. Whatever had happened in the past, it was plainly not his concern. He still considered, though, what promises his father had extracted from his friend to keep him so close to his son.

Leofwine again looked at Wulfstan's face. Its mistrustful look had not cleared, and he was now beginning to look a little green. Whatever he could not say about Wulfstan, this trip had taught him one thing; Wulfstan was more than awkward at sea. Good thing the day was so still.

Leofwine had been travelling on board with Wulfstan for most of their journey north. However, Olaf had announced last night, when they'd made camp, that today would be the day they sailed out of sight of land and headed across the sea towards the islands known as the Shetlands.

There was no landfall to be had between where they'd started the day and the islands of their destination. Instead, they'd stay on board ship and not camp on dry land for the night. So Leofwine had decided to ask for a place on Olaf's own ship for two reasons. Firstly, it was to foster links with Olaf and his own shipmen. Only at night had they been able to communicate on the voyage, and Leofwine wanted to watch Olaf at work to see how he commanded his men.

And secondly, if he were on-board Olaf's ship, they'd not be able to slip away from the English ship at night on the waters that were unknown to any of the men that Leofwine commanded. Wulfstan hadn't been happy about the decision; he'd made that clear. Still, it made good sense. Olaf was as slippery as a Thames caught eel when he wanted to be.

Of course, the request from Leofwine to Olaf has been couched in far more flattering terms. Olaf had readily accepted the change in plan and had sent Horic, his own second in command, to be a guest on board the 'English' ship, as Olaf and his men were calling her. Although they'd spoken derisively of her, they all viewed her with acquisitive eyes that could envisage the magnificent ship as their own.

Leofwine smirked at the memory of his ship's first appearance to the Raiders. They'd all been dumbstruck as the huge, menacing monster had been slowly oared into view in the estuary, with Leofwine at the helm and Wulfstan stood to the rear with the ship's captain, a burly westerner by the name of Ælfric.

Olaf's shipmen had tried to continue throwing underhand remarks his way, but when his own ship was at least a full half as long as their own ships and outfitted with eighty shipmen, they'd found little to ridicule. When the well-practised crew had effortlessly raised the huge mast, allowing the sail to billow in the gentle wind, Leofwine has been sure he'd heard low gasps of hastily stifled admiration.

The finishing touch had been when the mighty colourful sail unfurled. Many had not tried so hard to mask their appreciation. Against the better-seasoned ships of the Raiders, their wooden planks more grey than brown, she'd glowed an almost blinding gold – almost as if she was made from the weighty material instead of from solid oak from the forests of Mercia.

All that extra polishing on Ealdorman Æthelweard's orders had been worth the effort. Even Leofwine had given a hand to make the ship appear as magnificent as possible. After all, it represented his king, and it was his means of returning home from Norway, as well.

Leofwine didn't understand the derogatory remarks that most of the Northerners made about the English. After all, they'd long since defeated the many Raiders who came looking and even those who'd taken permanent hold, all apart from Olaf, and even he had paid to dissuade him from attacking again.

York was once more firmly reintegrated into the kingdom as a whole, and while there was a large population of Norse living within the old kingdoms of Northumbria and East Anglia, they'd all quickly adopted English customs, or at least the vast majority of them. England was a nation to be proud of, not laughed at. Still, Leofwine supposed the delusional way the men viewed England could only play into his hands. If they thought her weak and impoverished, they wouldn't bother to attack again.

The ship had worked her magic, showing the Raiders that although they may have stripped England of her movable wealth, she was still well endowed with ships and fighting men. The ship was also a threat from his own king to Olaf. Æthelred had power, and he'd use it; Olaf needed to remember that and to honour his promise never again to return to England's shores, a promise reinforced by his baptism into the Christian faith.

Leofwine smiled in remembered amusement. The Raiders had soon reappraised Leofwine's role on their journey to Norway. Leofwine was no weakling to stand alone amongst so many hostile shipmen. Leofwine had his ship and his shipmen, and they would fight to the death for him.

Along with Leofwine's first ship, the king had also assisted in the brokerage of his marriage to a wealthy Mercian noblewoman who brought further credibility to his newly promoted position with her own personal contacts within the old Hwiccan nobility.

This was the only area of his newly given ealdordom where any of his lands were, albeit briefly, open to the seacoast and, therefore, liable to attacks from the Raiders. Perhaps, Leofwine mused, he would position his great ship there, although his men would have to sail all around the southern coast and along the dragon's leg of Cornwall to bring her home. Leofwine thought it would be worth it.

Æthelflæd, his new wife, would love to see the ship. She was a truly beautiful woman with long lustrous chestnut hair and sparkling green eyes. She was quick to anger, and when she did, her eyes flashed dangerously. She was quite a woman to bed, and she'd either take some taming to his ways, or he would to hers. It depended on who ultimately won the battle of wills.

Leofwine had left her, happy and content to be married and bedded, and he hoped he'd return to her in the same state. He'd occasionally seen her at royal gatherings but had never thought she'd one day be his wife. Now she was, and Leofwine hoped that he'd left her with his child growing in her belly. He should like to go home and be a father.

Around him, the sky was starting to darken, and Leofwine realised that the time he'd been dreading was nearly upon him, his first night sleeping on a longship.

He'd thought that some of the shipmen would continue to row throughout the evening, but all around him, men were fixing their shields onto the shelf that ran the length of the ship on both sides so that they overlapped. He looked questioningly at the men in front of him, and a substantial burly man, known as Axe, smiled a huge gap of broken teeth before saying in heavily accented English,

'This helps to keep us dry at night. It's not a pleasant experience to be woken from your sleep by a giant, wet and freezing wave splashing you in the middle of the night!'

Axe continued to laugh a deep mocking sound as he returned to his night-time duties, still chuckling to himself and passing remarks in Norse to his shipmen. Axe took a lantern from under his war chest and quickly struck a tinder to light it before hanging it from the wolf's head of the ship.

'Don't worry. You'll be able to see, at least,' Axe chuckled again, making his way past Leofwine. Axe then returned to his war chest, pulled his cloak and sealskin outer cloak close to his body and, propping his head on his booty, and his body in the bottom of the ship rolled over and was, to all intents and purposes, asleep within mere moments.

Up and down the ship, the other men were following suit as the light rapidly faded from the sullen sky. Leofwine thought there was a little spare room with the oars now stowed down the centre of the ship, but everyone seemed to know their place. He wondered where his was, for there was now no room for him at the back of the ship, what with Sigismund and his opposite both already stretched out and asleep.

At that moment, Olaf called his name and beckoned him to the widest part of the ship, where the mast was currently residing. Leofwine gratefully rose from his cramped position at the back of the ship and, suppressing a groan from his protesting muscles, walked as confidently as he could between the two rows of sleeping or near sleeping men.

The ship rocked none too gently from side to side, with more movement than there'd been all day. Behind him, Leofwine heard a small chuckle but decided it wasn't worth seeing whom it came from. Like Wulfstan, he was no natural seaman, and he needed to concentrate on his actions to prevent a fall earning him further ridicule.

The ship was a spectacular specimen at just over twenty eels long. In the centre, she ballooned out to nearly two eels, and into that space, if he could avoid the mast and the end of the oars, Leofwine was being beckoned to sleep on a slightly raised platform by Olaf.

Leofwine had brought a good number of furs with him to make his journey as comfortable as possible but had foolishly left them on his own ship. He looked around frantically, hoping to catch Wulfstan's eye and get him to bring them over, but the light of the day was almost gone, and all he could see was a mass of gently bobbing lanterns floating eerily over the gently lapping sea. He'd have to hope that Olaf had some to spare.

Leofwine reached Olaf, who clasped his arm in greeting, even though they'd been in sight of each other all day and pointed to a comfortable-looking mass of furs. They filled a considerable space on the raised area of the centre of the ship. Leofwine sank gratefully onto them, fingering the soft coat of the now dead wolf. Olaf noticed,

'I'd like to say I caught him myself, but that would be lying. I simply found the trader who had the misfortune to meet me one day on his way to market. I didn't take everything, but this was too good to miss. I'll gift it to you when you leave to return home.'

Leofwine smiled in response, about to refuse the gift, before realising that Olaf might be offended if he did so. Instead, he responded, 'My lord, you're most kind. I can already envisage him on my marriage bed.'

Olaf smirked in response. 'I pray that he's not more attractive than your wife?' Olaf's voice was tinged with amusement.

'No, my lord. I think my wife is most beguiling and even softer than this beautiful beast.'

Olaf's laughter turned lighter. 'I wish I shared your good fortune. Now sleep, my friend. You dream of your wife, and perhaps, I will too.'

Leofwine shared in the congenial humour. It was no secret that Olaf's wife was not a beautiful woman. Even he'd picked up on the various comments Olaf's men threw his way. She had, however, brought Olaf wealth, which he'd desperately needed, or at least that was the rumour circulating. Leofwine was thankful his wife was both beautiful and wealthy.

Leofwine made himself comfortable lying down, remembering to swirl his sealskin cloak from around his neck to the top of the furs. In his raised position at the centre of the ship, he was likely to be the first to feel the cold hands of any stray waves slapping over the side.

The shipmen around him stilled as they all drifted off to sleep. Soon there was no noise apart from the soft snores of the exhausted men spent from their day of continuous rowing. He'd not been anywhere near as active, and so he lay awake staring up at the shining stars above his head and listening to the gentle slap of the waves against the sides of the ship. The clouds of daylight had dispersed, and the night sky sparkled clearly above him, bringing with it the promise of a cold night and perhaps an even colder tomorrow.

In the middle of nowhere, entirely at nature's mercy, the tales of mythical beasts and monsters seemed that little bit more real. Leofwine felt himself muttering a prayer under his breath to his Christian God, and the rhythmic, near-chanting eventually lulled him into an uneasy sleep.

Leofwine's dreams were filled with colossal sea monsters

he couldn't hope to battle, who tossed him into the freezing sea from his deep sleep, only too aware that he'd die there, so far from land, weighed down by his cloaks, sword and byrnie. Their game was a mere sport, and that was even more terrifying. If he'd been hunted for food, he could have understood their needs.

Leofwine woke abruptly, finally able to break free from his terrifying nightmares. He was drenched in sweat, and despite his many layers of fur, he was shivering uncontrollably. Sunrise hadn't yet come to the cloudless sky, but there was a faint lessening on the black horizon that meant it wouldn't be long until the daylight began to illuminate the sea around him.

The sounds from the ship were still those of gently splashing waves and both soft and thunderous snores from the shipmen. Leofwine concentrated on quieting his breathing and banishing the images from the dreams that had haunted his sleep.

His head hurt, and to warm himself, Leofwine pulled the furs higher around his shoulders. He'd not had nightmares since he was a small boy, apart from when his father had died. Then he'd experienced vivid dreams of his father calling for his assistance that he'd not been able to give. Leofwine had often woken from the dreams disorientated and crying. They'd lasted for a good few months, only finally banished when he'd taken to his bed a buxom local girl who'd made him forget almost everything.

With his breathing quieted, Leofwine gave up all pretext of sleep and rose to a sitting position, making sure the furs were pulled tight against his body. He rested his back against the base of the mast, careful not to disturb any of the sleepers.

Olaf was snoring loudly, and Leofwine would have liked nothing more than to nudge him to silence. He didn't, deciding it was better to tolerate the snoring than wake Olaf. He didn't want Olaf to realise how unnerved he was by the sea crossing.

In the near distance, he could faintly make out the shape of the other longships that made up Olaf's fleet. The ships made dark smudges on the horizon with specks of light at either end. He smiled with relief when he caught sight of his own ship. She'd stayed with the rest of the fleet all night, against their worst fears. Leofwine sincerely hoped that Wulfstan was starting to feel a little more at ease, for he was beginning to grow more unnerved with every oar stroke away from England.

Leofwine used the silent time to consider the lives the men on the ship led. They were seeking things he'd not have risked his life for. Out here, on the motionless ocean, the feeling of total hopelessness and isolation was terrible enough. What would it be like if a storm struck? How would it feel to know that you'd put your life in the hands of the faithless sea?

Leofwine was starting to admire the men's resolve where before he'd only felt contempt. Raiding was no easy way to make a fortune. He found himself wondering what conditions must be like at home for these men to force so many of them to leave home and take to the ships. He hoped now that his trip with Olaf would teach him more about the mindset of his enemies. Perhaps he'd learn things that would help his king and fellow countrymen.

Eventually, Leofwine stopped shivering and suddenly needed to relieve his bladder. Rising somewhat unsteadily to his feet, he walked the few steps to the side of the ship and gratefully emptied his bladder into the bleak steel sea. He winced at the loud noise his water made as it hit the infinite expanse. However, none of the shipmen stirred, and so his business finished, he returned to his place near the mast and his disquiet thoughts.

Leofwine's dreams last night had stirred up all the old memories of his father, and now in the half-light of early morning and the profound silence, not even broken by a cock crow as would have happened at home, he found himself assaulted by images of the time he'd spent with his father.

As a young boy learning to parry with his first wooden sword, to his time, when as an acknowledged man, he'd taken his father on as an equal. He couldn't beat him; his father was too good a tactician for that; Leofwine had to rely more on his brute strength. His father had assured him that his tactical skill would develop and grow with age. He had been right; pity he'd not been around to see it happen.

Leofwine had been no young boy when his father had gone to fight against the raiders in 991; he'd confidently taken control of his father's land while he'd been away. Only his father's failure to return had disturbed his state of mind. He'd grieved for months and, in that time, had been entirely reliant on Wulfstan to manage the land and people who supported his place in society.

His father wouldn't have approved, but then his own father's father had lived to a grand old age, well into his fifties, and was able to see his grandson grow to maturity, not just his son. His father wouldn't have understood the intense grief Leofwine had experienced, although he'd probably have been gratified by the knowledge that his only son had been so reliant on him as both father and friend.

Leofwine had never known his mother as she'd died

birthing him. His father had been his only family; his father and, of course, Wulfstan. Leofwine had enjoyed a peaceful upbringing but had not been shielded from the realities of the Court and the king. From his earliest days as a man, he'd attended the witan with his father and had watched and tried to learn the ways of the men and women who advised the king.

Leofwine became aware of movement around him at the same time as the snoring ceased. The entire crew of shipmen woke at the same time. They stood quickly and saw to their morning ablutions before removing their shields, extinguishing the two lamps and passing around some cold smoked pork for breakfast and drinking from a shared horn. With little conversation, they were soon again bent to the task of rowing, having un-stoppered the oar holes and reinserted the oars. Before the night gloom had fully cleared, the entire fleet had resumed the journey to the islands of their destination.

Olaf had assured Leofwine it would only take two days to reach their destination, and Leofwine hoped that meant they'd reach it that day. He didn't relish the idea of another night on board a silent ship with nothing to distract him from his nightmares.

However, the lack of wind had slowed them considerably, and Leofwine feared that Olaf's prediction of a two-day journey would prove to be wrong. He doubted that the men could power the ships as quickly as nature and decided he should resolve himself to a good few more days at sea.

The day, like that which preceded it, proved to be dull and gloomy, and about midday, or so he thought as it was difficult to tell without a clear view of the sun, he heard a shout from behind and turned to see that Wulfstan had ordered his ship to breach the gap between them. It made conversation possible, although far from private. Wulfstan looked more relaxed at the front of the ship, and Leofwine was pleased to note that the mild conditions were apparently increasing his confidence at sea. Leofwine wished he felt the same.

Wulfstan had nothing of import to tell him, so they shouted inconsequentialities at each other, and after only a short time, Wulfstan let his ship pull back into its original position, in the middle of the fleet, behind Olaf's own ship, which led the others.

The day was long and slow, and although the shipmen were in good spirits, Axe even allowing him to control the oar for some time, as night again fell, the land was nowhere in sight, and Leofwine's uneasiness at another night on board took hold of him. He had to dismiss it as irrational as he again joined Olaf in the middle of the ship to sleep but couldn't help noticing that the men's voices were unnaturally loud, and here and there, some had drunk slightly too much ale, and arguments had broken out at the front and rear of the ship.

Olaf contained his men and returned to his place by Leofwine muttering about bloody idiots and then, unlike the night before, set a watch. Leofwine couldn't help thinking it was more to keep an eye on the shipmen than a fear that they'd encounter another fleet at night. He doubted that any other fleet would have left their safe harbour when the sea was so becalmed.

Again, Leofwine struggled to sleep, even as comfortable and tired as he was, and even having spent some of the day rowing. His mind wouldn't shut down, and though his eyes stayed closed, he fought his busy mind as it went from childhood memories to concerns about the coming winter and then back to the erotic thought of his last night spent with his wife.

They'd only been married for a week before he'd left a month ago. He could vividly remember the image of her naked body, all long legs, flat stomach and perfectly proportioned breasts, and he found himself wishing over and over again that he was with her in a warm bed and not trapped here, on a ship journey that seemed to be going nowhere.

At some point in the long dreary night, and it had to be late because he'd heard the watchmen change more than once, he nodded off, lulled finally by the softly splashing waves and thoughts of how he'd celebrate his return with his wife.

Leofwine's dreams were quieter. His awakening was not. In his subconsciousness, he'd been aware for some time of a screeching wind and violent rocking of the ship, but it was the slap of frozen, cold seawater that finally woke him abruptly. His head was foggy from lack of sleep, and it took him precious moments to realise what was happening. The sky was still dark and menacing, but clouds were scudding quickly across the moon that was just beginning to drop lower in the sky. The wind had returned with a vengeance, and he feared rain wouldn't be long in joining it.

Up and down the ship, all the men were waking as Leofwine wiped the cold salt water from his face with the back of his hand before pulling his furs tighter. The temperature had dropped considerably as he'd slept, and his face felt raw from the wind it was exposed to.

His head finally clear and his eyes alert, Leofwine glanced to where Olaf was hastily assisting his men to unfurl the sail. He looked at Leofwine and winked.

'Now, we'll show you the exact speed of my beauty. We've signalled the fleet, and they're to follow our example. Do you think your men will be able to cope with a true wind from Hel?' he ended with a smug tone to his voice, and Leofwine, while not entirely sure that his shipmen would be able to, was stung into replying,

'Of course, they will, my lord. They're the king's finest shipmen.'

Olaf returned to his task, chuckling to himself, and Leofwine decided, in deference to maintaining good relations, to ignore the implied disbelief.

Leofwine scanned the horizon, hopefully looking for his ship, and was gratified to note, as the sun's first rays heralded the advent of the day, she was in place behind the ship he was on and that her sail was at the same stage of raising as Olaf's own. His men would not let him down. They'd trained for this, and they were prepared.

Leofwine caught sight of Wulfstan's grey head, bent to his tasks, and just stood and watched him until Wulfstan himself stood and waved in salute. By now, Olaf and his men had the sail up, and the wind immediately caught her. Leofwine lost his balance and stumbled back against one of the shipmen.

He offered him a steadying hand and no ridicule, which Leofwine was grateful for. Leofwine quickly made his way to the stern of the ship and settled in for what he hoped would be his last day at sea before reaching dry land. The oars were all neatly stacked in the middle of the ship from the night before, so space was a little tight to be overly comfortable for all the men.

Pleased to be having a day of rest, the men passed around a horn of ale and then, in small groups, took to playing games with wooden pieces and a board, polishing their swords and helmets, or just prowling through their own war chests to see what treasures they had not yet fully admired. The wooden pieces and board game were highly sought after, and Leofwine watched as many lost to one of the warriors, only for him to be beaten by Olaf himself.

The mood was jovial, for all the wind whipped around everyone's heads, and everything had to be firmly fastened down to prevent it from flying overboard.

Further down the ship, Leofwine could see one brown head bent forward as if in prayer to the Christian God, and finally, curiosity won, and he leant forward to tap Axe on the shoulder,

'What's that man doing?' as Leofwine pointed down the ship.

Axe followed his finger and shrugged his giant shoulders in response.

'It's just Finn. He's Olaf's scribe, although Gods know why he needs one. He's a useless fighter and can't row even when we tell him the Valkyrie are chasing us. Still, Olaf keeps him close and sees to his constant demands for parchment and ink.'

Axe returned immediately to polishing his mighty war hammer, and Leofwine was left to ponder the strange idea. Leofwine knew his own king kept scribes and churchmen to keep written records of grants and charters. He didn't think that a mere raider would have need of one. What did he need to write down? Leofwine certainly didn't believe that he kept written records of the people he killed and stole from.

Leofwine would have liked to have spoken to Finn; to see what he was writing now, but the violent motion of the ship prevented him and kept him firmly in the same place all day, only moving once when absolute necessity took him to the side of the ship to relieve his pressing bladder. He made it back to his place in one piece and then closed his eyes, head resting on the edge of the ship. The forceful sideways motion of the ship was less here, and he found himself able to sleep. He didn't dream, exhaustion from his two broken nights' sleep overwhelming him completely.

3
AD995

L eofwine woke later to the sound of 'Land ahead' and a profound feeling of relief. He wouldn't have to spend tonight on the wide-open sea.

Leofwine struggled to his feet from his prostrate position at the stern of the ship and watched with a mixture of intrigue and joy as the strange new land came into sight. A collection of islands slowly formed in front of him; the land coming into focus; the jagged coastline taking shape, while the smudges of smaller islands, further away, just became a little clearer as dusk slowly began to spread across the sky in a mixture of deep purples and crimsons, the clouds seemingly driven back from the landmass.

The island they were heading towards was backlit by the colours of sunset and appeared black in contrast, a total unknown quality but welcome for all that.

As they came within sight of the ragged cliffs, Olaf ordered the fleet to turn against the tide to the groans of the men, who took the sail down and began heaving on their heavy oars already in place. The men had been prepared for Olaf's commands, no matter their personal feelings.

On the land, Leofwine could see smoke rising into the darkening sky from some buildings and the occasional twinkle of a lit lamp. He didn't see anyone coming to meet them and wondered whether the inhabitants of the tiny isle were so used to the unexpected arrival of raiders that they didn't bother or whether they were merely expected.

The ship ran aground on a gently sloping beach with a thud that shuddered the entire length of the ship and moved from Leofwine's feet to the top of his head. He choked back a cry of euphoria. All around him, the other ships were mirroring the action, and he spied Wulfstan only a few ships over to his left. Wulfstan was at the front of his ship, the first to leap onto the greying sand. He shot Leofwine a grimace.

Up and down the ship, the men were stowing the oars and closing the oar holes. Leofwine squeezed past all the busy activity and, with exhilaration, jumped from the bow of the ship to be met by the softest sand he'd ever encountered. In the twilight, it appeared drab and dreary, but he imagined that with the sunrise, it would shine as golden as the sun itself. He hoped they'd still be here to see it. Leofwine didn't relish the idea of an early start in the morning; it would be nice to stop swaying in time to the sea, even if only for a moment. For now, he concentrated on staying upright.

Around him, the men were disembarking with their possessions for the night, and Olaf joined him on the beach.

'Come, we'll seek shelter for the night. The Jarl here, Sigurd, is an acquaintance of mine. He keeps a merry hall'.

'I'll just speak with Wulfstan and the men.'

'As you will. I'll see to my own men as well.'

With that, Olaf strode down the beach, his back towards

Leofwine, who took a moment for reorientation before walking on unsteady feet to where Wulfstan and his men were coming ashore.

Wulfstan greeted him with a lantern in one hand and an arm clasp with the other. 'Well met, my Lord. How have you fared?'

Leofwine's face contorted in response, and Wulfstan's face creased with a conciliatory grimace.

'And you feared for my sea legs, my Lord.' Wulfstan's words held no hint of amusement in them, and yet Leofwine smiled all the same.

Around him, Leofwine's shipmen were calling greetings as they carried their supplies from the ship to the beach above the high tide mark, evident from where the other shipmen were stowing their own possessions for the night and also from the grassy tufts amongst the sand.

The men all looked well, and Leofwine envied them their comfort on the open sea, although maybe they were as pleased as him to be on dry land. There were huge grins on the faces of most of the men, and only a few peered into the gloom with apprehension.

Fires were soon burning brightly, fuelled by the occasional piece of driftwood and hoarded dried animal dung, blues and greens, turning the yellow flames to rainbows. The Shetlands were notorious for their lack of trees, and so fuel for fires and cooking had been added to the ship's cargo.

Leofwine quickly took his leave of his men and Wulfstan, explaining Olaf's wish to seek out Sigurd. Wulfstan looked uneasy at the prospect, and so Leofwine took Wulfstan with him, needing his friend's advice. In Wulfstan's place, Godric was in charge of the men. He, like Wulfstan, was a remnant of Leofwine's father's own commended men, and his loyalty was guaranteed. Before they went, Wulfstan also ensured that the ship was correctly raised out of the water; it wouldn't do if it sailed away of its own accord when the tide rose.

The ground they walked upon was soft, and it was hard going as they strained to reach Olaf, who was awaiting them on the tufted grass bordering the beach. Leofwine knew it was a good sign, for if the sand was soft, the sea didn't often reach this far up the beach.

The captains of his own ships, a further twenty-three men in all, attended upon Olaf, and Leofwine was instantly glad he'd not come alone. He knew all the men by sight, from the menacingly huge figure of Gunnar to the much calmer, more even-tempered Thorkell; yet each of the men governed their crew with iron strength, and none would tolerate either shoddy work or outward shows of defiance.

Leofwine usually felt reassured by their presence, aware that while he was Æthelred's commended man, they respected that and would ensure their own men did. But here, on the island, seemingly at the end of the world, Leofwine was not so sure that they wouldn't let their own prejudices against him show.

Olaf's men all acknowledged his presence in some way and then turned inland. Many carried lanterns, as did Wulfstan, and by the twinkling procession, as full dark had descended, Leofwine was able to follow the narrow track towards the dark houses which Olaf assured him lay ahead. The men were talking in loud voices, in their native tongues, so Leofwine could only pick out the occasional word. Olaf walked beside him, happily regaling him with tales of the inhabitants of the island.

'She's called Mainland, for around her are more islands,

possibly nearly twenty in number, I can't remember the correct number, although I'm sure I'm told every time we journey here. She's cold in winter and warm in summer and serves as a stopping-off place for journeys from my homeland of Norway to Iceland and back again and for the many who travel along the coasts of the Picts, Scots and the Irish.'

Leofwine looked at him with disbelief on his face. He couldn't mask it, 'You mean the shipmen who bedevil the coast of my own lands, come from here? Surely it's too far to travel across the open seas? Surely it's too dangerous? And the risk too high? I understood that most of them came to England from across the narrow sea.'

Olaf smiled. 'My lord, we're a race of explorers. We travel far and wide, always seeking our fortune and our riches. Your land, it is on the farthest side of your king's land, is it not? Closest to the lands of the people of Dyfed?'

Leofwine nodded in agreement.

"Well then, my lord, the men from here usually travel down the far side of your country. There are many islands, and our ancestors have inhabited them all. They are a handy stop-off point along the way, and it means that we're never far from land and hopefully a friendly face. The way we have travelled with you is unusual, setting out across the open sea as we have, but you see, I'm overly keen to see my homeland, and the risk seems little in comparison to that.'

'Indeed, my lord, the risks seem high to me, but then I'm a novice at ship journeys, and I think I prefer it when the surface beneath my feet stays still.'

A long, loud laugh burst from Olaf's mouth at his rueful words, and Leofwine found himself joining in. Besides him, Wulfstan was almost smiling as well.

'I think I agree with Lord Leofwine, and I'm not new to

ships, having spent much of my time attempting to stop the Norsemen from raiding my king's land.'

Olaf continued to chuckle at Wulfstan's words.

'It's a dangerous life, but with the danger comes great rewards if you're lucky, and I consider myself lucky now. Now come! There'll be a warm fire burning tonight in the hearth, and I'll ensure that you're seated close to it. But a word of caution, these lands are much closer to your own than you think. The world we live in is much more intimately connected than I believe you and your king realise. We raiders are everywhere. Our alliances can be short, and we can change direction with or without the wind. I warn you, my Lord, don't underestimate us.'

Olaf turned abruptly away from Leofwine and Wulfstan to call to a man striding from the large hall that had finally materialised out of the dark murky night. Leofwine stopped walking, seeking time to prepare to meet another of the wealthy Viking Lords whom he was coming to realise were not just distant threats.

Olaf was correct in what he said. While his king recognised that not all Raiders stemmed from the same stock, he didn't fully appreciate just how far and wide they travelled. He'd need to inform his king of this; he didn't want him to assume that just because Olaf was gone, hopefully forever, that others wouldn't take his place.

Wulfstan stood quietly by, saying nothing, his presence itself a comfort. And then Olaf was back, bellowing and acting flamboyantly; his greying blonde hair blowing wildly in the steady breeze gusting in from the sea that surrounded them on at least three sides, the other being too shrouded in the black of night for Leofwine to see, although the sounds of the waves were loud enough.

Olaf introduced Leofwine to his Jarl of Shetland in sharp tones, which Leofwine assumed were meant to carry to the Jarl's men who'd come out of the hall to see who was arriving on the cusp of total darkness.

'Sigurd, I'd like to introduce you to Leofwine, Ealdorman of the Hwicce, and an ealdorman of Æthelred of England. Leofwine, this is Jarl Sigurd of the Shetlands. He holds sway over all that you see before you and much beyond the cusp of darkness. Sometimes, with the help of whoever might be calling themselves the King of Norway, and sometimes all alone.' Olaf, as flamboyant as ever, stretched both of his arms wide to indicate Jarl Sigurd's influence and reach.

Leofwine, impressed despite his intentions to the contrary, extended his arm toward Sigurd. They clasped hands in friendship, or so Leofwine hoped. It was difficult to see the man's facial expressions by the sparse lamplight, and so he could make out little of this man on whose hospitality he was intruding.

'My Jarl,' Leofwine said, 'let me introduce to you my second in command, Wulfstan. He served my father before me, God rest his soul, and now he leads my men on board our own ship.'

Sigurd looked surprised that Leofwine came with his own contingent of men. He looked at Olaf for what Leofwine assumed was confirmation, his dark eyebrows creasing as he thought, and at the same time, he extended his arm to Wulfstan so that they could also handclasp in friendship. Olaf responded as jovially as ever,

'I'm sure that my Lord Leofwine would attempt prettier words, but put quite frankly, I've been brought off with all of Æthelred's wealth and that of his subjects and the good Lord

Leofwine has been sent to ensure I leave the pleasant and easily plundered land of Æthelred. I'm never to return.'

Here Olaf again allowed hearty laughter to bellow from his mouth before continuing.

'Jarl Sigurd. I'm a bloody rich man, and all at Æthelred's expense. We must treat Leofwine with respect. I imagine,' and here he turned to Leofwine, 'that you'll be returning this way after you've seen me safely to Norway?'

Leofwine suppressed a scowl at the thought of more journeys across the sea but answered amiably enough,

'Yes, my Lord. It would please me to travel back this way if I can be assured of a friendly welcome?' His tone was inquiring, and for a moment, he thought he'd overstepped the boundaries of hospitality, but then the Jarl of Shetland's face scrunched in imitation of Olaf's own, and he laughed a deep booming noise that Leofwine thought could probably scare the strongest willed of men.

'Of course, my lord. You're most welcome. Now come, please enter my hall with your good man. I have an urge to hear more of Olaf's tales since last we met.'

Sigurd began walking back towards his hall, his large frame cast into darkness by the bright light pouring out of the open doorway. Leofwine looked to Wulfstan, but his face was impassive before shrugging in acquiescence, and then Leofwine, too, walked towards the hall. Almost anything had to be better than being tossed about by the whim of the sea.

Sigurd's own men had spilt from the hall when he'd left it, and now they formed up in a tightly fitting line, watching the new arrivals coil their own way inside. Leofwine would have felt even more intimidated if it hadn't been for the broad smiles on most of the faces and the hearty handclasps of men who were pleased to see each other again and counted each other as friends. Still, Wulfstan walked close behind him, a curled snake ready to leap if the situation presented itself.

Leofwine knew that Wulfstan had weapons secreted inside his cloak, not just the seax on display at his waist or even the glittering edge of a blade that he'd slipped inside his boots close to his ankle. Leofwine tried to chase away his unease. He was truly alone amongst strangers.

Smoke billowed from the deeply thatched roof, hanging almost to the floor in places. Leofwine attempted to determine just how big the mainly stone-built great hall was - only its edges continued past the limits of the illumination from the lamps, and he was left with the uncomfortable thought that he was about to step inside a massive stone coffin that hunkered almost deep inside the earth, as opposed to on top of it.

Once through the door, Leofwine relaxed a little. The hall looked formidable from the outside, but inside it shared many characteristics of his home. Amongst the sea of men, women, children and dogs, he could see great stone benches that fit snuggly under the massive outer walls and filling the space before him were wooden tables and benches. It looked as though they'd arrived in the middle of a feast, for surely the Jarl didn't regularly feed so many?

Somehow, Leofwine was pushed through the mass of bodies and seated on one of the stone benches, thickly strewn with furs, for comfort and to chase away the cold of the tomb. When he glanced up, Leofwine realised that in this position, all could see him. None had truly paid much mind to his shamble through the crowd, but now, sat so prominently, as if on display, he was aware of the many curious eyes turned his way.

Leofwine counted himself lucky that it was pure curiosity that turned the heads of the men, women, and children. He could not have thought that here, near what he considered to be the end of the world, visitors would be the norm, but that was plainly the case from their mild interest. Leofwine wondered what they thought of his wind-reddened face and his full beard, so conspicuous in a hall of large moustaches and cropped black hair.

A still wildly grinning Olaf pushed a huge welcome horn of mead into his hands. The returning noise and confusion, as everyone accepted the new arrivals, was disorientating after his few weeks at sea or on land, surrounded by none other than his own men and Olaf's shipmen. Leofwine tried to focus on more than just the level ground beneath his feet.

Leofwine gratefully swilled the sweet drink, unaware of just how thirsty he'd been. He passed the horn back to the lovely woman who stood patiently in front of him, swathed in rich furs, and she flashed a shy smile at him before turning to offer the drinking horn to Wulfstan.

Wulfstan drank less deeply of the cup, and Leofwine suppressed a sigh that he never ever seemed to let down his guard amongst strangers. Not that Leofwine wasn't pleased to have the man always at his side, but still, it would be good to know that Wulfstan was as delighted to be on dry land as he was. Secretly he doubted that Wulfstan's stony exterior would crack until they were back home and safe.

There was no formality to the feast, which appeared to have been in full swing for some time, the table before him piled high with half-eaten servings of more kinds of fish than Leofwine had ever seen before. He watched Olaf carve himself a slice of fish baked in dark bread before jamming it hungrily in his mouth and realised that up and down the bench, everyone was doing the same, even Wulfstan.

With a shrug, Leofwine too leaned forwards and helped himself to the fish and bread, luxuriating in the taste of hot, well-cooked food in his mouth. A less elaborately decorated feasting cup was passed his way, and he relished the strong flavours as he decided what to sample next. The food was certainly doing the job of settling his sea-sickened stomach.

All night the food kept coming, and the drinking horn passed from hand to hand with high frequency. As Leofwine slowly relaxed, the room finally stopped swaying, and he found himself looking around with as much curiosity as those who so openly stared at him, interest evident on their face.

It was a magnificently decorated hall that stretched off into a murky distance almost too far for him to see. He estimated that it must be virtually the equal length of his magnificent longship. Along the walls, people sat on raised platforms, eating and drinking in a huge swirling mass. Plainly there were no fixed rules as to who sat where and spoke to whom. A massive fire stretched across the midway point of the hall, blasting occasional smoky clouds across his view and warming the room to an almost unbearable heat.

Olaf and Sigurd had been deeply engrossed in conversation ever since their arrival, seated as they were to the left of him, and every so often, he heard a loud exclamation of surprise or annoyance from one or other of them that caused him to turn in shock. At his side, Wulfstan was vigilant and finally leaned over and spoke quietly to him.

'My lord, I'm not truly convinced that these two are such good friends as they are pretending. Olaf is plainly unhappy about something, and he's making Sigurd nervous. I could be wrong, but I think this is a pagan feast, and it's made Olaf aware that he could start his conversion toward Christianity here. I don't doubt his good intentions, but I think that if we're not careful, it could become a little too forced for our liking.'

Leofwine raised his head from listening to Wulfstan's carefully spoken words to look at the two men. It took only moments for him to realise that Wulfstan's assessment of the situation was correct.

The two men were overly loud in their heartiness, while both had their household warriors stood close by listening intently to the conversation. If Leofwine focused his attention on what they were saying, he realised that the men were having what could only be described as a drunken debate about the virtues of their respective Gods, and the more Sigurd swore his allegiance to the old Gods, the more Olaf pushed his version of the new Christianity on him. It would have been incredibly amusing if only the men had not sounded so tense and so determined that their viewpoint was the correct one.

And if Sigurd's pagan warriors hadn't been so keen to bloody the blades that hung from their waists. Few here were unarmed.

Leofwine leaned towards Wulfstan,

'I must agree with you. Will it become violent?'

'Let's hope not. We'll be caught in the middle, not only strangers to the vast majority of people here, but Christians at that.'

Leofwine turned to glance at the two increasingly angry men and their followers, and he couldn't help wishing that he was here with more than just Wulfstan as his support. He caught the eye of the physically dominating Axe and was surprised to see the hint of a smile playing about his lips. The man seemed to be enjoying this, his hand never far from the axe that hung at his waist. Leofwine swallowed convulsively. He didn't like this at all.

And then, above the cacophony of rioting noise, Leofwine heard a melodic voice and realised that everyone in the hall was quietening and paying respectful attendance to a well-dressed individual sitting close to the central hearth, a space opening up around him as his voice gained in sound.

Leofwine looked at the man with interest, noting his finely shaped face, elaborately curling moustache, and beautiful black fur draped down his back. He had a delicately shaped mouth, and Leofwine was struck by the disparity between the man's physical presence and the strength of his voice. This man was plainly admired and feted amongst these people.

Then Leofwine began to listen to the words the man spoke and realised that even Olaf and Sigurd had fallen into silence, allowing their argument to drain away. The words the man said were in the native tongue of the islanders so that Leofwine and Wulfstan couldn't understand all of what he spoke but the timbre of his voice and precise mode of imparting his speech was mesmerizing, and Leofwine found himself listening intently to the strangely different but familiar words and watching the almost silent and still audience.

The skald, for that was surely his profession, spoke for a long, long time, telling a plainly intricate story that these people had either never heard before or simply esteemed so much that they would not consider interrupting. Only as the massive fire burnt dangerously low did anyone stir, and even then, it was only to restock it from a handy pile of wood and then sit again and listen to the man. The skald was plainly as beguiling as the great churchmen Leofwine knew in his land. Perhaps this was someone that Olaf should approach to help him spread the word of Christianity.

Leofwine's eyes grew heavy as he listened, and he feared that he would ere in the worst possible way and sleep while the storyteller spoke. Leofwine nudged Wulfstan to alert him to the danger, and Wulfstan flickered his ever-vigilant eyes towards him and smiled. It was evident that he, too, was caught under the spell of the accomplished storyteller.

After what felt like the entire night had passed, the storyteller finally ceased speaking and bowed his head toward both Olaf and Sigurd. The two men moved as if in slow motion, but they showed their appreciation of the man's talent by gifting something of value to him. Olaf shrugged one of his silver armbands from his wrist, and Axe handed it to the man, bowing his head respectfully, while Sigurd ordered that something be brought to him from his war chest hidden, though barely, behind his ceremonial chair.

The massive ring that flashed under the dusty light looked magnificent, and Leofwine wondered if these plunderers understood the riches they stole from the church and the people they attacked. Such wealth for a mere story was astounding.

Stifling a massive yawn, Leofwine now saw Olaf rise from his place and offer his thanks to his host. Leofwine gratefully rose as well and walked to Sigurd to offer the same. Sigurd was quieter now, the argument of earlier forgotten, and as they left the hall through the rear door this time, as there were far too many people to make a path through to the door they'd entered by, Olaf smiled in joy and said.

'We'll return tomorrow. The feast is not yet done, but I most certainly am. I crave sleep and rest. Tomorrow evening we will listen to the great storyteller again. I see that you enjoyed listening to him.'

'Indeed, he was fascinating, although I didn't understand his words.'

Olaf opened his mouth and laughed again.

'I'll ask Finn to speak to you of it. He'll be able to tell you the story, albeit in a far less fanciful way.'

Their small party had found the beach by now, and they separated to find sleep amongst their men. As he lay down on the gently sloping beach, Leofwine breathed a sigh of contentment for the full night's sleep he hoped to gain, safe and flat on dry land, the sound of the sea a mere accompaniment to the gentle whisper of the wind.

4
AD995

Leofwine felt the white-hot stab of the steel as it sliced down his face. Agony exploded inside him. Only sheer gut reaction jerked him aside from the still flashing blade while he fumbled for the seax on his belt.

His sight was a sudden blur, and he could focus on nothing apart from the blood shrouding his left eye.

His other eye was filled with a glinting image of lightly armoured men in strange black helms and fire greedily licking outside its cage in the centre of the hall.

Leofwine tried to duck away from the shadowy blade as he felt a hand on his back. Grabbing it instinctively, he attempted to wrench it away while trying to avoid the flashing blade. Only the patterns of rings impressed on his hand stayed his action. It was Wulfstan. Leofwine turned his face towards his friend but failed to focus on him.

Instead, Leofwine felt himself behind Wulfstan's own body as he saw others surrounding him from Olaf's ships. There was Horic and there Axe, and he realised that Olaf, too, was fighting to protect him. The flashing blade had disappeared, and Leofwine didn't understand what had happened.

The hall was a blazing wreck, fire sneaking its way along any piece of exposed wood or fabric, and all around him, men fought for their lives. But who did they fight?

Leofwine tried to get Wulfstan's attention, but a cough formed in the space of his question, and then Leofwine could see for the space of a single blink. Wulfstan was engrossed fighting a massive man with long dark greasy hair and eyes that flashed red from the reflected fire sprouting along the walls of the mighty hall. Wulfstan's seax was busy at work, sweeping from side to side, while he shouted unintelligible instructions to those unhindered by the enemy.

Leofwine struggled to hear the commands over the roar of the fire, dimly aware that few remained within the hall. Where had all the other people gone?

Leofwine stumbled on the rough floor and felt hands lift him and place him back on his feet, not roughly, but not gently either. The heat in the area was overpowering, and sweat was dripping from his hairline. And as he licked his suddenly dry and cracked lips, he tasted his salt and iron. Along with his mouth, his throat burnt from the rising heat. Leofwine licked his lips again, trying desperately to think. How could he get out of the burning hall?

Leofwine angrily wiped his hand across his eyes to clear his vision. It didn't help, and as he watched his hand on its descent, he saw a vivid red streak and realised the iron he tasted was his blood. The knowledge sent a shiver up his spine. It was his blood, and it was leaking from a wound near his eye.

Sparks flared above his head, and he beat at his clothes to extinguish the few that landed on him. Abruptly Leofwine felt cold water wash over him, and he looked around further in confusion, blinking away water and blood until he could focus. Again, it was Wulfstan, purposefully covering him with a container of freezing water, having fought free from his enemy. Through the increasing noise of fight and fire, his friend muttered.

'It'll prevent the sparks from catching, my Lord. I apologise for the shock.'

Wulfstan turned and quickly parried another blade aimed at his face. Leofwine leaned forward, attempting to see around his friend, but found himself roughly shoved back.

'Please, my lord. It's for your own good,' a gruff voice stated out of the corner of Wulfstan's mouth.

As Leofwine glanced above, flames flickering amongst the grass roof caught his attention. Where there had been sparks, a fire now raged, raining down on him.

Panic took hold. There was nowhere for them to go. They were hemmed inside the great hall, as far from the doors as it was possible to be, and there were more and more men pouring through the two simultaneously open doorways, their black helms reflecting back the wave of fire.

Leofwine glanced at Olaf or what he could see of him. Olaf's face was sheened in sweat, and his blade didn't stop flashing in the greedy, golden flames edging their way steadily towards them. The heat was intolerable, and now the smoke was making it hard to breathe. Olaf turned and caught his eye,

'My Lord, I think we may have encountered a little resistance from the locals,' and then Olaf laughed, a deep thudding sound which reverberated up Leofwine's body.

Leofwine looked at him in shock. Olaf was enjoying this life and death struggle!

Axe had somehow heard the words and joined his own Lord in laughter, 'I think you might find you've upset Swein Forkbeard, not the locals.'

Olaf abruptly turned to his comrade with alarm, 'Swein?'

'Yes, my Lord. Is that not he by the door?'

Olaf turned to peer through the hazy, smoke-filled room in the direction that Axe had indicated. Leofwine tried to follow where he looked, but his eyes defeated him. He saw only smoke and shadow, rimmed with the fiery red of flames.

'Fuck. I believe you're right. Come, we must get out of here. Axe, if you would be so good as to make us an exit in this wall,' and here Olaf pointed to the wall at the farthest end of the long hall currently guarding their backs.

'I wondered when you'd ask.'

Axe raised his massive war axe and swung it at the part stone, part wooden wall, which shuddered under the onslaught. Olaf turned slightly in his defensive position so that he could protect the huge man as he swung, time and time again, at the thick wall behind them. Leofwine couldn't help thinking that it was a waste of effort. Axe didn't seem to be making any progress, and the enemy, so many of them, were gathering in an ever-tighter group around them, their eyes menacing and their swords and axes hungry for blood.

Then there was a loud crack, and Leofwine looked up to see a massive log that formed the ceiling struts crashing to the floor. It fell across the doorway on the left, and as one, the advancing men all looked back, concern registering on their faces. Olaf, Wulfstan, and Horic quickly took advantage, felling the men closest to them using their blood-red swords and smaller seaxes, all now luminous and glistening with gore. Above the roar of the fire, Leofwine heard a distinct bellow, and the men turned as one and quickly made their way back the way they'd come. Olaf chuckled, a dark sound full of contempt,

'Retreat he shouts. He'll never win when he's so ready to retreat.'

Leofwine gasped in relief and instantly coughed on the fumes, struggling to breathe in anything that was not hot sparks and choking ashy air. The men retreating towards the doorway were coughing as well, and as Leofwine watched in horror, blinking constantly to clear his vision, one of the men took a running jump over the burning log blocking the entrance, only to have another beam land on top of him, as the ceiling cracked again, the grass roof now fully ablaze the length and breadth of the hall. The man screamed in agony as he was caught between the white, hot logs. No one went to his rescue. Leofwine's gut twisted at the overpowering smell of burnt hair and flesh, but he controlled himself. It wouldn't do to vomit here; he would only draw more burning smoke into his air-starved lungs.

Abruptly, Leofwine felt cold fresh air wash over his face, and he turned to find Axe standing next to a gaping hole into the blackest of nights.

'My Lord,' he uttered, in a semi-mocking tone, bowing slightly and gesturing with his arm, 'your exit as requested.' Olaf smiled in slightly manic happiness beside him.

'Axe, you never fail to amaze me. I think an extra war chest for you, my friend.' Axe's grin widened further at the thought of more treasure, and Olaf rounded on Leofwine.

'I'll go first and check that no one is waiting to ambush us. We must be quiet, and then we can sneak back to our ships. Hopefully, they'll think us happily roasting to death in here.'

With that, Olaf was gone, and a few tense, almost silent moments passed. Wulfstan stood as Leofwine's guard, but the men who had attacked them were all gone, either dead or facing the wrath of the flames at the front of the hall.

A few grunts were heard from the men lying at their feet, and Wulfstan and Horic both checked to see if they were enemies or allies. The enemy they finished off with a seax to the throat; the wounded they either helped to their feet or equally ended their lives if the injuries were too significant, making sure they clasped either sword for the afterlife in Valhalla or crosses to ease their way into Heaven. All told, of the over thirty who'd entered the hall, only about ten staggered out under the whispered assurance of Olaf when it finally came.

Leofwine stumbled the few steps through the waist-high hole in the hall's wall that Axe had hewed with his mighty strength and huge axe. He was bent double, his knees almost meeting his face. Leofwine reeled, unable to see much, and felt hands steady him from both outside the hall and within.

Outside, the cold night air was a welcome change, and Leofwine felt his head clear as he breathed in fresh, uncontaminated air, and the burn in his lungs slowly eased, although the tension in his shoulders didn't abate. He still couldn't see clearly and swiped angrily at his eye, again and again. Every time he did so, more and more blood filled his vision, and eventually, Wulfstan leaned over and forcefully removed his fist from his eye, whispering, 'My Lord, you must leave it alone. It's severely injured, and you'll infect it.'

'But I can't bloody see anything,' Leofwine angrily whispered back, blinking and then blinking again. Wulfstan had followed Leofwine through the axe-hewn hole, and now they squatted together outside the remains of the hall.

'Then clasp my arm. I'll keep you safe. You can't see how bad the injury is. Please, my Lord. I fear for your sight if you don't do so.'

Leofwine purposefully held both arms downwards upon hearing Wulfstan's words. For all that, it hurt like Hell and was now starting to itch. He would do as his friend requested, even though he continued to blink, desperate to disprove his friend's words.

Olaf, Leofwine, Wulfstan, Horic, Axe and the few others who had all exited the building ran a short distance away to hide behind the animal shed, dodging behind the sauna Leofwine had been told to try but which now was never going to happen. The night was filled with the screeching complaint of collapsing wood, and in a whoosh of burning hot air, which reached them even where they huddled, the entire great hall collapsed before their eyes.

Leofwine closed his ears to the screams of agony he heard coming from inside and outside and turned resolutely to follow Olaf. He knew the sound would haunt him forever. What a way to die in the fires of Hell.

As Leofwine turned his head away, he caught a glimpse of men highlighted against the burning building and his breath caught, between one blink and the next, as he desperately tried to focus on the images he could see. But even though he was convinced they looked his way, they didn't hear the near-silent retreat over the roaring flames. Perhaps the men weren't looking for them, assuming that they too were inside the now collapsed building, Leofwine reasoned.

He greedily gulped air, which made him cough, a noise he quickly smothered in the crook of his elbow. Wulfstan looked at him in alarm. Leofwine angrily shook his head, forestalling any comment.

Olaf led them from behind the animal barn and down to the dunes closely bordering the sea and the Jarl's home as though he'd done this before.

Briefly, Leofwine muttered a question about what had become of the wife, children, servants and slaves of his host. It went unanswered, and then he forgot he had even asked, as he had to expend all his energy on crawling through the dunes, which Olaf had shepherded them toward. The sand constantly blew into his mouth and into his eye, making it sting horrifically. Still, Leofwine did nothing but blink away the pain.

In front, Olaf was acting as a guide and look-out, while at the rear, Horic watched for anyone following. The few injured men suppressed their groans and continued in determined silence. Leofwine didn't know how severely they were damaged but reasoned over and over, when the pain became too great, that if they could do it, so could he.

Leofwine was exhausted, half-blind, and riddled with pain from head to toe from injuries he couldn't remember receiving. But he would do it. He would make it back to his ship.

The night dragged on and on, relentlessly and at points, the wind blew fiercely into his face and eyes, bringing with it muck and ash from the fire that had so nearly killed them as they had to pass the burning longhall to make it back to their ships. As Leofwine crawled through the dunes closest to the blaze, all seemed quiet, and Leofwine wondered how the men who had appeared from nowhere had so effortlessly disappeared again.

At the front of the straggling line of crawling and

wounded men, Olaf abruptly stopped, and so did all the men, Leofwine only stopping when Wulfstan grabbed at his arm.

Leofwine found himself breathing harshly at precisely the moment they stopped, and the screeching wind died. His heart hammering in his chest, he held his breath for as long as he could. His heart sounded over loudly in his ears, and he was sure that whomever Olaf had heard would be able to hear it too.

Then the wind picked up once more, and Leofwine was able to breathe freely, and their journey continued. Only as the first muted pinks of dawn were starting to streak the sky and turn the vast deep ocean to an inviting blue, from the murkiness of inky blackness, did all the survivors return to their feet, and then only to make a fast run for their ships.

As Leofwine ran, Wulfstan at his side, he tried to focus on his ship. By turning his head to one side and trusting only his one eye, he could tell that there were only two ships left on the beach, whereas last night, they'd left over twenty. Leofwine noticed this depletion with shock, not so Olaf.

'Good,' Leofwine heard him mutter, 'They've left at the first sign of trouble. Only my ship and yours remain. My Lord, I'm truly sorry for what's happened here. I fear we must go our separate ways. Swein is obviously most upset with my treaty with your king, and I must get home to Norway before he does. I trust you'll be able to make it to England from here.' Olaf's voice was rushed, almost breathless. The first time Leofwine had heard anything but amusement ripple through the man.

Leofwine, just about dead on his feet, found he had trouble understanding Olaf and his intentions. He stood there mutely while the other wounded returned themselves either to his own ship or to Olaf's. There were fewer of them now, and he wondered whom they'd left for dead on the fraught journey across the sandy dunes. Olaf clasped his arm and turned to board his own ship.

'My Lord, are you leaving us? We don't know these waters. How will we return home?' Leofwine could feel panic starting to enter his voice, and he looked around frantically for Wulfstan, who'd chosen the moment to inopportunely leave his side. Wulfstan would know what to say and what to do.

'My Lord, with your leave, I'll see him safely home,' a deep voice answered from behind him. Leofwine turned in surprise, searching for the person who'd spoken with his restricted vision. Leofwine finally made out Horic's huge shape and realised that he was standing holding something substantial in both arms, his war chest. Horic had apparently given this some thought. Olaf's expression betrayed no surprise as he stared openly at his friend.

'You always had much more honour than I. I wish you well,' and with that, Olaf turned to his ship. A heavy rainstorm had blown in abruptly around them with the dawn, and it was suddenly so intense that the water puddled in long smoke-stained streaks down his face.

'We've had good hunting, my Lord, and I wish you well.' At Horic's shouted words, Olaf momentarily paused as he clamoured on board but then hauled himself inside his ship. He turned back when on board and shook one of his arm rings loose.

'A token of my esteem,' Olaf said, his voice gruff, as he handed it down to Horic.

'My Lord Leofwine. You're in supremely safe hands,' Olaf stated, emotion colouring his voice, and then the ship moved on the rising tide, the oars out already as Olaf's men rowed him quickly away without looking their way even once.

Leofwine was speechless. He was continually amazed by how quickly these Vikings could come and go, almost ghost-like in their abilities to appear and disappear. Then suddenly, he found himself staring at the sand on the gently sloping beach and could feel strong arms hauling him back to his feet,

'Get him on board. We must leave now. It'll only be moments more before search parties start looking for us with the sunrise. Get the men ready to row.' Horic barked his orders, his face uptight, as he and Wulfstan lifted Leofwine to the front of the ship with the aid of Edmund, one of the crew.

'My Lord, you need to lie down and rest. Your wound is severe, and you've lost much blood,' Wulfstan chided him.

Leofwine opened his mouth to respond but then shut it again abruptly. He was too tired to argue. He helped as much as he could as they lifted him inside the ship and then stumbled a few paces forwards. Wulfstan raced to the back of the ship, which was facing directly towards the open sea, and Horic dumped his war chest and nimbly took hold of the oar which had been placed through the oar-hole in preparation for the journey by the expectant crew. They'd plainly waited as long as they could for Leofwine to return, but the strain could be seen on pinched faces and in relieved cries on seeing their lord returned to them.

The ship hit the waves with a creek, and Leofwine felt his nausea return immediately. He realised even in his pain-wracked state that him being asleep would be the best thing for everyone involved. When he was asleep, the swaying of the ship didn't bother him.

Leofwine was tired, bruised, battered, bleeding and drenched with rainwater. As he faltered along the length of the ship, looking for somewhere to collapse, his men greeted him deferentially. He could not help but notice that some of them stared at him a little too long with horror on their faces. Just how ravaged was his face?

From his position at the back of the ship, Wulfstan was shouting commands, telling the men to follow Horic's orders.

'He knows the area. He'll keep us safe.'

'My lord,' Horic responded, inclining his head deferentially in Wulfstan's direction, 'I'll do my best. We need to avoid that bastard Swein Forkbeard and get the injured to safety. I'll give it some more thought, but I think it best that we travel back to your lands via a different route to the one that brought you here.'

'Swein won't be expecting that. He's possibly not even aware that you're not Olaf. They've always been uneasy allies, and I fear they'll now become even more awkward enemies. Now get to it, men. We need to row ourselves around the islands and change our course. Then we can raise our sails. It's certainly windy enough for us to make better time under sail than under oar power.'

Through all this, Horic didn't stop rowing from his place at the front of the ship, and Leofwine felt exhausted just watching him, blinking away sand, rainwater and blood from his injured eye.

Abruptly, Leofwine dropped into the bottom of the ship, amongst the legs of his shipmen, his eyes rolling in his head as sleep took him.

At some point, as he slept, Leofwine felt himself being lifted and laid to rest on a bed of dry furs, but he didn't stir, even when he was piled high with other furs up to the neck. At points, he was woken and forced to drink tepid ale. It burnt his throat as he swallowed, and he turned his head ineffectually away.

Leofwine felt so weak, and even though he stirred often, he couldn't bring himself to open his eyes because they, too, felt heavy, and the effort was too much to be expended on simply seeing where he was. He dully hoped that Wulfstan and his shipmen were caring for the other wounded. He was too drained to find out. Occasionally he thought the rain had stopped, while at others, he could feel cold rainwater soaking his face and chilling it so that he could feel nothing other than the dull throb behind his wounded eye.

Eventually, Leofwine became aware that the rocking motion of the ship had stopped, and he exerted his every effort to open his eyes. Slowly, the one opened, but not the other.

He fought his hands free from their place under the layers and layers of furs, and as he did, the smell of damp clothing filled his nostrils. It was mingled with the scent of sea and fire and smoke. God, he stank. He shrivelled his nose in disgust at himself. His left hand broke free from the covers with much effort, and he ran his hand over his eye that was closed, trying to determine if it was closed due to an accumulation of sleep, smoke or rainwater.

What he felt turned the pit of his stomach cold. His eye was swollen shut. However, there was also something else. His breath quickened, and he struggled to breathe. Panic set in as he probed his eye with his free hand. The other was still limp and encased in the furs that covered him.

Leofwine could feel it, though. It didn't matter how many times he calmed himself and touched it again. He could feel a cut that ran right through his eye socket and down his face as low as his chin. It was a deep, ragged gash with crusts of blood and sand all over it. It had to be cut to the bone!

Leofwine's chest hurt as he desperately tried to catch his breath. Such a wound could kill him. If it became infected, he'd die in agony, burning up with fever, and there was nothing anyone could do to save him. He had seen men die from infections before. It was torture, and it brought on fever and hallucinations. He'd never see his wife again or his home. He'd never know the child he hoped she carried in her belly.

A panicked sob erupted from his mouth. He looked around frantically with his good eye. Where was Wulfstan? Why had they stopped? Why wasn't the ship still rocking? Leofwine could see nothing but black. Was he dead already? Had they abandoned him for dead and left him in one of the ancient's burial mounds that dotted the remote islands which Olaf had brought them to?

The panic of moments ago was nothing compared to how he felt now. Now he actually couldn't breathe, and he sat bolt upright, wherever he was. Fresh pain erupted all over him as molten lead poured on his skin. His head spun from lack of oxygen, and he thought that these were his last moments.

Images of Æthelflæd and his father, of Wulfstan and his men, flashed quickly through his mind. He even saw a picture of his trusty hound, all grey-flecked muzzle and rheumy eyes, before he felt gentle hands on his shoulders and a soft voice speaking to him. He didn't recognise the words, but the touch of another person calmed him immediately, as did a fire being tended in the hearth. It must have been smothered or burnt so low that it had given off no light. He was not thought dead then and abandoned in the bowels of the earth.

Joy flooded through him, and as it did, Leofwine thought his legs were injured as well as he lost all sensation in them. The feeling returned momentarily, and he realised that it had only been the after-effects of the fear that had caused the loss of feeling.

There were quiet voices all around him now. The dim light meant he couldn't see well enough to discern who spoke or where he was. He felt a cup under his mouth, and he drank deeply of the warmed, spiced water he was offered. He felt gentle fingers probing his injury and warmed water cleaning the wound. He wanted to ask so many questions. Instead, he slept again. The drink laced with something. As he drifted back to sleep, he heard Wulfstan and Horic's muffled voices. The knowledge that he wasn't forsaken lulled him into a deep sleep without dreams.

THE ANGLO-SAXON CHRONICLE ENTRY FOR AD994

This year came Anlaf (Olaf) and Sweyne (Swein) to London, on the Nativity of St. Mary, with four and ninety-ships. And they closely besieged the city, and would fain have set it on fire; but they sustained more harm and evil than they ever supposed that any citizens could inflict on them. The holy mother of God on that day in her mercy considered the citizens, and ridded them of their enemies. Thence they advanced, and wrought the greatest evil that ever any army could do, in burning and plundering and manslaughter, not only on the sea-coast in Essex, but in Kent and in Sussex and in Hampshire. Next they took horse, and rode as wide as they would, and committed unspeakable evil. Then resolved the king and his council to send to them, and offer them tribute and provision, on condition that they desisted from plunder. The terms they accepted; and the whole army came to Southampton, and there fixed their winter- quarters; where they were fed by all the subjects of the West- Saxon kingdom. And they gave them 16,000 pounds in money. Then sent the king; after King Anlaf (Olaf) Bishop Elfheah and Ealdorman Æthelweard; and, hostages being left with the ships, they led Anlaf with great pomp to the king at Andover. And King Æthelred received him at episcopal hands, and honoured him with royal presents. In return Anlaf (Olaf) promised, as he also performed, that he never again would come in a hostile manner to England.

5
AD996

The door was heavy oak, with sturdy black hinges and a door lock to match. Leofwine eyed it speculatively with his good eye. He wanted to wrench it open and march proudly into the room.

Now that he'd decided he would, Leofwine was half-crazed with desperation to see her and his son. Yet he was also riven with indecision and momentarily doubtful.

He knew he looked different now and was a mere shadow of his former self; he hoped she'd still want him as her husband but knew she'd be well within her rights if she reneged on her promises to him. He'd honour her and provide for his son as was fit. But he was desperate for her to accept him back, and he'd dreamed of this throughout the crazed moments of his long illness.

The thought of seeing her again had kept him going; had made him recover; had made him want to get better even in his blackest times of depression when he'd finally accepted the full extent of his injuries.

Now Leofwine eyed the door apprehensively, aware that

Wulfstan was patiently waiting behind him to ensure he entered the room before retiring for the night himself. Taking a deep breath, Leofwine reached out with his right hand and, wincing at the slight noise from the massive black lock, opened it and pulled the door open.

Against all expectations, it made only a small squeaking noise, and Leofwine stepped inside the room, waving his hand to acknowledge his trusted friend and wish him a good night, before pulling the door closed and gently resetting the lock.

Finally letting the held breath out of his lungs, Leofwine turned to face the room before him. The first thing he noticed was the total silence apart from the occasional snap from the fire burning merrily in the small hearth. Secondly, he noticed the heat. It was hotter than he'd become accustomed to on his extended journey home in the depths of winter.

Leofwine quietly slipped the thick fur cloak from his shoulders and took a few steps into the room. It was dark apart from the light from a solitary candle. It made it difficult to see with his reduced sight, and he stayed still for a few heartbeats attempting to orientate in the nearly dark room that he'd never before been into.

Leofwine didn't want to fall over anything and have his reunion with his wife marred by the apparent disfigurement he now wore like a badge of office. He wondered why she'd not come to see who'd entered her room unannounced, but then he heard the soft snores. He smiled to himself.

Of course, it was late, and she'd only recently had the child. She was bound to be sleeping while the baby slept. Leofwine looked around for both the bed and the crib and alighted on the vast wooden box bed first. In the dim light, he could make out a shape and gingerly stepped around some discarded clothes that had been left on the raised wooden floor as he walked the few steps to the bed.

The sight that greeted him made his heart constrict, and for a moment, he felt unbalanced, both physically and emotionally. Leofwine took a few deep breaths, concentrating on his semi-naked wife asleep on her side, with a small bundle curled around her full breasts and still distended stomach, his child, and his wife. He didn't know where to look first and so stayed where he was as he fully absorbed the sight of both of them.

The child was well wrapped. Only his face was visible, and then only half of it. The rest was hidden by the breast he was absent-mindedly sucking as he slept, for his eyes were both firmly closed and other than the occasional noisy suckle, the child did not move.

His wife lay sprawled across the bed, her hair still braided and her shoes still on. He chuckled gently to himself. His son was apparently a handful if his mother had simply fallen asleep where she lay. He wanted to reach out to touch his son and to run his hands along the length of his wife's body, but he didn't. If sleep was such a precious commodity to be gained whenever the opportunity arose, he decided he didn't want to disturb either. In the soft light of the quietly crackling fire, he sat on the handily available stall and just watched them both sleep.

Neither of them was covered by furs, and although his son was firmly bound and his wife half dressed, he could see enough to know that they were both fit and well if exhausted. His wife's face looked relaxed as she slept, and he admired afresh her high forehead, perfectly proportioned face, and plum-red mouth. He wanted to kiss it, but every time he raised himself slightly from his stall, his son would stir in his sleep, and he'd sit back down again, afraid to disturb their slumbers.

Leofwine was unsure how long he sat there, staring at his son's tiny hand and small lips, and only when he felt his eye starting to close of its own accord did he realise that he, too, needed to sleep. Looking around the room, he could see a finely carved wooden backed chair silhouetted against the fire.

But Leofwine longed to spread out on the inviting bed next to his wife, and so instead, he slowly undressed and, grabbing his fur cloak from where he'd left it, for he could see no spare blankets, lowered himself onto the bed, wincing at every small sound his actions made.

Behind his wife, he was away from the merry fire and shielded from it by her body, and so he pulled his fur cloak tightly around his body as he inched himself closer and closer to her. She didn't stir, and eventually, he found himself spread along the length of her body and able to feel both her heat and her strength. The joy was intense. To be here with her had seemed impossible for so long, and as his eye closed in dreamy ecstasy, he felt tears prick it. He might not be home yet, but this was certainly close enough for him.

He luxuriated in the smell of her and curled her thick braid around his fingers, enjoying the scent of fresh flowers and a more musty milk smell. Slowly he put his arm around her enlarged waist and felt her tense posture relax at his touch and her weight shift so that she now lay with him instead of beside him.

Leofwine cushioned his head on his arm and fell asleep for the first time since that fateful night, with a smile on his face, instead of having to drown his worries with drugs or ale to gain the blessed release of oblivion.

HE WOKE TO THE SOUND OF THE COCKCROW AND A ROOM illuminated in the soft summer sunshine. It felt fresh, and he gratefully pulled his fur and an unexpected blanket further up his body so that it covered all of him instead of just the lower part of his body.

The room was quiet, and it took him a moment to remember where he was. When he did, Leofwine sat bolt upright, looking frantically around for the two other occupants of the bed who were no longer warming him with their body heat. With joy, he sighted Æthelflæd propped in the wooden chair near the fire, whose embers were still burning slightly. She was awake, and he was again dumbstruck by her beauty. She'd released her tightly curled braid, and her luxurious chestnut hair tumbled all around her, partly obscuring the child who lay noisily sucking at her breast.

Æthelflæd smiled at him as he glanced from her face to his son, and he returned her smile, rising quickly from the bed. Leofwine had thought of what he'd say to her ever since he'd decided that he'd go back to her, but now words failed him, and he merely found himself standing next to her, mirroring the radiant smile that lit her face.

She made the first move, reaching out and taking his hand and holding it to her face so that he could feel the silky soft skin of her cheek and so that she could turn and kiss his hand whenever she wanted. They stayed in that position for a long while until curiosity got the better of him, and he reached out with his other hand and gently pulled back her hair that had fallen over their son like a curtain.

His breath caught as he finally saw his son complete. The most piercing blue eyes he'd ever seen were staring at him, and the baby abruptly pulled away from his mother to stare at him. Æthelflæd laughed softly and then spoke in her soft voice,

'My Lords, may I introduce you to each other. Leofwine, this is your son, and my son, this is your father.'

Leofwine looked from Æthelflæd to his son and back again before laughing out loud in joy. The baby immediately jumped and turned back to his mother's breast for comfort, and Leofwine muttered to himself, 'Fantastic first impression.'

Æthelflæd chortled tenderly and held her hand out toward her husband. He grasped it gently but firmly, and she squeezed his fingers, her hand feeling soft under his own hardened, rowing hands. He found himself at a total loss for words and glanced away briefly while he tried to marshal his thoughts.

Leofwine's glance took in the corner of the room, and his eye was struck by the morning sun streaking through the small window and the dust motes dancing in the golden light. Perhaps he fancied it, but he was sure that he saw some lessening of the dark that continually clouded his damaged eye.

When he looked back, he was surprised to see that tears were streaking silently down his wife's face as she stared at him with saddened eyes. And then he remembered. While he was now used to the ravages of his face, this would be the first opportunity for her to look at him.

He wanted to flinch away from her scrutiny, but she held his hand tighter, and he couldn't break away from either her searching look or her lock on his hand. He also realised that he didn't want to. He'd rather let her see him now, with his injuries laid bare, and then she would make her choice, and he would accept that choice, no matter what it was and what it cost him.

Her eyes were an ocean of deepest green. He found himself mesmerised by what he saw there; so much compassion and love, his heart filled with hope. Then she broke their stare, released his hand and looked away.

Leofwine's confidence deflated, and he staggered back against the bed he'd only just risen from, his eye clouding and closing in grief. But then he felt soft, warm hands on his head and a hand gently stroking the damaged side of his face; the socket where his damaged eye stared blankly out and the cruel scar which ran the length of the left side of his face. He felt tears leak from his good eye and felt an equally soft hand wipe them away. The warmth on his face was a stark contrast to the months of harsh winter conditions he'd endured, and he gloried in the heat and felt soft lips on his face, gently covering the places where only moments before he'd felt soft, probing fingers.

Leofwine opened his eye now and his mouth to speak but felt a finger on his lips cautioning him to silence. He complied and closed his eye in bliss, more than content to enjoy this re-acquaintance. He found his arm resting gently on her hips and wanted to crush her to his own body. He resisted. She may not yet have decided on her response to his injuries.

Æthelflæd's lips brushed his forehead and his nose and then found his lips. It started innocently enough; a harmless warm, wet kiss, but suddenly passion flared within him, and his hands found her face and held her face level with his own; his mouth opened, and suddenly they were kissing so long and so deep it was as if they were trying to merge to become one person. Her body responded to his needs, and her hands cupped the back of his head, and she pushed forward with her weight, and he submitted to her wishes and leaned back across the bed; her body pressed against his, and her gentle weight on top of him.

His hands now explored further, tracing the contours of her full breasts, slightly distended stomach and the top of her thighs. Their kissing was intense; the reunion he had hoped it would be and dreamed it would be in his fever-induced state of recuperation.

Leofwine felt his excitement rise, and she responded, rubbing her body suggestively and sinuously against his own. He found himself gasping for air, and she pulled away from him, a smile of delight on her face. She straddled him with her legs and then undid her full braid that snaked down her back, allowing her luxurious river of thick chestnut hair to cover her as if a cloak. He reached up and ran his hands through the glorious robe, and she again grabbed his hands and kissed them, all the time moving her body against him, a smile of pleasure on her face.

Leofwine managed to untangle one hand from her own and reached out to run his fingers over her collarbone and shoulder and then down to her breast. She groaned in pleasure, and he reached out with his other hand to mirror the same action. A soft giggle escaped her mouth, which she stilled with the back of her hand, an urgent look going to the wooden cot where their son lay asleep.

Æthelflæd stood abruptly, and he glanced at her in surprise. She smiled in reassurance and undid the ties on her underdress before letting it drop to the ground, where it pooled at her feet. He could see her body in all its naked splendour, apart from her breasts that were tightly bound, he assumed to prevent her milk from flowing until it was needed. She smiled and undid the band. Her full, heavy breasts sprang free, and his desire grew even more.

Her figure was well-rounded and shaped by her recent pregnancy. Still, she looked as alluring as when he'd first met her, possibly more, for she had now filled out in places where before she'd been a little too skinny. She returned to the side of the bed, her clothing discarded, and his breath caught in his excitement. The sunlight arrayed her skin so that she shone, looking like he'd always assumed an angel from God would.

Æthelflæd took his hands and pulled him to his feet. He obliged and watched as she slowly began to disrobe him, first dragging his tunic over his head and then letting his trousers pool around his own feet. He was glad now that he'd at least managed to remove his heavy boots the night before. They would have made the moment incredibly awkward.

As soon as he was naked, Æthelflæd stepped close enough to him that he could feel the warmth of her body against his own, and he reached out eagerly to touch her and to reacquaint himself with her pliant body. She again giggled and stepped away from him. He looked at her quizzically, and she lowered her eyelashes coquettishly. She was trying to play hard to get, for all that she stood naked in front of him.

He reached out and guided her body firmly back to his so that he crushed her against him. Leofwine touched her lips with his own, and the desire between them instantly reignited. His need was now desperate, and he lifted her against his body, and she wrapped her legs tightly around his waist. As he stumbled his way back towards the bed, his lips staying firmly on hers, his hands exploring the available surfaces of her body; her neck, her back, her shoulders and where he could reach them, the delicious curve of her breasts, from which milk occasionally spilt. She tried to keep his hands away, but he patiently removed hers. He didn't care about the milk, wanting only to hold and touch as much of her as he could. He'd been deprived for long enough of her firm but accommodating body.

He lay her back on the bed gently. He didn't want to hurt her. After all, the babe was only weeks old, but she encouraged him on with her own touches and her groans of pleasure, the passion by no means spent as yet.

HE WOKE LATER TO GENTLE CANDLELIGHT AND THE DYING MUTED colours of the day. He was not aware of having slept so long. It seemed only moments ago that he'd made himself comfortable against his wife, his arms coming from around her back to rest gently on her soft stomach, her shining hair arrayed across his chest.

Now his arms were empty, and his wife again sat in the wooden chair near the fire, which crackled away in the hearth, adding its own dull glow to the dying light of the day. He was half-covered with his fur cloak, and where his skin was exposed, it felt chill, even in the warm room. He must have slept the night and most of the morning away.

He rolled onto his front and watched his wife and son. Æthelflæd smiled at him in a distracted way, and he wondered what had happened to mar the joy she'd shown initially on his return. He opened his mouth to speak, but she forestalled him.

'Your faithful hound has been looking for you. I think he had some concerns about your well-being in my care. What have you been saying about me? I hope it wasn't a concern regarding your injuries, my Lord. I'm sure I made my feelings towards you more than clear before you left on your journey.'

Æthelflæd's tone was acerbic, and he quickly grasped that his fears regarding her feelings for him had been entirely unfounded. Worse, he'd been more than honest with Wulfstan about his worries, and he cringed now at the tone he'd taken with the king and his advisors. All had been more than aware that he'd feared his loss of sight and scarred face would make her renounce her vows to him. He'd been wrong, hideously wrong, and he'd obviously hurt her deeply, and she only knew of his indiscretions voiced to Wulfstan. Leofwine could see that she was offended by his mistrust without another word uttered from her lips.

He rose from the bed, grateful to find his trousers waiting for him, folded neatly over the end of the wooden bed. He shrugged into them and walked the short distance to where Æthelflæd sat, eyes now averted from him, gazing into the fire, which looked to be in need of restocking.

Leofwine was tempted to fulfil the task as a means of distraction but realised it was a further wrong to visit upon his wife. Instead, he went to her side and knelt beside her, taking her hand in his, and examining her long slender fingers, crowned with the shining ruby red ring he'd given her on their wedding day. He would need to see about adding another to it, to mark the birth of their son.

The ring had been placed there by his infatuation for her and the joy that the king had given her to him. It had not been love that had made him gift her such a fabulous ring. Now it would be. He gently twisted the single golden circle from her finger, hearing her gasp of shock as he did so. Leofwine wanted to reassure her, but she'd not meet his eye. He lifted his hands and gently touched her cheek with his finger and turned her face towards his own. She moved it almost unwillingly, still refusing to meet his eye.

'When I was injured,' Leofwine began in a quiet voice, filled with sorrow, 'I feared that I'd die. There was so much blood and pain, and I could see nothing even with my good eye, and I knew that I'd likely die and never see you again, and my heart broke, there and then. The journey back on the ship was in the middle of a terrible storm, and all I could hear was the crash of thunder and the wind rattling the sail and the hard, heavy raindrops on my face. I felt as if they were my tears, as if I was crying for everything I'd had, and that was now lost to me. The storm seemed to last forever, and it was days before we reached dry land.'

'By then, I was so weak that I thought I'd not make it out of the ship alive. Wulfstan kept me going. He talked of you, and he held me through the nights when I shivered uncontrollably with fever, and when I slept, I cried your name in desperation, and he promised he would bring me back to you. My wounds were infected, and the fever racked my body for weeks, and all that time, he spoke of you; spoke your name for me and of my joy of being reunited with you. He never once doubted that you loved me and would love me. I'm afraid that was all me. As I healed and I realised the extent of the damage, that I'd be partially blind, I knew that when I returned, I'd not be the same man as before.'

Here she tried to speak, but Leofwine stopped her with a finger gently placed on her lips, as she'd done to him, only she kissed it in acceptance, her expression rapt as she listened intently to his words.

'I didn't want you to think you had to take me back, and I covered my own fear for the future by doubting you. It was wrong. I see that now. I owe you apologies that words cannot provide. The thought of being with you again kept me going, made me come home, and I love you with the essence of my being, and....'

His words were cut short as she leaned forward and kissed him firmly on his still-moving lips. The kiss started off gently, more reassurance and reaffirmation than anything else. It quickly grew in intensity, and reluctantly he broke away from her and again took her hand in his. He twirled the ring between his fingers and then, having watched the fire dance on the golden surface, placed it gently back on the finger he'd taken it from.

'I'd have given you a choice, and I'd have let you go, but now I see I was wrong. Now, I refuse to let you go. You're mine, and I will keep you always. '

Leofwine's voice sounded rough as he spoke, harsher than he'd intended, and she looked at him in pleased surprise. He reclaimed her lips briefly, wanting to soften the intent and then, his voice cracking with emotion, he whispered, 'I love you, and I need you. You're my healer.'

He kissed her again, and he felt her mouth curved in a

smile. She broke away from him and, in a soft voice, said, 'I love you always, you fool. You should have known that, but I'll forgive you as I thought you dead, and I'm overwhelmed to know that you're here, alive and breathing. Now, go and reassure Wulfstan that you're whole and complete, with your heart intact.'

Her tone was warm and loving, and he smiled, slightly self-depreciatingly in return, which quickly turned into a huge grin, making his scar tug uncomfortably. He ignored it and grabbed for the rest of his clothes. He felt lighter than he had since he'd been injured. There was nothing he could not accomplish as long as he had Æthelflæd, Wulfstan and his son at his side.

'Aren't you coming out as well? I'd like to introduce Wulfstan to my son.'

She smiled in memory at something and said, 'Oh no, Wulfstan has met your son already, and really, I shouldn't be seen in public just yet. You can take him with you, though.'

At that, Leofwine stopped in the act of pulling on his boots. He hadn't yet held his son. Yes, he'd admired him as he lay sleeping last night, and yes, he could see him now, again curled around his mother's breast and sucking noisily, oblivious to the emotions which had so recently charged the room. He'd like to hold him, to feel him real in his hands.

'If you just wait for a few moments, you can take him with you for a bit, and I can clean myself up and make myself more presentable for my Lord's return.'

Æthelflæd's tone was suggestive, and he felt himself stir with desire again. She raised her eyebrows at him as she placed the bundle in his arms. He was distracted from his thoughts of later by the slight weight he now held, and he gazed with wonder at the perfect round face and slight dark curls that framed it. Æthelflæd touched his damaged face gently as she walked past him, and he wondered what she felt as she saw it. She simply said,

'It may take some time to get used to, you know, but you're still a most handsome man. After all, it's only really your cheek that's affected. Your eye, though, will it never heal?' Her tone was matter-of-fact, with no trace of the disgust he'd thought she'd feel, and so he responded accordingly.

'No. Wulfstan sought out every healer we could find on the way back. They all said the same thing. The sight is gone forever. I'm lucky I still have my good eye to be awed by your beauty with.'

She chuckled softly at his attempts to lighten the mood.

'Now off you go. I need to organise a bath and get this fire rebuilt.'

She turned her back to him in dismissal, and he walked to the door he'd eyed so speculatively last night and threw it open. The late afternoon sun infused the hallway, and the serving women who had been gossiping in the corridor jumped guiltily. He smiled brightly at them, pleased to note that while they glanced at his face, they didn't stare for an over-long time.

'I think my lady requires a new fire and a hot bath.'

The women both dipped their heads and mumbled, 'My lord,' before scurrying away on their errands. Leofwine vaguely recalled them as his wife's ladies, but he'd need to make an effort to learn their names.

Leofwine walked the short length of the stone-built corridor and entered the main guest hall of the priory. It was made of stone, the roof stretching far above his head, with intricate stone arches holding the occasional lamp.

Wulfstan sat near the considerable hearth dominating the near wall, ale in his hand and his feet resting on a huge grey hunting hound. As he entered the room, the hound looked immediately towards him and slid energetically out from under Wulfstan's feet to rush to Leofwine.

Leofwine greeted his hunting hound enthusiastically but awkwardly with his one free hand, pleased to see that Æthelflæd had naturally adopted her as part of her household in his absence. Wulfstan was thrust forwards on the chair by the abruptness of the hound's departure, and ale spilt down his front. Horic, at his side, laughed good-naturedly as Wulfstan spluttered. Wulfstan made to stand, but Leofwine made a sit-down motion with his left hand, his right hand tightly holding his son. He walked the short distance to join his men.

A beautifully carved wooden backed chair was placed next to Wulfstan's by Horic, and Leofwine gratefully sat down, wary of carrying his bundle too far on the hard stone floor, dotted here and there with the occasional rug. Sometimes he felt as though he favoured his left side when he walked, and he did keep walking into things. He'd need to be careful when he walked with his son. The boy lay asleep on his arm, and his men came forward to admire him. He was soon stumped by Wulfstan's query of what the child's name was.

'You know Wulfstan. I haven't discussed it with Æthelflæd. I think, for now, we shall just have to call him 'baby'.'

Leofwine laughed in delighted joy, and his men joined him. He could still not believe that he was here now and safe, with assurances from his king that he'd keep his position and an apology from his father-in-law for banishing his wife away to the priory when he'd thought Leofwine dead at the hands of Swein and his shipmen. He had his first child in his arms and a beautiful wife who was waiting for him.

Leofwine's broad smile again split his face, pulling at his scar as Wulfstan pushed the trencher of cold roast meat towards him.

'I saved this from our dinner, my lord. I think that you've failed to break your fast this morning or eat your meal. This might keep your strength up until supper.'

Leofwine grabbed for the food, suddenly ravenous. It had been nearly an entire day since he'd last eaten.

His son slept peacefully in his arms as his men came to examine him. Leofwine smiled at each of them and joined in the good-hearted joking about the time to make more and how enjoyable it could be.

Those of his shipmen who had acted as his temporary war band when he'd returned to England and who had wives and children had not seen them for many a long month as they'd journeyed to see the king at Chelsea and then discovering Æthelflæd gone from the court, had hastened here with their lord. He must not linger too long here. He knew from his own sweet reunion with his wife and son that his men deserved the same opportunity and as soon as possible.

He resolved to speak to Æthelflæd about when she would be ready to travel. Perhaps he should send the men home in advance, especially those with families. They were now deep in his homeland, and it seemed nonsensical to keep the people from further west with him. He should send them on and have them meet up with the other shipmen whom he'd ordered to return to their port.

As Leofwine was pondering his next moves, he noticed

that his men had all risen from their benches and were bowing towards the figure walking towards them. He jumped to his feet, realising that the figure dressed in finest blue cloth was Æthelflæd. She looked freshly washed, with a healthy glow to her cheeks and her luxurious chestnut hair falling in a tight braid down her back.

She acknowledged the men, who then sat at their Lord's distracted command. His mind was centred entirely on the tall, graceful, beautiful woman walking toward him. She had apparently tightly bound her breasts under her dress, as they seemed much smaller than when he'd last seen them, and her overdress fell almost straight to the floor, with only a slight bump at her slightly swollen stomach.

She reached him and curtseyed before him, her eyes downcast and modest. He stepped forward and lifted her gently to his height before kissing her soft cheek and presenting her to his men.

'My men, I reintroduce you to the Lady Æthelflæd, mother of my heir.'

Æthelflæd flushed with pleasure at his proud words, and the men burst into cheers. They had perhaps enjoyed too much mead with their meal, but Leofwine let them give resounding cheers before realising that the still sleeping child he held was growing restless. Then he quieted his men whom all returned to their games and mead. It had been a long few months with little chance to relax since the attack, and he knew that his men were as grateful as he was to finally sleep secure in their beds, even if those beds were not yet at their homes.

Leofwine motioned for Æthelflæd to sit beside him on another wooden backed chair that Wulfstan had found in front of the roaring fire. It had been a beautiful summer day, from what he'd seen of it, but there was now a deep chill in the air.

As Æthelflæd sat, her clothing rustled, and a delicious smell washed over him of summer flowers and freshly grown grass. She still smiled and then inclined her head towards Wulfstan.

'Wulfstan, I believe I owe you somewhat of an apology for my harsh words earlier. My lord has explained himself to me now, and I'm most grateful for your constant attention upon him and for bringing him safely home. As you are no doubt aware, we had been informed at Court that he had perished in the attack.'

Æthelflæd spoke softly but with some heat to her cheeks, and Leofwine couldn't help wondering just what he'd slept through earlier. He knew that neither of them would enlighten him, and so he merely waited for Wulfstan's response.

'My lady, there is no need for apologies. I believe it was simply the stress of not knowing the fate of your husband. I was most remiss. I should have sent a messenger to assure you of his safety, but I thought it too dangerous with the marauders still actively seeking us.'

Again, Wulfstan inclined his head, his tone low and a little guarded. More colour spread over Æthelflæd's cheeks. She must have been more than unreasonable in her earlier demands. Leofwine felt remorse for both his wife and his friend.

When news of his death arrived, her family had abandoned her. It must have been crushing for her, both emotionally and politically. She was a woman more than aware of her importance within the old Hwiccan nobility, and to see it all snatched away on the cusp of her achievement of producing an heir, must have been soul-destroying.

He hoped that somewhere in there, she'd also grieved for him, the man, but knew they'd been married for too short a time for her feelings for him to have developed. Their protestations of love now came from the joy of their unexpected reunion.

For now, Leofwine did not want his wife and his friend to bicker, albeit very politely, about a situation which had arisen because of his ill-counselled ramblings. Luckily, at that moment, his son grumbled, and all attention returned to him. He was not fully awake, and Æthelflæd was served her own meal. The distraction worked, and the tension in the air evaporated. Leofwine was able to turn to his wife and conversationally ask about his son.

'I fear I was a little preoccupied earlier, for I failed to inquire as to my son's name.'

Æthelflæd looked up with shock from her meal of venison and scrutinised his face before responding,

'I may now have inappropriately named him, for he is to be known as Northman, with the hope that he would one day avenge your death at the hands of the Northmen.'

She spoke defiantly, her jaw firm, daring him to contradict her. He didn't need to, for their conversation had been overheard by Horic, who laughed loudly and long at her words. She looked between Leofwine and Horic, unsure who the man was. Leofwine again felt negligent in his duties to his wife before realising that he could not have imagined that such a simple request would cause problems.

'Æthelflæd,' Leofwine began, 'May I introduce to you the man who saved my life with his quick thinking. This is Horic, second to Olaf, and now my own commended man, when I find some land to gift him with.'

Æthelflæd's face really shouldn't have been able to turn any redder with embarrassment, yet somehow it did, and she faltered with her food, looking anywhere but at her husband and Horic.

Horic saved the moment.

'My lady, I fear we Northmen are not all as bad as you believe. For myself, I have decided to adopt the Christian God and your husband as my master and hopefully earn from him the name of Englishman instead of Northman. I think they're all robbing, murderous bastards.'

'It is a fitting name for your son. May he become a warrior akin to his name but tempered with your charming and delicate ways. I will gift to him a sword and promise to teach him to use it when he is older if my lady approves?'

Leofwine cast him a grateful look, and the men at the table, who had ceased in their activities to find out how the situation would resolve itself, returned, once again, to their own meals, drinks or games. Æthelflæd waited a moment and then too returned to her own meal. Leofwine could see the anger and humiliation in her eyes dying down, and he hoped that he would not find himself at the same end of her anger when they were alone again. She was an elegant woman, but the months of stress and thinking him dead had apparently had a detrimental effect on her typical good humour.

Moments passed, and his son stirred in his arms. His mother noticed immediately, and while Leofwine resettled him in a more comfortable position, her eyes strayed to her husband's face and the hideous scar that ran the length of his left side and which he imagined must be harshly cast in the candlelight that surrounded them. She stared for a moment more and then met his eyes, her own looking a little guilty to have been so blatantly caught in the act. He smiled in understanding,

'Believe me, every time I see my own reflection, I do a double take. I'm sure that one day I'll recognise myself again, but I think it'll be a long time.'

Æthelflæd opened her mouth to speak and then closed it abruptly, obviously deciding her words were unsuitable. Leofwine knew that she needed to ask her questions. As had been proved this evening, they'd not survive if they didn't know the truth about each other. He'd have to tell her all the details of his escape and survival. He didn't relish the thought of reliving the many moments he thought his life had nearly ended but realised he had no choice.

With his free hand, he reached toward his wife and tweaked her braid. She turned to look at him, and he used the opportunity to run his hand down her cheek, enjoying the feel of her soft skin and rounded cheek. They still felt a little warm, but her anger had cooled, and she seemed more at ease.

'My lady, I'm unsure when my son was born and how long you'll need to recover before returning home. The men are sick of travelling, and I'd like to make some plans if that's acceptable to you.'

'Your son was born twenty days ago. A Sunday. It was a difficult delivery. He was a big child for all that he was early. The Sisters here offered many prayers for the babe and me, and luckily they must have worked. I had also heard a faint rumour that you were alive and well, my lord, and that lent strength to my endeavours.'

His hand was still cradling her cheek, and he leaned forward and gently kissed it,

'You have my deepest thanks. He's a truly wonderful gift to return home to, and the child grows well. He is surely a handful. We must also thank the Sisters. I'll investigate and see how we can endow their foundation further.' She looked pleased with his words and continued to speak.

'I believe this is the longest he's ever slept away from me. He has lusty lungs and the appetite of a full warrior. All I do is feed him and sleep.'

'Then I'm glad to have returned. I'm sure that between us, we can keep the little brute happy. And you must eat more, or you will lose your lovely curves.'

'It's good to enjoy a full meal,' she offered, busily eating between her words. 'I've been grabbing bits here and there. I think this is my first meal away from my rooms and certainly, the first one to not be interrupted by raucous crying.'

As if on cue, the baby abruptly woke and began yelling at the top of his lungs. Leofwine looked at his son aghast. How could so much noise come from such a small bundle? He looked towards Æthelflæd. Panic etched onto his face, and she finished her mouthful and held her arms out for Northman.

'I'll take him, my lord. I think that he'll probably be more hungry than normal now that he's slept so long. I'll see you in our rooms.'

And with that, she cradled the wailing baby and walked from the great hall. Leofwine rose as she went, as did his men, and only as the wailing disappeared down the corridor, echoing painfully around the stone space, did he regain his seat. He looked to Wulfstan and Horic with dismay.

'Are they always so noisy?' Horic laughed heartily at Leofwine's evident consternation.

'Aye, my lord, they can be. Mind, his lungs are surely huge. I pity you, my lord, while admiring your good fortune. You may not gain much sleep tonight,' Horic announced. Wulfstan unexpectedly joined him in the good-natured banter. Leofwine looked at him in surprise. Could it be that the man had a softer side after all?

6

AD996

Home at last and feeling safe, Leofwine found himself seeking the company of his men that first night. Æthelflæd had worn herself out with her determination to make it home to Deerhurst in only one day. No sooner had she returned and bathed than she'd fallen asleep feeding their son.

Northman, too had bizarrely stayed awake for most of the day, and the old nurse had whispered to Leofwine, her scratchy chin close to his ear, that she didn't doubt the babe would sleep all night for the first time. She'd chuckled and then added that he'd be starving in the morning and none too quiet in his demands. Her plain words had made him chortle in amused outrage at the implication in her words.

Leofwine had found himself too energised to seek his bed and had instead sought the company of his hall and his own men. He was pleased to note that in his absence, his servants and slaves had maintained his home well, seeing to a good and thorough cleansing after the cold and dark winter months and maintaining the wood stores. As

Leofwine had ridden through his fields on the final leg of his journey home, he'd been gladdened by the sight of green shoots showing and the oxen out ploughing the fields that were still brown and barren.

Life had continued regardless of his absence. Leofwine was relieved and a little melancholic at the thought that if he'd died on his journey to the north, none of those he passed by would have been affected in any way other than having a new landlord and owing their sake and soke to another man. Leofwine had shrugged the feeling away. No matter. Today was a time for luxuriating in the sharp early summer air and the thrill of finally being home and on dry land.

His father's house, now his own, was at least a hundred feet long, made of sturdy oaks and roofed in thatch and grass. It was a thing of beauty with a large central wooden door on the side that faced the small trackway that led to it. Leofwine eyed it critically with his restricted sight and found he was pleased with its upkeep.

Neither did it stand alone, having a stable and a smithy close to it as well as more ramshackle dwellings behind it for the servants who had families.

It was situated in the generous curve of a river on a slightly raised hill so that it wouldn't flood. Leofwine had grown up here. It was his home, and it always would be. He appreciated that he'd need to use Æthelflæd's home, part of her wedding gift, for some of the year but for now, he was just heartened by the sight of so much familiarity.

Here he'd not have to worry about furniture inappropriately placed or unknown and uneven floor surfaces. His eye wouldn't trick with shadows and half-light. Leofwine knew the location of all the rickety floorboards and where puddles formed when it rained. He'd be more at ease than at any time since his injury.

Leofwine came upon Wulfstan seated on the benches near his own chair. Only, he shied away from his wooden backed chair and instead inserted himself into Wulfstan's small group of comrades. Most he knew as members of his war band, but there were two he didn't know, and he turned a questioning eye towards Wulfstan. Wulfstan shook his head at his unspoken question, indicating he would explain later, and just introduced the two youths as Wulfhelm and Wulf.

There was something about them that was familiar, and as the evening wore on, as well as the consumption of ale, Leofwine finally put his finger on where he'd seen them before, or rather in whom, for they were surely Wulfstan's own sons. They shared the shape of his face, even though his was hidden by a long beard and unruly, silvering hair. The young men were clean-shaven with flashing grey eyes.

Leofwine was unsure how to approach Wulfstan on the subject. The young men, evidently of an age with him, had been merely introduced by their names, and it was long rumoured that Wulfstan didn't wish to draw attention to anyone sharing a kinship with him. Leofwine was genuinely intrigued. Knowing Wulfstan as he did, there would be a reason for his actions, and he decided to leave it for now. He needn't interfere in Wulfstan's affairs.

Leofwine was shocked, though. He'd not known that Wulfstan had his own children. He'd considered it before but had never voiced his questions.

Eventually, the rest of the men took their leave and retired to their beds or chose to lie on the wooden floor closest to the central hearth, including the two strangers.

Wulfstan made no effort to move, and Leofwine remained sitting with him. There was silence apart from the odd crackle from the fire and soft snores emanating from those who already slept within the hall.

Wulfstan's eyes were glazed from too much ale, and Leofwine was none too sober either. Leofwine didn't speak, content to enjoy the silence. Finally, the comfort and quietness of his home lulled him, his eye closed, and he slumped forwards, head on the arms where they rested on the table, and slept.

Leofwine woke sometime later, in the predawn light, as he felt soft hands around his neck and a fur blanket being gently wrapped around him. He blearily opened his eyes and saw that Wulfstan was still wide-awake, staring into space. He, too, had a warm fur around his shoulders but didn't seem to be aware of the soft covering around him, even as a servant noisily prodded the fire into life.

Nor had Wulfstan noticed that Æthelflæd had joined Leofwine and sat inside the fur cover with him, her gentle hands tracing the lines of his face, a look of tenderness on her face. He raised his head from the table and gently took her hands in his. They didn't speak, just shared a conspiratorial smile. He placed his arm around her shoulders, and she leaned into him. He inhaled deeply of her aroma of an early summer day and sleep. She looked fresh, and he hoped she'd rested well after their journey.

A few loud crackles came from the fire as more logs were added to it. When the quiet of the predawn had been restored, Wulfstan began to speak in a low, urgent voice, his voice rough.

'I'm sure you've guessed, but these young men are my sons, born of my wife before you were born. Your father and mother knew of them, although I'm aware you were probably ignorant. They're good boys and always have been. They honour me although their mother does not, and all these years, they've stood by her and cared for her.'

'They've come to me now with grave news of her ill health and have begged for my help. I don't know what to do. She's always been a cantankerous woman. I was attracted to her because of it. I thought I'd be able to tame her wild ways, and for a time, I thought I had.'

'I was wrong. When your father and mother married, my wife became unbearable and used her marriage rights to dissolve our marriage. I supported her, but I wasn't allowed to visit, and so I became your father's commended man. As the boys grew, they'd sneak out and visit me, and my old neighbours helped as much as they could. Even so, it's been difficult.'

'She'd not let them train to be fighting men, and they loved her too much to go against her wishes. So they're farmers through and through, but the land they work is poor, and she'll not live on my property. I've strangers who work it for me. It's ridiculous, but I can't force her, and now the boys have come to tell me that she's sick.'

'She was afflicted by some ailment that laid her low for days, and now she's even more unreasonable, and she's lost the use of her right arm. They fear for her, and so do I. I've always loved her for all that she'll no longer have me. I've had no other woman since.'

'She doesn't want the boys with her anymore and has sent them to me. But she can't look after herself. I'm heartsick and powerless. The boys say she lives in squalor and cares more for her lands than she does for herself. What am I to do?' His voice cracked in despair.

Leofwine was thunderstruck. He'd not known that Wulfstan carried such worries with him. He speculated, not for the first time, what else he didn't know about his friend. Leofwine decided there and then that he'd make more effort to draw his friend out and learn about his past.

Æthelflæd stirred against his side, and he looked briefly at her. She was gazing intently at Wulfstan, her expression pensive. When she spoke, her voice was charismatic. 'Have there been rumours about her? Do people talk about her? What are your real fears?'

Wulfstan glanced sharply at her, his expression intent as if he tried to decipher the meaning behind her words just by looking at her. When he spoke, his tone was matter-of-fact.

'There have been rumours about her, yes. But in the past, they've been manageable, for she always went to church and observed the Saint's Days. Now she does neither, and I'm only too aware of the damage she does to herself,' Wulfstan's tone turned steely. 'I'll protect her whether she wants me to or not.'

Leofwine wasn't sure what they were talking about, and he looked questioningly at his young wife. She shook her head at him, so he didn't ask his question outright. Instead, he joined the conversation.

'Is your land nearby, or rather, your lady's land? Does it owe its tithes to me or to another?'

'It's another, my Lord. It's land from her own family and is further west.'

'Do you commend yourself to that Lord, or do your sons?'

'It's always been my wife who commended herself. Though now, I don't know what will happen. I fear he'll demand she gives up her land if it's not being managed correctly. I'll need to set the boys on my own land here.

Wulfhelm has a family to support and can't be without land to farm, or his family will starve.'

'Have you considered sending her to the monastery? Surely they'll care for her there, and then the boys could farm the land.'

Wulfstan looked pained at the idea, and Leofwine opened his mouth to utter another solution, but Æthelflæd lightly touched his arm to forestall him.

'I'll think on this, Wulfstan. I'm sure there must be a solution; it simply eludes me at the moment. I'd suggest you take no action immediately. There's time yet.'

And with that, Æthelflæd rose from the table, taking the fur with her still wrapped around her narrow shoulders. Leofwine shivered as the chill air of the morning attacked his suddenly exposed body. She stood by him and eyed him with a meaningful look. She was waiting for him. Rising clumsily from the bench, Leofwine hastened to join her, although his leg was stiff from sitting down for too long.

Leofwine turned to speak to Wulfstan, but Wulfstan was locked deep in his own thoughts again. He decided not to speak as he could do little but offer platitudes, and his friend deserved more than that.

As Leofwine half staggered to his private room, his hound rose from her disturbed sleep by the rekindled fire and brushed past his leg to beat him to his room. The movement inadvertently knocked him off balance, and Leofwine struggled to right himself in the slowly easing gloom of predawn. He cursed quietly under his breath. His loss of eyesight was deeply problematic when the lighting was dim.

He'd hoped that here, in his own home, he'd not be beset by problems of balance. He was disappointed to have been proved wrong so soon.

Eyeing his hound, Hunter, with some annoyance, Leofwine was struck by the thought that perhaps it was merely about training. He'd have to teach her to watch her steps more closely. The idea brought him comfort, and he gladly slipped into bed beside his warm and pliant wife.

He'd barely closed his eye when a loud, raucous cry echoed around his private room. He groaned and was relieved to feel Æthelflæd slide gently from the bed to hush his hungry son. There were a few near frantic moments before he heard hasty snuffling and the greedy gulps of his boy.

'Go to sleep, my lord. I'm sure you're no good to anyone half dead with lack of it,' Æthelflæd whispered to him. Too exhausted to reply, Leofwine resettled himself into the warm bed and let sleep take him. His home had survived almost a year without him, and he was sure another day would make little difference. Still, he didn't wish to sleep the day away and hoped that Æthelflæd would wake him before night fell again. He didn't intend to let his days and nights muddle as they had during his illness.

Leofwine got his wish, as sometime later, he felt soft hands shake him roughly and then gentle kisses trail across his face. He smiled as he woke, enjoying the comfort that only came when he was home.

The air reverberated with the noises of his household, and through the sturdy wooden walls, he could hear the soft shuffle of the horses and the scampering feet of the hens as they moved around outside. Leofwine reached out to touch Æthelflæd's face, but she was gone, distracted by the quiet whimpers of his son, her back to him, and her attention on the cradle, she spoke.

'My lord, I think you should wake. Your men believe that

you've disappeared and I, for one, am more than ready for my dinner. The young man keeps draining me dry, and I must keep my strength up.'

Æthelflæd's tone was light and teasing, but for all that, he knew she was right. His eye still felt heavy from lack of sleep, but he'd have to see to that later by sleeping at a reasonable time. His body was only recently healed, and he couldn't undo all the long, slow months of recuperation by messing it all up now.

Leofwine sat upright on the bed and swung his legs clear. Æthelflæd returned to him, their son again in her arms.

'Besides, you have a visitor, and Wulfstan hasn't been seen since early morning.'

Both reports were unwelcome, and Leofwine couldn't suppress a groan as he stepped into his trousers and bent to pull on his boots. The hound came and stuck her face in the way of his hands, and he good-naturedly moved her away. She stalked off, and he was struck again by his thoughts of last night while being grateful that even in his long absence, her loyalty towards him hadn't diminished.

'Who's my visitor? I assume someone I probably don't want to see as you're not telling me who it is until I'm dressed.'

She turned to face him and offered a small smile,

'How well you know me already, Leofwine. I think, perhaps, I'll let you wait and see now.' Her voice was airy and tinged with humour. He groaned deeply in response.

'It must be someone I don't want to see. Just assure me that it's not the abbot. I don't think I can face the abbot today.'

Æthelflæd walked towards where he was shrugging on his tunic, and she lightly touched his face.

'I only wish I could.'

Now his groan was heartfelt, and Æthelflæd giggled at the pained expression on his face.

'I've been home for barely a day. What does he want?' Leofwine whispered over loudly.

'What holy men always want, only now, I think he may have a good point to make, and I believe that you might not be able to refuse him.'

'Ah, you wake me from my sleep under false pretences, and then you play the coquette with me when you obviously know what he wants and why he's here. You're a terrible wife.'

She gave him a mock look of horror at his slightly aggrieved words and shrugged a shoulder even more coquettishly.

'I wasn't aware that there was a list of acceptable and unacceptable guests to this house. Perhaps, if you informed me, I could turn them away at the door at your insistence.'

He groaned even louder now, looking to her for some pity but seeing none on her teasing face.

'Come on, let's get this over and done with and then, maybe, I can enjoy my dinner too.'

'You needn't fear so. The good man is staying for his dinner.'

'Of course,' Leofwine muttered darkly, 'Of course he is. Well, maybe we should get there first before he eats the whole bloody lot.'

This time, Æthelflæd's peal of laughter was long and loud, and he stood abruptly and kissed her almost roughly on the lips to silence her. Still, her eyes danced with merriment, and he turned to walk away dejectedly. At least he'd get it over and done with.

And then he tripped over Hunter, who'd been lurking around the corner, and he fell, heavily, to the floor. Æthelflæd let out a small scream of shock, and the dog squealed as Leofwine just managed to avoid landing entirely on her and caught only her back leg. Instantly he manoeuvred himself off her, and she skulked around to breathe in his face, contrition in her actions.

'Come on, silly girl. It's not your fault, but we're going to have to work something out to stop that from happening again.' Leofwine stroked her head as he worked his own legs straight, barely managing to hold back a loud curse.

There was a polite cough from behind their closed door, and Æthelflæd recovered enough to shout an assurance that all was well. She bent to help him up, and he took her hand willingly before pulling a little harder on her hand and propelling her into his lap. She chuckled as she fell towards him, clutching the baby tightly, and he caught her effortlessly and planted a kiss on her forehead.

'And you, you can stop panicking every time I fall over or trip or make a fool of myself. It'll take me time to get used to my lack of sight, but I have an idea that the damn dog might be able to help me if she ever stops getting in the way. Now come on, the Abbot is waiting and is probably wondering what we're doing in here and looking all disapproving.'

Æthelflæd kissed him on the nose as she stumbled to her feet and looked a little shamefaced before squaring her shoulders in defiance.

'Well, I'll stop squealing when you stop falling.' She

glared at him, daring him to defy her words, and he held her gaze steady for a few moments, and then he stuck his tongue out at her and lurched to his feet and scampered through the doorway in a way he expected his son to do one day.

He patently ignored her huff of annoyance as he straightened his dishevelled tunic. The dog slinked out too, and he called her to his side. She came briskly toward him, and together they walked the short distance to where the abbot was indulging in a goblet of fine wine.

The Abbot stood to greet him, a wild smile of welcome on his standard ramrod straight face. Leofwine paused briefly as he walked towards the man, an equally broad smile on his face but one that was usually there. What was this? A new way to beguile more land and grants out of him? The abbot didn't even flinch at the sight of the ragged wound that sliced Leofwine's face almost in half and which caused his smile to feel and appear lopsided.

As the Abbot effusively greeted him, Leofwine heard a soft tread behind him, and Æthelflæd joined the small group. He looked around for Wulfstan but didn't see him with the other men who were waiting for their dinner somewhat impatiently. Horic offered Leofwine a smile of welcome and a slightly sardonic nod towards the abbot. Leofwine tried not to grin in response and turned to listen to the abbot who was praising the Lord for his safe and miraculous return.

Now Leofwine realised what the man was here for, and he turned amused eyes towards Æthelflæd, who was demurely listening to the abbot. He wondered if this was something that they'd already communicated about, only perhaps concerning the birth of his son before she knew he'd lived.

Leofwine was going to have to watch her if she thought it was acceptable to give thanks to God for anything by giving away all their land to the church. They already took much of his portable wealth, and while he realised it would be expected of him to reward the Church, he'd need to get something in return. Perhaps here, he could assist Wulfstan with the problem of his long-ago wife. He wondered again why Wulfstan had disappeared.

Leofwine's servants worked quietly around him, serving the dinner and ale to all within the room. He drank from his own elaborately decorated and bejewelled flagon with relish. He was thirsty after his interrupted night's sleep, and his stomach rumbled in anticipation. His wife was speaking co-conspiratorially to the priest, and he realised it was probably in his best interests to listen to their conversation. He was also mulling over which land he could gift to the Abbot if he chose to.

While he'd been endowed with a certain amount of land by the king when he became ealdorman, much of the land around his father's old home he held on his own and, as such, was able to disperse it as he saw fit, without asking the king for permission. Leofwine hoped it was some of this land that the Abbot would be sated with. He didn't relish the thought of protracted negotiations with the king about gifting land the king classified as his own.

Indeed, the king was only recently reconciled with many of the country's churchmen following certain infringements of their rights while the king had been a youth and unable to govern fully in his own name. Leofwine knew, without having to give it much thought, that any gift to the abbot would have to come from his family's landed interests.

Leofwine wondered if he could merely gift a small piece of land close to the Church that could then be used to increase the consecrated burial grounds, but immediately he thought better of it. For his life, he'd need to make a significant gesture, not a few plough lengths but perhaps the area that could be worked by oxen in a few days or maybe even a week.

Æthelflæd was wrapped up in conversation with Abbot Cenhelm discussing the changes he was planning on making to the interior of his Church and the items he felt he needed to add to it. Cenhelm was quite animated when he talked about the possibility of obtaining a new relic for the church and often mentioned the protracted discussions taking place between him and the Priory that currently held the piece. There was mention of land and exchange, and Leofwine groaned inwardly. The abbot had plainly decided that Leofwine was the person to assist in the purchase of the piece.

It was evident Cenhelm was after his weighty support as opposed to more land, although Leofwine was sure that at some point in the future, money or property would also become attached to his name.

Leofwine sighed inwardly. He was a deeply religious man himself, and yet he didn't necessarily agree with the vast wealth the Church already hoarded and the great stock all churchmen placed in relics and pilgrimage.

For himself, he believed firmly in his God, and he felt it was enough to live a Christian life. He didn't think that he had to buy remission for his sins. Æthelflæd knew his feelings on the subject because they'd briefly discussed it. However, she'd assured him that it was the duty of rich young ealdormen and thegns to gift to the Church.

Leofwine had not informed her that it was this portable wealth that the Raiders he'd encountered sought and that all they were doing was allowing the problem to develop and the raids to escalate by continually gifting more and more to the religious houses.

Perhaps, when they'd spent more time together, he'd have a reasoned discussion with her about it. As Leofwine watched her now, delicately picking at her platter of roasted fish and with a heightened intensity about her as she spoke of the possible gifts she could procure for the church, he didn't think that he would ever convince her to do otherwise.

Leofwine ate carefully but quickly, refraining from stuffing the delicious trout into his mouth. The fish was so well cooked it crumbled at his touch, and he noticed with not a little humour that the abbot, stick thin as he was, had already devoured one fish and was moving swiftly onto the next. Leofwine envied him for his ability to eat so much without gaining weight, for all that he spent long hours within his Church both sermonising and writing, and little time practising his fighting skills.

The fish was accompanied by servings of a mix of early summer vegetables, deliciously seasoned with herbs from the small garden that his servants and slaves cultivated near to the river bend. He assumed his fish had been freshly caught that morning in the nets that were routinely strung along the curve of the river.

Wulfstan took that moment to walk through the door-way. His expression was sour, and he cast barely a glance at Leofwine before sitting with the men at the end of the bench.

Horic shuffled along to make room for him without

comment, and Leofwine purposefully did not call him over. Wulfstan seemed to have the cares of the world on his shoulders, and the quick way he ate his fill and then departed again made Leofwine realise he'd only come to sate his hunger. Wulfstan had no intention of making small talk with the abbot, whom he didn't seem to get on with.

Leofwine was not a little jealous. He wished to distance himself from the meeting in a similar way. He'd much rather be out and about, surveying his property and seeing where repairs needed to be carried out on the roads and bridges which crisscrossed his land and helped all his tenants to traverse the river.

'My lord, my lord Leofwine, I must beg your pardon. I hadn't realised that you only returned yesterday. Otherwise, I'd not yet have come calling on you.'

The Abbot's sincere voice penetrated his reverie, and Leofwine turned a smile towards the man.

'It's of no great concern. I'm well rested from my journey home, having first visited the king at Chelsea and then finding Æthelflæd not there; I travelled to retrieve her from the nunnery at Winchcombe.'

'Of course, my lord, of course. However, news of your survival reached me nearly a week ago, and I wrongly assumed that you'd come straight home. I visited merely with the intention of wishing you well but also begging for details of your survival from yourself. I appreciate that now is perhaps not the best of time.'

Leofwine appraised the man before him. He didn't look calculating, simply intrigued, as did Æthelflæd, and he supposed it was perhaps better to get the retelling out of the way sooner rather than later. He would, however, have felt better with Wulfstan at his side.

Leofwine turned to where the remaining men of his war band were joking and laughing as they ate, and he caught sight of Horic again. Perhaps he would help him fill in the gaps? Calling his servant, he bid her ask Horic to join them and proceeded to explain to him what he wanted. Horic frowned at his words, a facial expression Leofwine had not seen on the jovial man before. He was lost in thought for a few moments and then shrugged his shoulders in acquiescence.

'Aye, my lord. I'll do my best to help you out with some of the details, but mind, much of it must be your recounting.'

Leofwine grunted quietly in agreement and took some time to collect his thoughts. He felt Hunter press closer to his leg and soft hands clasp his own suddenly lifeless ones, and then he began to speak, his voice quiet and clear for all that it was about to tell of his worst moments.

'We'd sailed to the farthest of the Outer Isles, the Mainland of Shetland, in poor weather, as there was little wind, but made good time nonetheless. I was aboard Olaf's ship while Wulfstan commanded my own. I didn't enjoy the journey at all, feeling not a little seasick even though the ship barely bobbed in the becalmed water.'

Horic chuckled at his words and interjected.

'Aye, it's perhaps the smoothest crossing I've ever had, but then, I'm used to the mighty waves of the great ocean, and you, my lord, are used to nothing more than a river.' Horic smiled as he spoke, taking the edge from his words. Horic had often teased all of the English men on their journey home when they'd been ravaged by terrible storms, and all had felt seasick. None had been able to walk around the deck as nonchalantly as the giant northern man.

'I was pleased to see dry land, and that first night, we

feasted in the hall of a great Northern Jarl by the name of Sigurd. I confess, it was a pagan festival, and a skald recited many ancient tales of the Northerners, and there was a horde of people all eating and drinking and mildly interested in us. But nothing more.'

'We slept late the next day, overwhelmed with too much mead and fine food, and then Olaf announced that we would return to Sigurd's hall as he wished to discuss his conversion to Christianity with him. All seemed to be fairly cordial in tone, and again we enjoyed a fine feast and the words of a wonderful poet. Not that I understood his words, but the way he spoke them conjured up images that told their story in my head.'

'He told the tales of the Pagan Gods and the World Tree, and he did a mighty fine job of it as well.' Horic provided, by way of an explanation.

'Unbeknown to me, that night, Olaf and Sigurd quarrelled violently about Sigurd's possible conversion. All I heard was a few raised voices, but I understand now that we left the feast that night under less than cordial terms so that when we returned the next night again, Sigurd had called on some of his allies.'

'While we feasted and drank and listened to more fantastic tales, Swein of Denmark and his ship army descended on us from some of the Inner Isles. By chance, they'd been there, and when Sigurd had sent word of his by now unwelcome guests, Swein had been only too pleased to respond.'

I don't know if he was aware that we were there as well, but in the fighting that ensured I was injured and escaped only through the efforts of the appropriately named Axe who hewed a hole in the wall of the Jarl's great farmhouse. We snuck back to our ships as though we were criminals, and then the winds and the rain came, and Olaf left us there with Horic to guide us home. Thankfully. I think we would still be less than halfway home if it had not been for his sea knowledge, and I'd probably have been dead.'

'Knowing that Olaf had gone north and that Swein had probably already gone that way, we set off for the inner Isles of Orkney. I remember little of the journey, for I spent it bleeding and in pain, lying in the ship as it was tossed about by a storm which had been threatening for days.'

'Horic and Wulfstan rallied the men and carved us a path through the seas. I remember none of it, only pain and agony. The next thing I knew, I was alone in a darkened room, and there I stayed, ministered to by a healer from the islands until my fever had passed and my wounds had started to heal.'

'She stopped my eye wound from festering and destroying my face further, and she attempted to save my sight. None were allowed to bring bright lights near me, and so I spent what felt like months and months in semi-darkness, barely able to move and with only Wulfstan or Horic for company. The rest of the men made themselves useful around the strange little community who'd helped me. Only when I was recovering was I allowed to walk outside and see where I was.'

'Indeed, my lord, and you were a crotchety and ill-tempered patient. Be warned, my lady, if he's ever ill under your ministrations, he's an ungrateful fool.'

Leofwine smiled sadly at Horic's words.

'Indeed, I am. Not that I remember much of it. Often I didn't know if I lived or died, if I was dreaming or awake, and if you were really with me or not, Æthelflæd. I felt lost and alone and with only the gentle words of the healing woman to guide me, and when I became violent, Wulfstan would sit with me and tell me of you, my lady. He was exquisite at describing you and telling me how I must live so that I could see my child. He was much more than just my commended man during those days, and so were all the men.'

'Well, not quite *all* of them, my lord,' the stress clearly on the word 'all'.

Now Leofwine laughed out loud, the visions of his near-deathbed temporarily forgotten.

'The poor man couldn't help it. That vixen of a woman smote him, and he cared more for her than for me, but I don't blame him. She was a lovely thing.'

Æthelflæd shot a meaningful glare at him and indicated the Abbot to the side of her. Leofwine offered a small apology and explained that they'd been forced to leave behind Sigurd for he'd been too enamoured with a girl from the village, and she'd refused to leave her family.

'Let's just be pleased that he found happiness, even if it felt like the end of the world to us. The place where we stopped was known to Horic, or rather vaguely known through such a complicated arrangement that I'm still unsure how you think yourself related to them.'

'Well, my lord, on the Inner and Outer Isles, it's always necessary to claim a kinship of sorts, no matter how long-winded it might be. The be-all and end-all were that I had stopped there before with Olaf, and I might also have gifted them some of your treasure, and your men helped re-turf the structure.'

'So, it wasn't just an act of good faith?'

'Absolutely not. I had to barter hard and fast to get us taken in there.'

'I can't deny that we must have been a massive burden for them. Did we double the numbers in their homes?'

'I'd say so, and with it, we doubled their need for food but added our strength and skills. We were lucky the weather wasn't more bitter.'

Horic spoke with a twinkle in his eye for a good reason, as the weather had been horrendous. The storm had raged for almost as long as Leofwine's fever, and as soon as it had gone, a deep chill had settled over the land, which had forced all the men to wear all their clothes all at once.

'Sorry to interrupt, but can you describe the place for me? I'm very anxious to know how our heathen neighbour lives.'

Horic spluttered into the drinking horn at the abbot's fascinated words.

'I can describe it, of course, but you need to realise that they're as interested in their Gods as you are in your God. They're as deeply reverent as you, my good man. Only they serve many Gods and not just your Lord God.'

The Abbot looked even more intrigued now, and Horic swallowed a mouthful from the drinking horn before passing it on to Leofwine. Then he opened his mouth and began to build a picture of their lodging.

'We came across the place as I was seeking shelter from the rolling seas. There had been many, many islands I could have chosen, but I wanted to choose somewhere that I knew to be more sheltered from the sea.'

'As such, when I reached the Inner Isles, I directed the ship to be pulled around the tip of Mainland Orkney, and we sailed through a tricky patch of the sea for all that there was another island besides us and another one situated between the two. The currents were wicked, but soon I'd managed to steer the ship towards a beautiful sandy bay, and from there, it was but a small walk to the village I vaguely recalled.'

'We were pelted with rain as we walked; Leofwine stretched out on three shields which we lashed together. He was mumbling and incoherent, but I was determined to get him to the warmth and shelter I'd seen.'

'A few of the men came to greet us, loosely armed with spears and daggers, but when they took in our bedraggled state, they ran on and made us welcome within the small village. It was built of old stone and must have been there for many long years. The stones were only thin, but they used them as a decent wall, and then they built up through layer upon layer to form the chief's house, and they were roofed with thatch.'

'The chief's house was on different levels with stairs leading upwards. Leofwine was taken up these stairs and tended to. It was dark and smoky on the lower floor, with a fire and a pit for keeping fish under the wooden floorboards. There were a further five or six houses nestled close to the main one.'

'Each house had beds of stone, a small hearth and most curiously, small pools that they kept filled with seawater and stored fish within. I thought it a strange thing to do until I realised that some days it was impossible to fish because of the strong current and the terrible winds, and therefore it was best to have a store of food within the houses.'

'They all spoke a dialect of the Northern tongue, and I could make myself understood and explain who we were and what we wanted. And there we spent the terrible winter months. The rains lashed the houses, and the wood and peat became damp and smoked, and still, they did not demand we leave and neither did I. Better to be a little cold and wet than dead at the bottom of the sea.'

'And I was oblivious to most of what went on,' Leofwine interjected. 'Slowly, I healed, and slowly, the year began to pass. In the darkest days of winter, word came that Swein was looking for me, knowing that I had escaped.'

'When the news was brought to Wulfstan and Horic, they weren't asked to leave even though it was evident that the people who sheltered us were unhappy that we might have brought a war to their door. Instead, we moved on, taking the healer with us, and found refuge in another village similar to the one we'd been using. Only this one was abandoned and hidden on the near side of one of the other islands.'

'We hoped that its remoteness would prevent Swein from finding us, and we were lucky enough that it worked. The men kept constant guard, and there was the tiniest harbour possible where we were able to draw our ship inside it so as to be hidden from the sea. It could have worked both ways. It could have been our downfall if Swein had come and blockaded the small space. Luckily, he didn't come, but we were effectively marooned waiting for me to recover enough to risk a run for home.'

'Yes, my lord, and Wulfstan was like a bear with a sore head. He couldn't rest and prowled endlessly around our confined quarters. Every slap of the waves and every screech of a seabird sent him running to check that attack was not imminent.'

'I must confess that he sorely tried the patience of us all. It was a combined relief whenever he sat down and slept but a torture when he awoke and realised he'd been less than vigilant. In my defence, I ensured I was always alert when he slept. I wasn't about to let Swein capture us, and nor were the rest of the men. None of us much fancied a sword fight when we'd managed to survive for so long.'

'In the darkest of days, at the turning of the year, we were all struck down by some form of contagion which left us shivering in all the clothes we possessed and then casting them aside only moments later. We coughed, and we sweated, and we sneezed, and we croaked, and the healer cared for us all without complaint. The only ones to stay free of the contagion were Leofwine and the healer, and I think that was because they did not go outside at all. They didn't endure the freezing winds followed by the indoor heat.' Horic ended almost with a question, lost in thought.

'When they were all well again, I was finally deemed healed enough to begin moving around. We'd heard new rumours of Swein, and this time, the healer asked us to leave. She didn't want any more trouble for her people and could only hope that they'd not been discovered as our saviours. We watched her sail away in a tiny fishing vessel she'd summoned from her village across the narrow sea, and when she sailed out of sight, we turned in the opposite direction. We heard nothing more from her or her people.'

'I still wasn't fully healed, although my physical wounds had long since knit over. My dreams were filled with night-mares, and I was weak and seasick. To prevent undoing all the good that my months of inactivity had done, we were forced to make short journeys and find shelter where we could. Luckily, the outer isles are littered with caves and long abandoned shelters. Still, it was a long and painful process for the men as much as for me. We relied exclusively on Horic's knowledge.'

'And sometimes it was misremembered,' Horic commented sourly.

'Yes, sometimes it wasn't correct, but still, we're here, aren't we? And only thanks to you.'

Horic looked a little taken aback by the unexpected praise.

'Well, I'd not considered it like that.'

'No, I didn't think you had. You and Wulfstan are very alike, you know, both far too keen to blame yourselves when things don't quite go as you've planned. You don't appreciate that you still accomplish what you set out to do.'

Horic shrugged in embarrassment at the praise, and Æthelflæd smiled at his obvious discomfort. Horic shot her a glance, and she instantly sobered.

'You have my heartfelt thanks for all you did in ensuring he came home,' Æthelflæd said with grave seriousness.

Now Horic looked even more embarrassed, and Leofwine found himself grinning at the man's discomfort as his face coloured the brightest red, and he fumbled the drinking horn, splashing himself with the ale. Leofwine relieved him of the drinking horn as he spluttered and stood to allow the fluid to drip onto the floor.

At that moment, Wulfstan re-entered the room and walked towards them, a quizzical look on his face at the scene before him. Horic stepped aside as if to move away, but Wulfstan beckoned him to stay.

'We were just trying to offer an accounting of what happened to us after we were attacked,' Leofwine offered by way of explanation, 'and Æthelflæd was thanking Horic, which caused him some embarrassment.'

A ghost of a smile crossed Wulfstan's tired-looking face.

'Indeed, without him, I'd not have known where to look for help.'

Leofwine looked at him in concern. Wulfstan seemed maudlin that day. Naturally, worry for his sons gnawed at him. Horic took heart from the other man's thanks, and a great smile covered his face, replacing the self-consciousness that had been there previously.

'And I'll need to reward you with a little more than silver armbands, which I see you wearing most handsomely. Perhaps now that we're safely home, and all is well, you'll reconsider my offer to become my thegn. I hope you can see that I do have the requisite wealth to support you.'

Horic looked Leofwine straight in the face as he instantly sobered.

'It would be my greatest honour.'

'And obviously, I'll gift you with land to allow you to meet the requirement for the status of a thegn.'

'Land, my lord. Why ever do I need land if I'm to be your thegn?'

Leofwine was surprised by Horic's question.

'It's part of our laws. Our thegns must hold at least five hides of land, and I must in turn gift you with horse, saddle, helmet, byrnie, spear and shield.'

'It seems like a great deal to gift me with.'

'Not at all, not at all. For the man who guided me home, nothing is too much. Have the other thegns not spoken to you of their commitments to me and mine to them? I'm surprised, but I suppose, like me, they simply assumed you knew. But for now, I'll think of where your land can be, and I'll ask Wulfstan to instruct the smith to outfit you. And for you, abbot, we must discuss how I can best endow your monastery as a thank you for my safe return.'

The Abbot bowed deeply at his words and opened his mouth to speak, but Leofwine forestalled him.

'I'd like to see some more of my lands if no one has further need of me here. My lady, will that be acceptable?'

'Of course, my lord, but please take some of the men with you. The Raiders have been coming ever closer, and I'd not like you to take any risks. And you should take Horic with you, too. Perhaps he may have an idea of what land he'd like. Only take Wulfstan, too, as he will stop you from gifting excessively, as is your way. I'll discuss options with the Abbot about how we obtain this relic he so desires.'

Instantly Æthelflæd turned back to the Abbot and began a complicated discussion with him. Leofwine bowed slightly to her back, accepting she'd dismissed him, and sent his servant to fetch his great cloak. He could feel the chill air even inside his home every time the door opened and shut. Calling his hound to him, he stepped carefully outside and felt a little warmth from the sun on his face.

Wulfstan had gone ahead to see to the saddling of the horses, and for a few moments, Leofwine just took in his surroundings before him. To the left of his doorway were about five buildings, with their foundations dug deep into the earth, which the servants used to store grain and carry out any activity they didn't wish to do outside or inside the hall itself.

Leofwine could hear the grate of the quern stones as they ground the wheat and the soft conversation of two of the women as they sorted through what provisions were left from the last winter, deciding whether they were good enough to keep or whether they should be fed to the pigs. For now, the pigs had been guided toward the woodland not far from the house.

A few small children ran around in the area enclosed by the ditch playing, and Leofwine watched them wistfully, remembering his carefree days and wondering when his son would be joining in with them.

It was a beautiful early summer's day with the smell of fresh growth and dampness all around. The sun was a pleasant warmth on his back, and when Wulfstan had the horses brought round, they were a little frisky and keen.

Once mounted, Leofwine kicked his horse to a walk and followed the path that led to the open gateway. He'd decided he wished to ride across his lands, and he felt confident enough with Wulfstan, Horic and a few others of his men to do so. Hunter followed him as well, no doubt keen for the exercise.

Leofwine chose to ride the path that followed the river back upstream, in the opposite direction to the way he'd travelled yesterday. Before he'd gone away, one of the wealthiest thegns had been having a water mill built, and he had a fancy to see if it was complete, as well as to scout out any changes that the long winter may have inflicted on the people who called him Lord, and their land. It would be better to know now if there was likely to be any shortfall in the harvest so that he could start to plan for the coming year.

The men behind him murmured amongst themselves as they allowed the horses a lazy walk. It had been some time since any of them had ridden their beasts, having left them behind when they'd travelled with Olaf. Leofwine would need to ensure the horses the king had lent him to journey home were returned sooner rather than later. He wondered if Horic would like the honour of the trip. He'd have to send him with another, though, as he'd not know the way to the king's stables at Wantage.

Leofwine had found the king at Chelsea on his return, but it was not there that he would want his horses returning to him. The king would be moving onto another of his residences now that he'd called together his witan and arranged for a review of his laws to be undertaken next year and for his coinage to be recalled.

Leofwine had played very little part in the proceedings, much of the work already having been conducted. His king had, however, insisted that he take a higher honour in ratifying the charters from the witan, well, some of them at least, while Ælfhelm of Northumbria had been temporarily either absent from the witan or out of sorts with his king.

Ælfhelm had been restored soon enough, and the king had forgotten his initial delight at Leofwine's recovery and pushed him further down his witness list. Leofwine had not been too concerned. He'd merely wanted to leave as soon as possible to seek out his wife.

He'd been a little mollified to know that while his wife had been sent away from Court, he'd not himself yet been replaced. Perhaps, with Æthelflæd out of the way, it had been easier to think that Leofwine was maybe coming back.

That said, Æthelred was not always the most dynamic of rulers. It had taken him many years to name an ealdorman for the Hwicce. Leofwine wondered if he'd initially planned on giving the position to his father and had then needed to reconsider in the wake of his untimely death. Or perhaps, after all, he'd merely seen in Leofwine a willing tool to do his work in getting rid of Olaf.

Whatever it was, the king had reconfirmed Leofwine in his position gladly enough, making it known to all that his infirmity did not preclude him from being an Ealdorman. In fact, if anything, his wound made him more credible and able to offer a more reliable opinion on the Raiders and their desires and needs. Leofwine wondered how long that would last.

For now, he pushed the thoughts aside. He was home and almost whole. The future he'd hoped for was still before him and achievable. Leofwine was more than happy as he let the sunlight warm his face.

7
AD996

The summer began in earnest once he was home, and Leofwine found himself spending hours with his son, his wife, and, when they slept, with Hunter. He was determined to train her to help guide him in places he didn't know well.

It was a long and fruitless attempt at first. Hunter simply refused to walk before him, having been trained from a young age that her place was behind her master. Leofwine almost gave up on the attempt on numerous occasions, but every time he did, he slipped or tripped or walked through a muddy puddle, which Hunter had the cheek to walk around, her expression at his anger showing that she simply didn't understand what he wanted from her.

In frustration, Leofwine finally took the advice of Wulfstan, and on a bright sunny day, he took to his horse with only Horic and Wulfstan and their squires, and of course, Hunter, and journeyed to one of the more affluent sheep farmers, in the gently rolling hills to the east of Deerhurst.

As they rode along the farm track, Leofwine became

aware of piercing whistles coming from the far field and gazed in surprise to see a man standing in an open gateway while two dogs ran rings around a herd of sheep.

Leofwine watched eagerly as Burgheard used whistles and hand signals to make his dogs do his bidding in rounding up the sheep.

'My lord.' If Burgheard was surprised by the arrival of the local lord and two of his mounted warriors, he showed no signs.

'Good day,' Leofwine called, shielding his face from the harsh sunlight that seemed to penetrate his remaining eye with fierce intensity, forcing his eye to water.

'Tell me, how do you train your animals so well.' Leofwine was relieved that Burgheard didn't stare at his mangled face but rather settled into a relaxed position, hands resting on his slightly bulging belly.

'I train them from a young age, from pups. I have some now, in fact, just waiting to start the process. The older dog helps, of course, but the youngsters pick it up quickly enough.'

Burgheard didn't seem at all concerned that Leofwine had more interest in his dogs than in him. Leofwine smirked just a little. The man was proud of his dogs; that much was evident. He no doubt found it strange that his lord hadn't visited him before to discover the secrets of their training.

Hunter had at least learnt that she must always stay by her master's side and sat patiently and attentively by, even though there was a field full of sheep she would in the past have been happy to chase. Indeed, every so often, her head turned toward them as though dreaming of a time she could have chased the other animals.

'She's a fine animal,' Burgheard informed Leofwine as he

bent to examine her and make her acquaintance. 'Already fiercely loyal. She just needs to understand what you expect from her better.'

Leofwine nodded but waited for Burgheard to explain further, noticing that Hunter was attentive at his side, no matter the enticements of Burgheard and an entire flock of sheep.

'They respond to rewards and punishments. It sounds harsh, but good behaviour should be rewarded, and those actions you don't want her to take should be punished. Nothing too severe,' Burgheard scratched his grizzled chin as he spoke. 'She won't like it if you're cruel to her. Not that I think you would be,' Burgheard quickly corrected himself, but Leofwine smiled.

'I'm perhaps both too kind and then too cruel. I get frustrated,' he explained, as Burgheard nodded, paying more attention to Hunter than to Leofwine. Leofwine considered how quickly the situation had been reversed.

Leofwine smirked. He's been warned that he could expect nothing else from the man.

'Start by having her walk at your side, closely. Hold her tight, on a short leash, and reward her when you reach your destination. If she runs off or tried to run off, then let her go and ignore her, no matter what she does, to regain your attention. She'll quickly learn, as my own dogs do, that doing what you want is going to get her what she wants.'

'Of course, if you find she won't do as you desire, I have my own pups being trained at the moment. One of those could serve you in the fullness of time.'

Leofwine eyed the black and white bundle of paws and furs, which he could now see in a small pen close to the farmer's open gate, with a smirk of amusement. The farmer's dogs were perhaps not as majestic as Hunter, but if a dog was the way forward, and Hunter proved impossible, he would welcome one of the smaller animals.

'My thanks, good man. I'll do as you suggest and see how we progress. I would sooner keep her close.'

'Aye, I'd want to do the same, my lord,' Burgheard grinned as he absentmindedly chewed a piece of hay. 'These beasties are good with the sheep. I'm not sure what they'd think of the king's court.'

Waving good day to Burgheard, Leofwine returned home, his mind busy with the new information, although he wasn't distracted enough that he didn't notice the relieved look that Wulfstan shared with Horic.

The next day, Leofwine took Hunter to task, one of the horse's harnesses being adjusted to fit the hound. While Hunter whined whenever the harness was attached to her, it allowed Leofwine to direct her as he wanted, and certainly, she appreciated the pieces of dried meat he rewarded her with.

Leofwine persevered, though, and by the time the harvest was being collected and stored, his hound was used to leading him and showing him where it was safe to step, even guiding him around darkened rooms, and all without the aid of the harness, which Leofwine had discarded, and replaced with a fine collar that proclaimed Hunter as his animal.

Æthelflæd was amazed at the dog's usefulness and quickly stopped complaining about her loud snores that echoed around the still night when they slept. Initially, Æthelflæd had complained that Hunter woke Northman each night, but when Leofwine spent a week away from home attending the king's witan, she realised that

Northman naturally woke throughout the night anyway. He was a hungry, active baby, seemingly even when he slept.

The real test for Hunter came when they left Deerhurst to visit Æthelflæd's family at their home closer to the market settlement of Winchcombe. Hunter stayed close by Leofwine's horse the entire journey there, for all that the horse clearly resented her presence, and when Leofwine dismounted, Hunter appeared at his side and guided him into the prosperous hall avoiding the many puddles from the recent rain storm.

Æthelflæd's parents, Ælfnoth and Alta were overjoyed to see their grandson, and throughout the gathering, both Leofwine and Æthelflæd managed not to mention the way she'd been treated by her parents when they'd thought him dead. Leofwine couldn't say that he found either of them to be good company, and they were often rude and ill-mannered toward him.

Alta had a tendency to stare at his face and moan at the smell of Hunter, and Ælfnoth wouldn't look him in the eye. It was a strained three-day visit, at the end of which Leofwine was pleased to leave and overjoyed with the success of his training of Hunter. Not once had he fallen or knocked or bumped anything, giving his relatives no excuse to complain about his injury.

Æthelflæd was quiet as they left her family home. She'd been anxious about visiting and was keener than he was to go. That night as they lay entwined in each other's arms in Deerhurst, she spoke vehemently about them and was reduced to tears, something he'd never witnessed before.

Æthelflæd's shame at her parents was evident, and Leofwine tried his hardest to show her that he was not distressed by it all, finally having to take her in his arms and kiss her until she no longer thought of crying but only of pleasure.

The only good thing to come about at their ill-fortuned meeting was the opportunity to discuss the problems of Wulfstan's wife, for it was Æthelflæd's mother who owned her land. Alta wouldn't have responded well to Leofwine's own discussion of the subject, but Æthelflæd managed to get her to exchange the land with some of her own. Æthelflæd might well have lost out on the arrangement, but for Wulfstan, Leofwine knew she wouldn't object.

So Æthelflæd became the owner of the land and assured Wulfstan that provided it was maintained to a reasonable standard, she'd overlook the slightly irregular situation. She also spoke to the local cleric and had him turn a blind eye to the less-than-Christian attitude of the woman.

Æthelflæd also made provision for one of Wulfstan's sons to hold the land next to his mother's. Wulfstan was left speechless by her actions, and finally, she hugged him and told him that it was little when he'd brought about the safe return of her husband. Wulfstan had been stoically quiet up until this point, apparently worried about what the future held for his wife and sons. A week later, he was heard laughing, and Æthelflæd spent the day with a grin of pleasure on her own face.

And there was more excitement when Horic announced that his own family was moving to England. He'd arranged via such a complicated string of accomplices to get news to them of his survival and whereabouts that Leofwine's head hurt whenever Horic discussed it. It didn't help that so many of Horic's contacts had either the same name or a multitude of strange nicknames. Leofwine didn't think he'd ever heard of so many men named after their beards, moustaches, or teeth.

Agata arrived just as the winter was turning the leaves to a golden brown and set up home on the hideage that Horic had chosen near to the coast. Horic had joked that as much as he loved his wife and ship full of children, he wanted a decent excuse to spend some time away from them if he needed to, and being just over a day's journey from Leofwine's home near Deerhurst was ideal.

When Leofwine met Agata, he was unsurprised to find her as robust as her husband.

'My lord,' she bowed her head to him, just enough to show her respect. 'So, this is what you've bribed my husband with,' she complained next, her hands high as she took in the substantial hall and outbuildings that now belonged to Horic. Before Leofwine could open his mouth to offer anything, she continued.

'I don't deny the land is good, but the salt from the sea impoverishes the soil, and that ox is next to useless.' Horic looked horrified at the whip-sharp comments while Wulfstan, stood behind both Horic and his wife and their mass of children, couldn't keep the grin from his face. Leofwine couldn't deny that it was good to see that Horic was not a master everywhere.

'I can do nothing about the salt,' Leofwine finally managed to interject. 'Of course, I could provide the coin for a better ox, provided you keep the old beast as well. He's served for too long to be cast aside.' A roll of the eyes from Agata and Leofwine knew to expect the next tirade.

'Bloody men growing too fond of useless old animals.'

Horic's slack jaw was too much for Leofwine, and laughter billowed from his mouth as Agata glared at him.

With her hands on her hips, she opened her mouth once more, only for three of her sons to dash between Leofwine and her, half naked and streaked in mud from the coastline.

Rucking her skirt in one hand, Agata took off after her sons, allowing Leofwine to laugh even louder, while Horic shrugged his shoulders as though he had no control at all.

'A northern woman is a thing of beauty,' Horic grumbled, while Wulfstan and Leofwine both chuckled.

'At least I know whom to call on next time you refuse to obey my orders,' Leofwine eventually gasped, only to laugh again when the sad old ox bellowed in rage as Agata turned her fury on him.

'You poor old men,' Wulfstan offered without sympathy, a hand on Horic's shoulder, as he angled his head toward the waiting horse, his intentions clear. Leofwine turned smartly to make good his own escape, as Agata's shrill voice could be heard berating her sons, the ox, and anything else that irritated her.

'I think I might send her back,' Horic said, only half in jest.

There was also a celebration when Leofwine's shipmen sailed the ship back around the leg of Cornwall and docked near the coast. Leofwine rode out, pleased to see the mighty beast again.

In the early winter sun, she'd shone as beautifully russet as he'd remembered, looking magnificent with her newly made sails, now in his own colours of blue and yellow. Even the dour old ship's captain had been pleased to see the man he'd termed his 'pestilence' when the ship had been given to Leofwine, and a few fine days of feasting and drinking had followed.

Leofwine had already rewarded the shipmen with gold

and silver for their part in bringing him home, and it was clear that even though they were to stay as part of the king's own fleet, they now felt themselves Leofwine's men. Many of them went down on one knee and offered him allegiance.

They were a ragtag collection of men with land stretching almost from one end of England to the other, and their acceptance of him as their commended lord meant that he'd need to learn about the places where they held land and the other lords close by to them. Leofwine almost wished the men hadn't acted so but realised that it was an honour to be chosen by the majority of them all, even if it might give him a headache if, and when, he needed to act on their behalf.

Before the winter storms could blow up, the men returned to his ship and sailed back to the western lands and made their winter port at London. Once there, half of the men returned to their homes while the others stayed to be ready should the king call upon them.

At mid-winter, they swapped positions so that all the men had time away from the ship and time to be with their families. Leofwine was filled with respect for the shipmen. They were conscientious in their duty and unfailingly loyal to their king and to him. Their undeserved loyalty, as he saw it, made him realise that other men might turn to him as their lord through choice now that he was gaining a reputation for fairness and equanimity. He hoped they would.

8

AD997

When the summons came to attend his king at the Easter witan the following year, it jarred Leofwine from his happy winter routine. While not necessarily locked up tight against the ravages of the inclement weather, he was at least comfortable in the knowledge that while the heavens leaked snow, ice and rain, there was little to be done about his father's domain.

For a few days, Leofwine sulked and was unbearable company for everyone. No one chastised him. He'd wondered if it was his position that had made everyone so quiet in the face of his temper.

Only once Leofwine had accepted that he had to go no matter what and he'd spoken more optimistically to the men of his household troop and his wife about the coming witan had he realised that they'd all understood his trepidation and had let him deal with it in his way. Leofwine was grateful to them all, and it had made him realise how well they all knew each other now.

Only three years as the leader of his household troop and their squires, and already he felt responsible for them.

Still, it was with a reserve that he set out on a daylong journey to Calne, surrounded by half of his men, leaving the other half to protect his wife and child. He'd wanted to leave Horic and Wulfstan, his best fighter and his best strategist, but Æthelflæd had insisted he needed them more than she did.

The Raiders had not ventured near to Deerhurst, and she'd argued persuasively that he was the one most in need of protection, and sound advice at the witan. Leofwine had given in with ill grace, and Æthelflæd laughed at his bad humour, before taking him to bed and making him think that going was an even worse idea, as he'd be away from his enticing wife.

There was small consolation in the fact there was a royal palace at Calne, and he'd visited it before. He knew his way around and hopefully wouldn't embarrass himself in front of the other ealdormen. And that was the crux of his problem. He'd not been tested in the witan last year. He'd arrived, spoken with the king's mother and young Athelstan, and shown he was alive and affixed his name to some charters that had already been agreed.

This year, he'd need to choose a point of view and argument and use them to persuade his equals and his king, not to mention the herd of royal officials who were always busy snapping at the heels of the few ealdormen. It was a tricky road to tread and one that he had little experience of. Leofwine desperately didn't want to humiliate himself.

Easter fell early, and so the king summoned them to arrive before the festivities commenced. Æthelred had ordered a High Mass and had decreed that he'd wear his ceremonial crown. Leofwine idly considered what else would be on the agenda. The Raiders, no doubt, as there had been reports of small skirmishes along the dragon's leg of Cornwall.

Leofwine wondered if they'd hear news of Olaf in Norway and whether any of the priests who'd escorted him on his journey north and who'd stayed with Olaf had returned home with news of the conversion.

Leofwine also imagined that the new dies for the coinage would be issued, and he'd need to deliver them to moneyers in the hundreds he governed for the king. He'd need to be heavily armoured when he did so. The official dies were priceless and almost a means of making money with the correct precious metals and the right inclination.

In the past, the Raiders had stolen the king's coin dies and used them to produce substandard coins. It had caused no end of problems for the king and for traders in particular.

The winter had been harsh, and summer was still not upon them as they rode to Calne. Although his horse and hound were now well trained to compensate for his sightlessness in the left eye, Wulfstan always rode level with him to keep them all on track. Horic always took the right because he said as the more handsome of the men, his lord should look at him the most often.

When Horic had first said it, while profoundly drunk, the men had roared with laughter. Only when they'd realised that he didn't even remember saying it had it become a real source of amusement. Horic was good-natured about the jibes he received, considering it was every time they rode out together.

Calne had long been a royal palace, and all the kings

since its first building had maintained the palace and the church to make it, perhaps, the most homely of the king's estates. Leofwine assumed that they'd all be forced to hunt with the king, and he only hoped his horse and hound were up to the task.

They arrived late in the evening and were greeted warmly by the steward, and feasted on a selection of fine meats before being shown to a room for the night. The king was not yet in attendance, having decided to make a grand entrance the following morning, but nearly all of the ealdormen and churchmen were there, ready to fawn on their king during his crown-wearing but willing to discuss real issues when the witan was officially opened the day after.

The king's palace was something of a rarity, a two-storied wooden structure built with individual rooms to house the king and his family on the second floor, above the feasting hall below. It was comfortably warm even though it only had fires downstairs, and while Leofwine felt welcomed to a tidy box bed, his men were expected to make do and lie where they could on the wooden floor.

Considering how many people were gathered, Leofwine was happy enough to have at least a door he could close on himself for a little privacy, and he closed his eyes to sleep, glad to have arrived, even if uncertain of what the witan would bring.

The other ealdormen who constituted the king's witan were a mixed bag. Some old, some nearly young, while some were foolish and some almost own too intelligent for their good. At the forefront and most trusted of them all was Ealdorman Æthelweard. A wizened old man, now almost more a monk than a warrior, he had control of the Western

Provinces and had done so since before Æthelred had succeeded to the throne in the murky intrigue of the events of 978.

Leofwine tried not to think about what had happened then. After all, the king had been a young boy of not yet ten. What could he have done to prevent the manoeuvring of powerful men and women? That the king's mother had also been implicated in the murder of Æthelred's half-brother, Edward, and predecessor on the throne, made the situation even more difficult. After all, Leofwine owed his position to the king's mother. It was she who'd spoken for Leofwine when the king was looking for new ealdormen.

Through all the intrigue, Æthelweard had stood proud, a descendant of a king in his own right, or so it was believed, and an intellectual man at that. If he'd once thought he should have been made king after Edward's murder, the idea had long since been abandoned.

But Æthelweard had grown old and weary in his duties. He'd served his king and his predecessors for over twenty years as an ealdorman and before that had been involved in court politics, through his sister's brief marriage to Æthelred's long-dead uncle, the tragic king Eadwig, king for only a handful of years, and hated for almost all of them, even by his own grandmother.

There was not a day that went by that Leofwine didn't fear he'd hear of Ealdorman Æthelweard's death. Æthelweard was a steadying force, and when he did die, there would be a void that would be impossible to fill. His son, Æthelmær, was not yet the man his father was, and Leofwine doubted that he'd be called on to fill the vacant position caused by his father's death. Leofwine wondered who could fill the gap left by Æthelweard in the Western

Provinces and also as the king's most influential ealdorman.

Certainly, there was little choice.

Ælfric of Hampshire was the next most powerful ealdorman, and he'd certainly weathered many storms with his lord and king. He'd been the first ealdorman specifically chosen by the young king when he'd attained his majority.

Ælfric had proven to be a poor choice, standing accused of informing the Raiders that they were to be attacked at sea six years ago. His son had been blinded for his father's treachery, and yet somehow, Ælfric was still deep in the king's confidences and likely to be forgiven for any transgression, no matter how treasonous it was.

Ælfric was a wily old fox with no remorse for his son's blinding. Leofwine had thought at the beginning that Ælfric would be the most sympathetic ealdorman to his plight, but exactly the opposite had been the case. It was almost as if Leofwine's presence affronted him, with the constant reminder of what he'd caused to happen to his son.

Leofwine had long learned to stay as far away from the grizzled ealdorman as possible. His presence was something to be avoided whenever possible. They made wary neighbours of each other. Leofwine knew he had to be strong to hold what was his by right against the grabbing hands of the avarice of the man.

Ælfhelm had succeeded to the ealdordom of Northumbria on the removal of Æthelred's father-in-law after the disastrous campaign in which Ælfric had turned traitor.

Ælfhelm had long been a chosen thegn of Æthelred's and, again, closely allied with Lady Elfrida, the king's mother. He had landed interests in Mercia, for all that he held power in Northumbria. He was to be found either as an ally of Leofwine's or as an antagonist. The swing from one to the other could be remarkably quick, and it was Leofwine's own ability to keep track of their many conflicts over land, jurisdiction and men, which was his strongest point in his dealings with Ælfhelm and his sons, and brother, Wulfric Spot.

Half blind Leofwine might be, but his eye for detail was immense. Æthelflæd and Wulfstan were always teasing him for being able to remember the tiniest detail of any treaty or point of law.

Ealdorman Leofsige was, in many ways, Leofwine's own personal mirror and torture. Appointed at the same time as Leofwine, he held power over Essex and its surrounding lands.

On occasion, Leofwine felt bitter recriminations welling up inside him. If only Æthelred had thought to send Leofsige with Olaf in Leofwine's place, it would be him who was blinded and not he.

Leofwine tried to keep such thoughts at bay, but sometimes, especially when Leofsige was vying for some position of prestige and gained it with the king's blessing just because he had two eyes, Leofwine felt bitter hatred for the man.

The few ealdormen were just the most powerful of the secular lords at the king's court. His bishops, archbishops, abbots and abbesses also counselled him. They were almost as varied in their nature as the ealdormen; for all that, they professed to be leaders of the true faith.

Many of the holy men fell into two categories. Either those who just wanted to die in peace and worship their God until that happened or those who were fighting their advanced age and trying to hold on to as much power as possible while couching their every act in terms of saving souls for their God. That Leofwine shared their God didn't stop him from seeing the truth of their actions.

Wulfstan, the bishop of London, was the most energetic and also the youngest of all the churchmen. Leofwine believed that the faith he professed was perhaps the most sincere of them all. Wulfstan honestly saw his people and his king for what they were, and he noted the injustices committed in the name of the king, the law or of God and worked to circumvent them all. Leofwine respected him immensely while hoping that he'd never be subjected to one of his pointed wrath-filled sermons.

For all that he'd only been a bishop for a year, he'd certainly made his mark on all who attended the witan. Leofwine thought that he'd prove to be an influential man in his own right in time.

The Archbishop of Canterbury was also in attendance, Ælfric. He'd only recently come into his position, as had Ealdulf of York, but they'd both weathered many storms under the rule of Æthelred. They were used to their king's difficult ways.

The other churchmen, Ælfheah of Winchester, Wulfsige of Sherborne and Ælfheah of Lichfield, were little known to Leofwine. It was Athulf of Hereford he had the most contact with as his local bishop. He was a young and passionate man of God, often overzealous with his good works and advancing his own diocese. Leofwine held him with high regard all the same.

The abbot of Glastonbury, Ælfweard, was a man of unbounded enthusiasm for his God and his work. Thin almost to the point of breaking, he wore his magnificent robes with dignity and had already witnessed any number of tricky situations the country had endured. He knew his king well, and Leofwine often found himself studying the man's expressions and alliances with interest.

Ælfsige, the abbot of the New Minster at Winchester, was similarly a veteran of the king's councils, whereas Wulfgar, abbot of Abingdon, was a relatively recent addition to the king's advisors, like Leofwine himself, only receiving his position of power five years previously. Similar to Leofwine, Wulfgar was still finding his feet amongst the sea of conflict and self-interest that dominated whenever all the most potent men of the kingdom met.

And then there was the king's mother. She was truly magnificent for all the rumours that surrounded her actions when Æthelred became king. Leofwine honestly wanted to say that he didn't think her capable of killing a young man in cold blood, but sometimes, when she cast her steely eyes his way, he knew that she was perfectly capable of doing that, even if she was one of his most loyal supporters.

Lady Elfrida, the king's mother as she liked to be termed, although her official position was queen dowager, had protected England and her son for decades. When Æthelred had fought free from her overzealous guardianship, she'd plotted her way back into his confidences and had the task of caring for the king's children on the king's estate at Dean. She had the ear of the king for much of the time, and she advised him accordingly, although Leofwine knew she also had half a mind to the future.

The king had many sons. One of them would rule after him, and he would have been prepared by Lady Elfrida for such a responsibility. She had been the wife of Edgar, known as the peaceable. Leofwine sometimes considered what she thought of her son's ability to rule. Certainly, England was far less stable than when her husband had ruled.

Leofwine was pleased she was his ally rather than his enemy.

Lady Elfrida supervised the æthelings at the witan. The oldest of them, Athelstan, Ecgberht, Edmund and Eadred, had been merely boys when they'd first attended the witan, and they'd stumbled alongside Leofwine as they'd tried to learn how everything worked.

Leofwine found them all engaging boys on the cusp of manhood, perhaps more confident in who they were than their father had ever been, but then, Æthelred had been king at their ages. They'd hopefully have many long years to grow into the position they would one day take on. Æthelred had not had that luxury.

The witan, when it finally convened the day after the king's crown-wearing ceremony, was far from taxing regarding decision-making, but the tense atmosphere and intended sly remarks regarding Leofwine's ability to perform as ealdorman were destabilising, no matter Hunter stood at his side, with Wulfstan and Horic to advise him.

'My lords and ladies,' the king greeted them all on the morning of the witan, his face keen with his desire to have his decisions ratified.

'First, we will talk about the new law codes. As you know, there has long been a discrepancy between the way laws are determined in the Mercian, Wessex and Northumbrian lands as opposed to in those areas that once fell under the name of the Danelaw. I wish to make their laws follow the ways of their own traditions rather than our own. The men and women of the Danelaw live by a mostly similar set of laws, but not in all aspects.'

'I am convinced that such an undertaking would ensure their loyalty if the Raiders were ever to attack there.'

The king allowed his ealdormen and other royal officials to debate the matter, but mostly he expected them to agree, and Leofwine was unsurprised when the king ordered his chancery to formulate the laws and have them brought before the next witan for ratification.

The king then turned his attention to old difficulties with the lands of the Old Minster in Winchester, keen to have more of his wishes enacted, as he ordered the return of land to the Old Minster, which he'd previously granted to his followers, even though he shouldn't have done.

This was a holdover from when the king had been youthful and only just in command of his kingdom, when his mother, uncle and bishop Æthelwold had stepped aside to let the king rule alone, and he'd been under the influence of Ealdorman Æthelwine, a man who'd been too ambitious for his own good. The king had since apologised for his actions toward the religious houses of England, but it was a slow process to ensure that all land grants were retracted.

Leofwine had no recollection of those times, but Wulfstan grumbled at his side about it being 'about time,' and Leofwine was content to witness the charter for the king. Leofwine tried not to let it bother him that of all the ealdormen, he was accorded the lowest status, signing the charter last of them. The king, as ever, had almost shunned him, and the news of attacks, as shared by Ealdorman Æthelweard, on the western coast was a worry.

Neither was Lady Elfrida as involved in her son's witan as Leofwine might have expected. She seemed content to guard her grandsons, and although the attacks on the western coasts were close to her birthplace and her brother's sphere of influence, she seemed almost as unconcerned as her son.

The witan was a far from pleasant environment. Nothing anyone ever did was unseen, and he found it difficult to tolerate the constant scrutiny. Even Horic was infected by Leofwine's bad mood, and his usual good cheer drained away.

The weather stayed chill as Leofwine huddled deep in his cloak as well as in his miserable mood. Wulfstan and Hunter were vigilant at his side, and so were his men, who travelled in silence but in full armour following the news of Raiders. Wulfstan didn't want to take any chances.

As they trotted through the woodlands and open fields heading back toward Deerhurst, Leofwine absently noted the small green shoots. He watched the farmers at work, the great oxen ploughing the heavy soils and the few early lambs already skipping self-consciously around the fields, their anxious mothers calling nervously to them when they strayed too far.

None of the hope of the coming summer could raise him from his despair.

Two of his men, Leofgar and Ælfnoth, were sent ahead to scout, more out of the desire to please Wulfstan than the fear of a threat. Yet, they quickly returned, hooves flying over the dew-soaked land, concern etched into their faces.

'We can see smoke, far to the west,' Leofgar spoke calmly but with an edge of excitement to his voice.

'Raiders?' Wulfstan demanded to know.

'I'd assume so.'

Leofwine shook himself from his stupor and looked towards Wulfstan, a question in his dull eye.

'Should we investigate?'

'Of course, my lord. Leofgar, Ælfnoth and Eadred, you ride on ahead quickly and determine the numbers and what's happening. But first, make sure you've armed adequately.' Wulfstan spoke as the three made to ride off with their weapons still sheathed.

The three men quickly removed their shields from their horses' backs and drew their weapon of choice from their scabbards snaking down their backs. Tugging their helms closed around their faces, ensuring the neck guards were in place, they kicked their horses to a quick gallop, spraying the men who were too close behind them with mud and ruts.

'Wighard and Oscetel, I know you won't thank me for this, but head back to Wantage. The king needs to hear of this in case the Raiders turn further inland.'

Both men groaned at the unwelcome news, and Horic laughed heartily at their disappointment, his hand around his war axe and a look of purpose already on his face.

'Don't worry, lads. I'll be sure to save you a few. Now hurry. We're barely halfway home, and that was at a slow trot. I'm sure you can cover the distance in a fraction of the time and be back here for the actual skirmish.'

Without another word, both men turned tail and headed back along the path they'd just travelled, once more kicking ruts at the immobile horsemen.

'And us, my lord?' Horic queried, his tongue licking his lips with his desire to encounter the enemy.

'We armour ourselves too and follow on behind the scouts, ready for anything these Raiders throw at us. We must be vigilant. The fires may be in the west, but we don't know how long they've been burning. The Raiders may even now be much closer than we think.'

Leofwine suddenly felt more alive than he had since his

arrival at the witan. This attack would be his opportunity. He'd rout the Raiders, and those detractors at the witan would then have to treat him with more respect.

Wulfstan and Horic nodded agreement at his words, and his other four men, Brithelm, Wulfsige, Lyfing and Ælfhun readied themselves, as Leofgar, Ælfnoth and Eadred had only moments before, fingering weapons from their belts or from down their backs, and ensuring their shields were easy to grab, should they be forced to hand to hand combat.

The household troop showed no signs of panic or concern as they raised their shields and ensured their swords, spears and seaxes were ready. This was what they trained for, day in and day out, in Leofwine's dusty yard and in the fields close to his home. This was their very purpose in life, to protect their land and their lord and their king, and in that order, if they were lucky enough.

There was little wind on the chill day, and even though Leofwine sniffed, he couldn't smell the smoke, even when he could detect it off in the far distance when they'd thundered down the trackway for a few more miles. The smoke billowed blackly into the sky, and Leofwine offered a silent prayer for any who'd been injured or killed by the Raiders.

At that moment, he vowed he'd make a new gift to his church in memory of all those who had been killed. Leofwine would ensure that their deaths were not simply forgotten about.

Leofgar was waiting for them on a rise.

'The others have gone ahead, my lord. I waited here because the path is a little tricky down this hill.'

Leofwine nodded to show he understood, and Leofgar quickly turned and allowed his horse to pick his way down the steep and rocky incline. In front of them, the shapes of the settlement under attack were starting to take form.

'How many do you count?' Wulfstan called to the men.

'At least seventy,' Leofgar responded, 'and some of them seem to be on horses. But not all.'

That was mixed news. The men on horseback were often able to make a quick retreat, and that just made the men without horses more desperate and their fighting more determined. Leofwine knew as much from all he'd heard about Raider tactics and from what he'd experienced in Shetland.

Leofwine didn't feel reassured knowing how the men would fight. He'd rather have known how to defeat them, but he couldn't recall any reliable conclusions drawn from those discussions. Some solutions had been suggested, but none of them seemed relevant when he had only nine men with him and his hound.

The odds were not in his favour, but they had no choice but to attack and hope that their superior equipment and near-constant training ensured a victory.

The settlement loomed before them, and Leofwine had his men push the horses to race across the flat land before reining them in. Arriving with horses foaming at the mouth would be counterproductive.

Ælfnoth and Eadred were readying themselves before Leofwine's force, and the Raiders appeared oblivious that their attack was going unnoticed.

As his scouts trotted through the fields to meet them, Leofwine spied villagers cowering amongst the early summer crops and shouted, urging them to seek safety along the hill they'd only just ridden down. From there, he urged them to travel towards Wantage and the safety of the king's palace if need be.

The villages were stoic in their resolve, some even beckoning to him to report on where they'd seen the Raiders. The consensus was clear; it was the small wooden church that burned because it had not contained the vast riches the Raiders had expected. They'd set fire to it in disgust and were now attempting to take what they could from the inhabitants of the settlement. One woman closed her eyes in grief and just whispered, 'my daughter.'

Leofwine felt his blood run cold and tried to offer reassurance that he'd get her back, but the words died unspoken on his lips. He couldn't give an assurance that wasn't guaranteed. That was just more cruelty than what she'd already witnessed.

Urging his horse onwards towards the settlement, Wulfstan directed them all to aim, not for the burning building but for the largest of the dwellings, a long hall surrounded by a motley collection of horses, tied haphazardly together and with a mass of swirling men surrounding them.

A strangled cry rang through the air, and Leofwine's head swung around to see an indeterminable figure fleeing from the burning building. In their wake, the entire church building come crashing down in a flurry of sparks and sneaking flame, its single solitary window of coloured glass glowing menacingly red as the flames inside consumed the wooden structure with a roar.

Leofwine hoped that it wouldn't spread to the other houses.

But he had no more time for thought, for the enemy had finally seen them. Men rushed his household troop, screaming in rage and brandishing vicious-looking axes and massive swords. The Raiders had abandoned their horses and so ran at Leofwine's horse, axes and swords at the ready, hoping to wound the horses and so drive Leofwine and his men from their saddles.

'Dismount,' the word ripped through the air as he slid to the wet ground with a muffled thud. Immediately, a huge man lunged at him, his axe held high above his helmeted head, only black eyes visible between the reinforced leather sides of the leather helm.

The enemy's veins stood out starkly on his forearms. Leofwine just managed to raise his shield on his left arm to deflect the force of the blow, which ricocheted painfully up his arm. Leofwine was pleased that long practice had made the manoeuvre instinctive.

And then Horic was by his right side, which made Leofwine quirk a brief smile, and Wulfstan was at his left. Leofwine had ordered Hunter to stay with his horse and had noted with satisfaction that horse and hound had cantered briskly away, back the way they'd come. He hoped that some of the villagers would catch them before they strayed too far.

The rest of the horses did the same.

Then there was no time for talk. The colossal man facing Leofwine let forth an ungodly war cry as he repositioned himself for another strike, and there were men everywhere. His household troop formed swiftly into three small fighting groups to protect each other's backs as they clashed, and the wild Raiders threw themselves with vigour at the English force, sharp blades glittering in the overcast day, helms obscuring nearly all but eyes and stubborn chins.

Leofwine lowered his protective shield and risked a strike at the huge man's belly with his heavy sword, now released from its housing behind his shoulder. The sword easily sliced through the man's leather padded byrnie, showing red spots of blood, all while the warrior still had his lethal-looking war axe raised above his head.

The warrior howled in rage or fear or both and swung his axe as blood seeped more quickly from the open wound. The action only served to open the wound further. Leofwine repelled the new blow with his shield that he'd hastily raised to cover himself, and as the man went to swing again, Horic stepped forward and used his tremendous strength to drive his war axe through the man's exposed neck.

Blood sprayed everywhere while Horic laughed as the blow nearly severed the warrior's head. The already dead man stood a moment longer, his head canted uncomfortably to the side, the grey of broken flesh causing Leofwine to swallow down his bile as the body finally began collapsing to the damp ground with a clash of dropped weaponry.

Leofwine turned to look at Horic, trying to focus on him with his good eye, but there was no time for more than a nod of thanks as behind the dead man Leofwine detected more Raiders running to join the battle.

The men who came were no smaller than the Raider, who lay dead and twitching at their feet. They were, however, better armed with shields on their arms and swords in their hands.

Leofwine slid his sword into its holder along his back and fumbled for his short fighting seax, wrenching it free from his weapons belt. Taking temporary refuge behind his shield, Leofwine waited for the first of the men to step forward, his sword raised and his shield slightly too high. As he did, Leofwine danced forwards and sliced his seax across the man's exposed stomach.

The Raider screamed in agony as the blade sheared

underneath the byrnie the man wore, too short to be efficient and no doubt stolen. Leofwine felt hot blood gush over his striking hand before he could finish his slicing motion.

The blue eyes of the warrior widened in shock and disbelief as he dropped his sword and clutched his wound. He fell slowly to his knees, and Leofwine finished him off with a vicious slice across his throat, left exposed by his helm, which had plainly been made for a smaller man and didn't protect his neck for all that it had neck guards.

Next to him, Wulfstan fought sword on sword with one of the other men, a smaller man, wirier and more nimble on his feet. The enemy held his shield tight to his chest but, in his haste, had forgotten to don his helm. As the Raider danced closer to Wulfstan, Leofwine stepped out of formation and ran his bloodied seax down the man's face, blinding him with the blood that leaked from the wound.

Leofwine felt small satisfaction in seeing the move that had so injured him inflicted on another, and then he was back in position beside Horic and Wulfstan as the wounded man staggered around in blind fear.

Wulfstan's opponent stumbled backwards slightly, and as he did so, one of his comrades pierced him with a spear thrown from near the longhouse. Leofwine gasped at the suddenness of the attack and looked up quickly to mark the man who had thrown it, noticing a small band of about five, all holding spears and taking aim at him and his men. Leofwine shouted a warning, which Horic bellowed to all around.

The dead Raider was still upright, pinned to the ground by the spear, but any life had fled his eyes, and he remained now as a haunting scarecrow. With a precise movement, Wulfstan kicked the man down, keeping a wary eye on the

Raiders racing towards them and those who continued to throw spears.

Leofwine took a moment to check his other men and saw them all fighting competently against the Raiders. The two separate groups of three men were fighting in a similar formation to him, Wulfstan and Horic, and he could see men dead or dying, lying at their feet.

Leofwine realised that he needed to thank Wulfstan for training the men so well, but then he was raising his shield to counter a heavy blow from yet another axe. It seemed that just like Horic, these Raiders favoured the weapon.

This man had both his shield and helm correctly placed, and Leofwine was momentarily stumped by how he could defeat the Raider. He looked to be the same size as him, and Leofwine frantically searched for a weakness as he stepped forward to meet his attack.

A mocking smile played around the man's face beneath the tarnished helm he wore, and Leofwine noticed the collection of silver armrings that extended almost to his elbow on both arms. This man was a true Viking Raider, and he knew it. The man had lived through many attacks before to earn so much silver from his lord.

Fear twisted Leofwine's stomach as he looked the confident well-armed man over. He was determined to make the first move and use the element of surprise.

At his sides, Wulfstan and Horic fought against equally well-armoured men, and Leofwine knew he couldn't expect them to help him as they had before.

The Raider raised his arm and threw something at Leofwine. Instinctively he raised his shield and felt something heavy thwack against the reinforced wood. The object hit off-centre, towards the left, and Leofwine quickly tried to claw back his grip that had loosened under the weight of what he could only assume was the battle-axe.

Lowering his shield slightly, Leofwine was not surprised to see the man suddenly directly before him, his smile now condescending.

At that moment, Leofwine realised that the man knew who he was and was playing to his weakness. In picking the left side of Leofwine's shield, he'd purposefully forced him off balance, and that, coupled with his sightlessness in his left eye, was weakening his ability to fight effectively, as he'd re-taught himself last year.

Leofwine hefted his shield again and took a step backwards. The warrior smirked and came ever forwards, his eyes glinting a vicious grey. The Raider thought he'd won already.

Leofwine moved cautiously again, making sure he edged over the dead men at his feet. The Raider didn't notice but skirted ever closer, swinging his long sword from side to side in a taunting manner. Leofwine hadn't even seen him remove it from the straps on his back, so concerned with determining a way to beat him.

And then it happened. Overconfident and off balance because of the weight of his massive sword, the enemy warrior slipped on the blood and guts of the dead.

As the Raider slid ungracefully forward, confusion on his face. Leofwine attacked with a sharp blow from his seax and slit straight across the now exposed throat of the man as he slipped forwards and his head shot backwards.

The man gurgled as the blood poured from his wound and clenched his sword firmly between his two hands as he toppled to the ground. Leofwine took a moment to be amazed at the man, who was assuring his eternity in Valhalla instead of raging against his death.

Leofwine's looked at the man, noticing his wispy brown hair visible under the helm. Leofwine vaguely wondered what the man had been called and if he had family and how, by God, he knew Leofwine's identity.

As his casualties mounted to three, Leofwine felt sweat bead his face. His breath was coming hot and fast, and he could hear Horic's laboured breathing even over his battle cries and the noise of metal on metal or wood or flesh.

Leofwine watched his war band with pride, aware of the swish of the few spears that flew through the air from the warriors still near the long wooden house but also mindful of the fact that they were falling short of the actual fighting. He assumed they must have shortened their range to not kill one of their own again.

Wulfstan fought mechanically and precisely. He didn't let the various fighting techniques of his enemy sway his fighting stance. Wulfstan attacked with his sword and his shield, and no amount of spears or seaxes was going to change that style.

Wulfstan had at least three warriors dead at his feet, and his face, where it was exposed, was covered in the blood and gore of his kills. It made Wulfstan look a little crazed, especially when combined with his precise strokes and mechanical fighting stance.

To the right of him, Horic was wildly attacking with his huge war-axe, literally chopping at the men who came towards him as though they were trees to be felled. First, he went for their legs, and if that failed, he aimed higher, at their stomachs, and then, if they still stood their neck.

Leofwine watched in grim satisfaction as Horic's current opponent lunged forwards to attack with his sword, only to have his hand severed at the wrist by the war axe.

Holding his now useless hand with his still whole hand, the Raider didn't notice the second blow that severed both lower arms just below the elbow.

The Raider screamed with rage, blood soaking into his clothes and running in an ever-faster torrent down his trousers. Horic bellowed in triumph as his next blow hacked at the disorientated man's neck. The Raiders went down with a wet gurgle, and Horic winked at his lord, noticing his scrutiny.

'Now that's how to do it,' Horic shouted with exuberance. Leofwine hid his shock to see the brute strength of his household warrior. He hoped he'd never have to face the man in a rage.

Into the space, another man ran at Leofwine, and he couldn't help but admire the Raider's cohesive fighting force. For all that it looked ramshackle, someone must be directing them because none of his men was ever left without an opponent for longer than it took to almost recover their breath and strength.

This Raiders carried a shield and seax and had an elaborate helm on his head, apparently made to fit and decorated with interchanging bright flashes of highly polished iron and dull pieces, distracting in the brightening day, forcing Leofwine to blink his only eye.

The helm was equipped with a neck guard as well, and long curling brown hair sneaked under its edges. The Raiders' eyes glared at Leofwine, blind to anything happening around them.

Leofwine offered him a mocking smile, daring him to come closer, and the Raider readily accepted the challenge, treading carefully around the dead men without ever taking his eyes from Leofwine's face.

A cold fear snaked inside Leofwine's chest. This man looked competent and lethal, efficiently handling his seax. Perhaps the Raiders had saved the best until last and not the worst, as he'd hoped.

Horic and Wulfstan both fought men with large decisive strikes, parrying away at them and waiting for an opportunity to break through the well-practised stance of the Raiders they faced. Leofwine's opponent threw his head back and laughed a strangely elongated gurgle.

Leofwine swallowed the acidic bitterness of terror at the back of his throat. He'd already killed three men. He must not falter now, even though this man was by far the most capable he'd faced.

The man stalked him, coming ever closer until he could prod at him with his seax, his shield perfectly balanced on his other arm. The enemy laughed while he glared at Leofwine with dead eyes, entirely at odds with the mirth escaping his mouth. Leofwine finally understood the horror that a warrior grown cold with the berserk madness could inflict on a well-trained man without even raising his sword or axe in a fight.

Around him, the sound seemed to mute as Leofwine focused exclusively on the man. How could he beat him? How could he kill him? What advantages did he have over the Raider?

Leofwine thought of nothing else in the long silence before the Raider almost languidly stepped forward and offered a mocking bow,

'My lord Leofwine. My lord Swein sends his greetings. He'll pay me handsomely for your death.'

Without pause, the Raider whipped his sword across Leofwine's battered shield, still encumbered with the axe from his previous opponent. Leofwine felt the weight increase on his inordinately tired arm, and he staggered slightly, trying to adjust his balance as the import of the words sank in.

Swein? What did he have to do with this? In Leofwine's distracted state, the Raider took full advantage of the slight lowering of his shield arm to rush forwards and slice at his exposed face. Leofwine no longer wore a full helm since his injury, finding the usual side padding too distracting when he fought. The sides of the helm had initially caused him to anticipate someone at the periphery of his vision who wasn't there. Without the sides, his limited vision was not so constricted, but he was vulnerable to a facial attack.

Before Leofwine could even process how the man had managed to switch seax and sword so quickly, he'd changed back again, and the Raider was swinging the seax at Leofwine's exposed face.

His good eye was abruptly blinded by a sheet of blood, as delayed pain shot down his face, all Leofwine could do was raise his shield to ward off the rest of the blow, trying to knock the arm of the Raider away from his body.

Leofwine had no time to attempt a retaliatory strike and just cowered behind his shield as blow after heavy blow rained down on his shield. He hoped the man wouldn't think to rush him and attack him from above, as his shield, even at the canted angle he was holding it at, didn't wholly cover his head.

He could sense Wulfstan and Horic coming to his side, but Leofwine could no longer see anything as the blood from his face wound ran freely down his sweat-slicked face. He still grasped his sword in his left hand and so was unable to wipe the curtain of red from before his eyes.

Panic filled Leofwine, and his body felt heavy with fear, his heart pounding in his chest. He didn't want to die here, but he was trapped, and he knew it.

Still, the mad laughter echoed all around him, the only sound now audible to his sound-muted ears. He offered up a whispered prayer to his God as more and more blows hammered the shield, each accompanied by a burst of gurgling glee.

And then Leofwine felt arms around his waist, pulling him back as shouted words penetrated his dull state. It was Oscetel, back from his journey to the king's palace.

Unable to see much beyond his own feet, Leofwine allowed Oscetel to lead him back towards his horse that Oscetel had retrieved on the way to the battlefront. Oscetel helped him into the saddle as all around him, the noise of battle continued to thunder.

'The king's household troops? Are they here?'

'Yes, my lord, although it doesn't look like you need them.'

'Why have we defeated them all so soon?'

'Nearly, my lord, nearly. Now stay in the saddle, and Wighard and I will accompany you back up the hillside to safety. Don't even think about complaining. You're wounded, and you've fought well. How many did you kill?'

'Three. Has Horic beaten that brute? I can't see.'

'Nearly my lord, nearly,' came a quiet response from Oscetel as he walked swiftly away from him to mount his horse.

Beneath him, Leofwine's horse started to move forward at a quick canter, and he grabbed hold of the mane tightly to stay upright. Not being able to see properly was making him not only disorientated but also sick to his stomach. The usual sway of the horse's movements jarred his head up and down.

The sound of the battle quickly faded as they started to ride uphill, and soon the noise was non-existent. Pain lashed Leofwine's face, and he desperately wanted to be able to remove his helm and wipe the sweat and blood to clear his sight, but it was all he could do to stay upright.

Oscetel was silent as they went, but Wighard must have been watching the battle behind them because he offered a running commentary on how the fighting was going. As they reached the top of the hill and turned to look at the scene before them, he let out a yelp of pleasure and then babbled.

'My lord, Horic has beaten the man. He lies even now with a severed arm. It was a long fight, but I was never doubtful of the outcome. Now come, we can remove your helm and look at the damage.' Wighard's voice was fast and loud with excitement. Leofwine could only assume that the man was disappointed to have missed out on bloodying his sword.

First, Leofwine slithered from his horse, all fingers and thumbs but pleased to have his feet on the ground. Then he reached up and tugged lose his helm, releasing it from his head with a gentle noise and finally rubbing his face with a piece of soft material Oscetel had handed to him. The rag came away saturated with blood, but at least he could see a little.

Leofwine squinted into the day grown bright and saw Oscetel studying him intently while Wighard, still mounted, kept his eye on what was happening below.

'Is it bad?'

'Not as bad as the other side,' came the slightly sarcastic reply from Oscetel. He could be a dour man and not likely to soften his words because he thought they might wound, despite their childhood friendship. A smile tugged on Leofwine's face, and he called up to Wighard.

'Is it bad? My injury.'

Wighard turned to study him intently, and Leofwine was mollified to notice that he didn't flinch.

'No, just superficial, I think. It's just that head wounds have a tendency to bleed a lot. It looks worse than it is. Although you better check with a herbalist.'

Leofwine felt a little better at the news and decided to ignore the gaunter face of Oscetel. Until he made it home, he'd much rather think it was superficial.

Leofwine fumbled for his water bottle on the saddle and gulped greedily before covering his cloth in some of the water and attempting to wipe his face clear of all the blood. Already the blood flow was much less.

Still a little unsteady on his feet, Leofwine used his horse as a walking aid and moved to where Wighard sat on his horse, watching the scene below him.

'Are the Raiders retreating?'

'It looks that way. It won't be much longer, and we can speak to the commander of the king's troops and get you home. I'm sure they'll be only too happy to pillage the dead and bury them.'

In the near distance, the fire from the church was smouldering, blowing smoke across the small battlefield, but even with his limited vision, it was evident that his men and the king's men were driving the Raiders back. Wighard's continuing commentary was filling in many of the gaps in Leofwine's knowledge.

Ideally, Leofwine would have liked to follow the Raiders to see where they went, but he supposed he'd have to let the king's household troop do that. Leofwine couldn't command his men as he was, and he needed to go home and think about his injury and the best way he could prevent it from happening again.

Oscetel had taken the respite to reach for his saddlebag and pull some bread and cold meat from it, pillaged from the king's table that morning. Oscetel was cramming the food in his mouth while offering some to Leofwine and Wighard. Gratefully Leofwine took a chunky piece of browned bread. He needed to eat to steady his shaking body.

Leofwine ate with relish and then heard the jangle of the other horses coming their way. Wulfstan rode at the front of the line, and Horic at the back of their now slightly ragtag war band. The men were slumped in their saddles but sat more upright, smiles on tired faces as they saw Leofwine standing by his horse.

There was no need for them to know that the horse was the only thing keeping him upright.

'My lord,' Wulfstan bowed, his head low, his voice gravelly, 'the Raiders have retreated, those who yet live anyway, and the king's household troop have split themselves in two, half to harry them and the other half to bury the dead here. We're welcome to leave, and they'll finish up and scout the area for signs of more Raiders.'

'Thanks, Wulfstan, and thank you to you all. You certainly know how to beat the Raiders. It's just me who let the side down.' Leofwine tried to keep the self-criticism from his voice, if not his words.

A cry of protest rose from all the tired men's mouths.

'I don't ask for your sympathy. I just state a fact. I'm the one with the injury. None of you even seems to have a scratch. Now come, we'll need to make it home and reassure

Lady Æthelflæd that all is well, and I'll need to see to a reward for you all. You fight well, and we're a cohesive force. I was pleased to see us finally tested.'

'Yes, my lord. But there are distinct ways that we could improve,' Wulfstan stated starkly.

Leofwine gave him a look of utter disbelief.

'Come, Wulfstan. We can discuss that at length tomorrow. For now, we should be pleased with our bravery and skills. More than pleased. We should be ecstatic and calling for strong ale.'

Half of the men cheered to hear that, but then Horic intervened.

'My lord, we're all very aware of how well we fight, but Wulfstan is correct to say there are lessons to be learnt. This was our first real battle, but I doubt it'll be our last.'

'Even with my skills and knowledge of how the Raiders fight, I confess that I'm a little rusty and was surprised by their tactics. I don't think it was just me who found the men becoming more skilled as the fight intensified. I fear they're sending their weakest against us first and then saving the skilled warriors to come at us when we're exhausted and thinking we've gained an easy victory. Do you all agree?'

Weary words of agreement were spoken by the men, while Leofwine also nodded in agreement.

'We must talk to the others who encounter the Raiders and see if they've had the same experiences. Now come, we should leave. Are the men managing down there?'

Wighard was still watching the scene below them intently.

'Yes, my lord. As Wulfstan said, half bury the dead, an unpleasant task, but necessary, and the others have raced after the retreating Raiders.'

Using his horse as a prop, Leofwine staggered back to his saddle and raised his foot to the stirrup. He was pleased that all was well, even if he couldn't include himself in that assertion.

A loud roar sounded in his ear, and Leofwine felt himself sway a little uncertainly. A steadying hand on his shoulder and Leofwine realised that Horic had moved his horse to stand opposite his own and was shielding his precarious state from the majority of his household troop. Leofwine was grateful for the action but didn't acknowledge the man, being too intent on just mounting up and remaining upright.

With resolve, Leofwine heaved himself up into the saddle and spent a few moments seeing to his comfort. He could see again, but his eye was always running and felt as though something was stuck in it. He repeatedly blinked, trying to clear it without touching it with his filthy hands, before finally accepting that he merely needed to tolerate the discomfort for now if he wanted any vision.

Wearily he noticed the men had formed up in a paired line, and Horic shunted him towards the middle of the line. He raised his eyebrow a little at that. He was usually at the front.

'It's for your safety, my lord,' Horic offered gently while Wulfstan finished relaying his wishes to his comrades.

'Where's Hunter?' Leofwine demanded, his injury making his voice too harsh.

'She's coming , my lord. I can see her,' Wighard shouted, still keeping a cursory eye on the actions of the king's household troop. But only when Leofwine felt Hunter's snout in his hand did he feel better.

With grudging acceptance of Horic's wishes, Leofwine kneed his horse into position, and they set out for home.

They arrived home when the sun had long since set, and a cold wind had sprung up, forcing Leofwine to sit huddled and miserable in his saddle. His horse was tired and plodding, and he could feel himself nodding off with the gentle sway of the beast.

Unfortunately, his shivering was, on occasion, so intense that it was keeping him awake, and his eye was stinging as intermittent raindrops flashed across his face.

Leofwine thought he'd never felt so miserable and beaten as he did now. His arms ached from holding his shield and sword in battle, and his legs had grown stiff with the after-effects of his exertion.

As they'd neared home, Wulfstan had instructed Oscetel to ride on ahead and inform the household of their return and their need for hot food, boiling water and the healer. Leofwine had been vaguely aware of the concerned glances being shot his way by Wulfstan but had not offered him any information on how he felt. Neither had Wulfstan asked.

Leofwine wondered how terrible he must look for even Wulfstan to be looking so concerned. He was usually so stoic in everything he did that it was rare to see concern on his face, but Leofwine could certainly see it now when his eye worked well enough for him to see anything.

As they plodded through the common fields of his father's home, more of his household troop road out to escort them in. Leofwine was too tired to care and barely noticed when they pulled up to the front door of his steading, and Horic and Wulfstan both rushed to his side as he more fell than slid from the horse's back.

Wulfstan and Horic held him upright as they walked into the main room and assisted Leofwine as he sank into his high-backed chair before the roaring fire. Leofwine noticed with satisfaction that there was a massive meal of pottage and that flatbreads were already laid out on the bench his household troop always sat at.

There were also at least four jugs of ale, and the servants were bustling around the men who walked inside, assisting them to remove their helms and byrnies and letting the two young boys run outside with them to see to their cleaning.

Leofwine also heard the slightly distant creak of the gateway into the steading being closed, a rare occurrence. Wulfstan was plainly taking no chances, even though they'd left the Raiders a good half a day's ride behind.

Æthelflæd appeared before him; concern etched on her young face. Her hair was neatly tied back, and he saw that she'd added a clean apron to her usual attire. He grimaced at its intent. In her hand, she held a piece of soft cloth and a small container of what he assumed held warmed salted water.

Leofwine offered her a lopsided smile, and she raised her querying eyebrows at him. He opened his mouth to speak and then closed it again. He was too exhausted. With a soft kiss on his head, she bent before him and extended the cloth to wipe the area around his wound carefully. She tut-tutted softly as she worked and did ask gently, 'Just what exactly he'd done to himself now.' Leofwine shrugged an apology, and she laughed softly.

'I think it's probably not as bad as it feels. The skin is cut above your eye and then on your cheeks, but it's missed the eye itself. I imagine if the healer stitches it cleanly, it will look well and good in a short space of time. She should be here soon, but this will work for now.' Æthelflæd handed him a welcome horn of ale, which he drank deeply from and felt it work its magic at loosening his aching muscles and pounding head, laced as it was with something to soothe him.

Leofwine drank his fill and then handed the horn back to Æthelflæd. She still held the cloth over his eye, but he could see her watching how her servants acquitted themselves in the aftermath of a small battle. She didn't issue any commands, and he assumed she was pleased with the men and women who served her home.

A shout at the gate and a scuffle at the door signified the arrival of the healer, who quickly set about stitching Leofwine's face with small neat movements. He tried to smile his thanks, but by then, his eye was rolling with exhaustion, and he was grateful when Horic and Wulfstan heaved him to his feet and carried him to his bed. As Æthelflæd tugged his boots from his feet, he closed his eye and drifted away to oblivion where there was no pain.

Leofwine woke stiff and sore at some point during the night, taking a moment to remember where he was and why he hurt and why his entire body was so lethargic.

Besides him, Æthelflæd slept curled up on her side. Her hair splayed behind her. Shifting on the bed, he shuffled to the side and took a moment to consider his next actions. He needed to empty his bladder desperately and heaved himself unsteadily to his feet before staggering uncertainly out of his room and through the main room. His men all slept, but Hunter slunk up to him and, seeming to sense what he wanted, walked beside him to the small latrine outside.

It was the middle of the night, and it was almost pitch black, with only a sliver of the moon showing. Leofwine could hear two of his men whispering to each other as they kept watch through the long night, and he called out a hello as he went about his business.

They responded but didn't bother him with further conversation, and he sank gratefully back into his bed with the help of Hunter, only moments later. Æthelflæd hadn't even moved in his absence.

He thought he'd drop straight back to sleep, but instead, he laid there and recalled his brief battle of yesterday. Unease was clawing at his innards, and he wanted to try and rationalise it away. He'd fought well. He'd retrained himself in a way to seek to compensate for his lack of sight, and yet it seemed as though it was not good enough.

While he could fight against Raiders who were clearly unskilled, the abler of the warriors was too much for him and saw his lack of vision as his weakness. He'd need to determine if there was another way to protect himself should he face them in battle again, and he was concerned by the fact that the final two warriors had plainly known who he was. Could Swein still be interested in killing him? It was not a pleasant thought.

Leofwine felt his heart beat rising in his chest and a moment of full panic. He'd assumed that back in England, he'd be safe from Swein's clutches, mainly as Swein was supposedly busy fighting Olaf in Norway. It seemed as though Swein might have alerted other Raiders of his intention to finish the job he'd started so well in Shetland. Leofwine hoped that he'd not offered some monetary incentive to the Raiders to kill him.

Now he felt his breathing coming short and shallow, and it was aggravating the pain from his wound. He could feel the stitches tugging on his face with each shallow breath, and unintentionally he moaned low in his throat. Instantly, Æthelflæd was wide-awake beside him. She looked at him in concern from the low light seeping through the slightly open door from the main room, and he tried to offer a smile of reassurance, but he could barely catch his breath. Leofwine didn't want her to see him not facing his deepest fears, but he couldn't bring himself under control.

Seeing his distress, Æthelflæd sprinted from the bed and quickly poured him what he assumed was water from a weathered jug on the sideboard. She handed it to him, and he was disappointed to see that his hands were shaking violently. She steadied his hands in her own and helped him raise a simple wooden cup to his lips. He swallowed the liquid, surprised by its sweet taste, and she explained.

'The healer left it for you. She said it would calm you and offer some relief from the pain.'

Gratefully, Leofwine drank it all and then asked for more. In no time at all, he'd drunk three full cups and felt his breathing calm and the tightness in his chest easing. His fears now seemed a little ridiculous. He was sure that Swein could not be interested in him. Perhaps the Raider had just made a calculated comment to knock him off his stride.

Æthelflæd took the cup from him and returned it to the sideboard. As she walked, he found himself admiring her gently swaying form from behind. When she turned around to come back to him, he gasped in pleasure, feeling desire stir. Her full breasts curved invitingly in the gentle light. She quirked him an amused smile and slid back under the bedclothes, turning to face him with a question on her face.

Leaning towards her, he carefully kissed her waiting lips, and she responded as gently. He stretched out his hand to cup her breasts, and she moaned slightly under his touch, arching to meet his hand. His desire ran molten hot, and he reached for her and pulled her against his body.

Leofwine could feel every curve and dip of her chest and

waist, and she giggled mischievously as the kiss deepened. She was running her hands over his body, and he moaned in pleasure, the pain and discomfort of his wound temporarily forgotten. It was perhaps, after all, time that they gave their son a playmate, and if it made his pain diminish at the same time, then he could think of no reason why he shouldn't indulge in a little after-battle enjoyment.

But even that didn't distract him entirely from his newfound fear. Would he be safe nowhere? Was Swein determined to finish the job he'd started two years ago?

9
AD997

The weeks that followed were a hubbub of activity and frenzy. Reports had to be sent to the king and men assigned to monitor the scant coastline of Leofwine's lands and also along the many rivers.

Reports also filtered through of raids in the south-west, most notably when the king's uncle's establishment at Tavistock was burned to the ground and the lands across the disputed borders with Dyfed and Gwynedd. There was a feeling of quiet panic amongst everyone. The farmers hoped their crops would grow quicker, and the sheep fatten more quickly than normal, so they could be harvested or slaughtered sooner, and stores could be laid in for the hopefully more peaceful winter.

There were occasional scares when smoke marked the horizon, and Wulfstan and the household troop trained harder and longer and faster than ever before under the blazing sun of perfect summer weather.

Leofwine walked almost ghostlike through all the activity. His wound had soured and grown infected, and he'd been confined to his bed for some weeks, and even then, his recovery had been tortuously slow.

While he might give his assent to the actions Wulfstan was taking on his behalf, Leofwine could hardly have said he was instrumental in ordering scouting parties and in assuring his people that they would be protected should an attack come.

Leofwine reassured himself that his wound caused it all, but in his heart, he knew that he fretted about Swein and that it was his fear that caused him to turn away from the work he should be doing.

As Leofwine's strength slowly returned, he took to training with his men for the same long sessions, trying to rid himself entirely of his weakness caused by his partial sight. Somehow he hoped that a new technique would present itself to him if he just trained often enough.

He went to his bed each night, exhausted having trained all day, and pleasured his wife in the hope that she'd carry another son for him soon, and every night he had nightmares similar to those when he'd first been wounded in Shetland.

Sometimes Leofwine cried out in his sleep, and he always woke dripping with sweat. The frequency of his baths became something of a burden to his household used to only provide hot water for such needs once a week, but in the increased heat of the summer, he could not stand to be around himself unless he bathed.

He also demanded his clothes washed more often, occasioning Æthelflæd to decry the amount of soap they were buying from the market.

Leofwine tried to take everything in good spirits but knew he was failing to fool Wulfstan, and his gaze became increasingly concerned when he watched Leofwine fighting or feasting or drinking too much. Leofwine found himself almost desperate to avoid spending time with the man even though it was a physical impossibility. Wulfstan was his man by oath as well as the leader of his household troop.

The matter came to a head when Leofwine received a summons to attend a witan the king had convened to discuss the Raiders and the planned response. Arranging to leave his newly pregnant wife at home with some of his most experienced warriors, worry gnawed at him throughout the journey to Cookham, a royal palace built by King Alfred, along the Thames but closer than London.

The nearness of the vast river throughout their journey slowly gnawed at his resolution to beat his nightmares about Swein. By the time his cavalcade arrived, Leofwine was jumpy and ill-tempered, none of which was helped by his overhearing of Wulfstan issuing orders about ensuring he was safe to the men, amongst them Oscetel and Horic, and advising them to tread carefully around him before they'd even left his father's hall.

Throughout the day-long journey, Leofwine allowed his anger and frustration to fester so that after he'd been greeted by the king's servants and shown to a room he could call his own, within the grand two-storied wooden hall, he called Wulfstan to him and asked everyone else to leave them alone.

His men filed out of the room like naughty children, and to further fuel the flame, Wulfstan didn't look at all concerned about what Leofwine might have to say to him, and then, before Leofwine could even speak, Wulfstan began to talk in a calm, controlled voice.

'I've compiled information about Swein and have also

had Horic send out some feelers to men he knows and trusts in the Northern kingdoms. The reports received back are less than reassuring. Swein has decided that you're as much his enemy as Olaf. My lord, your fears are, regrettably, well-founded.'

Leofwine felt his anger ebb at the news he'd so feared. Wulfstan looked at him reassuringly, and Leofwine suddenly felt weak. He stood his ground, helping himself to some water from his water bottle as he took time to consider how he should react. He walked towards the closed door, suddenly desperate to be outside again and feel the wind of the warm day on his face. But he stopped; a further, terrifying thought had taken hold.

'What about Æthelflæd and my boy?'

'My lord, there's no mention of them. It's you he detests. You and Olaf and no doubt many more men who've attempted to go against his wishes.'

Leofwine looked sharply at Wulfstan.

'You and Horic have discussed this at length?'

'Yes, my lord. We felt it was only prudent. We both heard what that man said to you before he tried to kill you, and we both know why your recovery has taken so long.'

Leofwine nodded to show he understood. And then he straightened himself and stood tall. Hearing his worst fears confirmed was a calming balm. To know that Swein wanted him dead suddenly gave him the impetus never to let it happen, which had been so lacking while he fretted and fussed.

'Thank you, Wulfstan,' Leofwine spoke, turning to face the man. Wulfstan looked a little shrunken, and suddenly his years seemed to have attached themselves to him, like heavyweights pulling on his eyes and shoulders, turning his hair ever greyer.

Wulfstan looked up at Leofwine in surprise at the words, and the flicker of a smile flashed across Leofwine's face.

'My lord?' Wulfstan asked, concern evident on his face at Leofwine's unexpected response.

'Well, now we know the bastard is out to get me, we'll just have to make sure that he never succeeds, won't we? Now come. There should be ale and food in the hall below. Let us drown our sorrows and not think of the bloody Raiders for one night. No doubt the king will have our heads full of them tomorrow.'

Wulfstan raised his eyebrows in a show of almost disbelief. Slowly a grin spread across his face, a rare show of pleasure, and then he was laughing out loud.

'Leofwine, you surprise me again. And that is your greatest strength. Don't forget that.'

With that, Wulfstan strode from the room, uncharacteristically before Leofwine, and could be heard laughing softly to himself as he made his way to the king's hall. Leofwine felt a genuine smile grace his face, testing his newly healed scar and finding that it held, he realised this was his first real smile since his slow recovery.

10

AD997

The king was concerned with the news that Raiders were ransacking his lands, showing real annoyance that it was distracting everyone from the new law code he wished to promulgate and which had been his main concern earlier in the year.

The irony was not lost on Leofwine. The king's projected law code was intended to regulate conditions in the eastern kingdoms settled by the first wave of Raiders during King Alfred's reign, while a new wave of Raiders was now causing similar issues.

Still, Leofwine's recent encounter with the Raiders was sobering enough that he, too, felt the need to pressure the king into further action. It was time to deal a blow to the Raiders. They could no longer come and take what they wanted when they wanted. They needed to be stopped.

The attacks on the Western Provinces, and Lord Ordulf's lands, had been severe and almost constant. Leofwine understood that Tavistock abbey was little more than a burned-out ruin, and that saddened him, for it was the family abbey of Lady Elfrida, and he knew she would grieve for the destruction.

Leofwine was also aware that Lady Elfrida grieved for another of her allies, Lady Ælfflæd. He was unsurprised to find her absent from the king's witan. No doubt, she had other concerns on her mind.

The king also had worrying news to share with the witan. There were rumours that the Duke of Normandy was aiding the Raiders, providing them with a ready base before they launched their attacks on the exposed coastline of the land. That, compounded with Leofwine's knowledge that the Raiders could also sneak down from the Outer Islands, hopping from island to island, even colluding with the Irish kings, made the situation in England critical.

It meant that for all that England was an island, potential enemies, even from the northern lands, effectively surrounded it. While the ealdorman of Northumbria tried to hold the peace with the inhabitants of the land of the Scots, Leofwine was kept busy ensuring that the border area with the Welsh kingdoms was also free from unrest.

While the ealdormen and king's thegns all diligently listened to the sermon given by the bishop of London, Wulfstan, there was an undercurrent of unease amongst all the men. Æthelred seemed oblivious to it all, sitting patiently through the sermon of the cleric and feasting his men in his hall later. While the rumours rushed through the assembled dignitaries, none of it seemed to touch the king, or if it did, the king was unconcerned.

A cold fear built within Leofwine. Could the king be so blind to what was happening around him? Surely he must realise the danger the country was in? He'd been prepared to offer a geld to the Raiders only a handful of years ago in order to achieve a peace. In fact, he'd done so twice now – on both occasions to Lord Olaf. Did Æthelred not appreciate by now that more decisive action was needed? That money couldn't buy the sort of peace England needed. No, England needed warriors to protect her, men who could be relied upon to drive fear into the hearts of the Raiders, to make them think twice about attacking an enemy who was most likely to kill them.

Leofwine indulged with the ealdormen, clerics, and the most minor noblemen who jostled for position, including Wulfheah and Ufegat, allies from when he'd been a youth at court, during the feast the king gave that evening.

All the minor officials hoped to one day be given a position of responsibility as a reeve or a port-reeve, or even if they were lucky enough, a sheriff or even an ealdorman, and all were keen to have allies amongst the select group of ealdormen that the king seemed loath to increase.

Leofwine remained jovial and well-tempered throughout the evening, trying not to let the gossip and unease in the room show on his face while absorbing as much information as possible. People were keen to speak to him about the attack earlier in the year, and even though he'd rather not have relived those moments, it was impossible not to.

The king's uncle had refused to attend the witan, informing the king his place was protecting the people of his lands. While Ealdorman Æthelweard was attending, it was only because he'd left his son to guard the Western Provinces and because Lord Ordulf could be relied upon to race to the protection of any area that needed it.

That night, Leofwine struggled to sleep, and when he did finally manage to sleep, it was not the sort of rest that would stand him in good stead for the morning and whatever arguments were to be had in the witan that day.

The morning was dull and overcast, serving a too-ready reminder of Leofwine's sour mood. The looks and whispered comments that reached his ears and which his men regrettably relayed to him helped further to undermine his already shaky confidence in his abilities. While people were pleasant enough when he spoke to them, as soon as his back was turned, there were those plotting to undermine him and, if possible, replace him as the ealdorman of the Hwicce.

The king was full of good cheer and strove to discuss at even greater length his new law code. Leofwine was mildly pleased to see the king in his element, happily discussing and offering counter suggestions to comments that the other ealdormen submitted on what was and what wasn't acceptable.

The king was particularly respectful of the words provided by bishop Wulfstan and his eldest ealdorman, Æthelweard, but at heart, much of what he was doing was merely reiterating the already current status quo, only now it would have the king's seal of approval on it.

There was some minor discussion about the Raiders, but nothing more than that, with the king seeking some reassurance from his ealdormen that they would call on the fyrd to protect the land if need be. Leofwine didn't miss the look of consternation on the face of Ealdorman Æthelweard, but without Lord Ordulf, or the queen dowager at the witan, there was little that could be done to force the king to greater action.

Eventually, the king asked all those assembled to witness his charter granting back land to the Old Minster at Winchester. This was another occasion when the king was undoing an injustice from earlier in his reign when he said he'd been poorly guided. No one said, but all knew that the king meant by the now dead Ealdorman Æthelwine.

As Leofwine stepped forward, Hunter at his side and under his outstretched hand, to add his mark to the charter, he stumbled on the uneven and unknown floor of the wooden hall. He fell heavily on his left side. Where one moment he'd been standing, the next he was flat on the floor and struggling to regain his feet. He was aware, as his cheeks flushed bright red, that there was a stunned silence of disbelief all around him.

Silence swept through the hall, and then a cacophony of whispers, louder than the roar of battle, and time seemed to drag. Leofwine felt as though it took him almost an entire day to stand once more, and only with the aid of Wulfstan did Leofwine find his feet.

Leofwine knew great damage had been done. He'd shown yet another weakness in front of all the assembled ealdormen, clerics and members of the king's court. Even the king favoured him with a pensive look. He knew then that it wouldn't matter that he was the only one to have faced the Raiders and defeated them. It was his fall that they'd all be discussing.

When Leofwine finally made it to the elegant wooden table at the front of the great king's hall, he was unsurprised to find his name at the bottom of all the other ealdormen's, Leofsige above him That the witness list had been written before his fall, only added to his fears.

Leofwine hastily scratched his mark on the vellum and turned to walk through the crowd of men and women who were still to add their mark. He looked neither left nor right as he walked, concentrating on putting one foot in front of the other. Hunter was at his side, and he hovered his hand over where her head was to determine if she veered from her path without clinging to her, like a drowning man to a piece of floating wreckage. Wulfstan walked behind him, proud and tall in his bearing.

At the end of the long press of people, Leofwine turned and bowed toward his king. Æthelred had plainly been watching him and nodded his assent to his most lowly ealdorman's request to be excused. Leofwine could see, even with his half vision, that the king's expression was still thoughtful.

Once outside in the clear air, he felt Wulfstan grab his right shoulder and Hunter slink under his hand to guide him more fully. He finally acknowledged the pain that was running up and down the left side of his leg and his arm, on the side he'd fallen, and with a quiet gasp of pain, he stumbled away from the witan, feeling more a fraud than ever before. Wulfstan didn't speak or offer words of encouragement. There was no need. They both knew that his fall would always be marked against him, even more damaging than his injuries sustained at the hands of Swein of Denmark.

THE ANGLO SAXON CHRONICLE ENTRY FOR AD997

This year went the army about Devonshire into Severn-mouth, and equally plundered the people of Cornwall, North-Wales, and Devon. Then went they up at Watchet, and there much evil wrought in burning and manslaughter. Afterwards they coasted back about Penwithstert on the south side, and, turning into the mouth of the Tamer, went up till they came to Liddyford, burning and slaying everything that they met. Moreover, Ordulf's minster at Tavistock they burned to the ground, and brought to their ships incalculable plunder. This year Archbishop Ælfric went to Rome after his staff.

11
AD998

Leofwine received an unwelcome summons from his king as summer attempted to rear its head from the bitter cold of the long winter months. It filled his heart with dread but equally, he couldn't help but think that the king was right to order his ealdormen to his side.

The Raiders would simply not leave the country alone. After his encounters with them last year, when he'd been moved to doubt his abilities to defend his own people, they'd kept up a steady presence, even staying for the winter on the Isle of Wight. It was an outrage, and it needed to be dealt with.

The meeting had been called for the festival of Easter at Oxford, a strategic location for it was far away from the Raiders and their enclave to the south, and while it did lie on the River Thames, the Raiders would be forced to travel in plain sight of many settlements along the way. It was unlikely that they'd make the journey without first being spotted, by which time Oxford could be reinforced or abandoned, depending on the size of the attacking force.

The Raiders didn't like to leave their ships untended. But by now, Leofwine had also realised that the Raiders were not after the king. They wanted more of the portable wealth that Lord Olaf had robbed from the kingdom. Olaf's successes in Norway after his treaty with the king had made others jealous, and they wanted nothing more than to harvest the same wealth and claim their own land in an imitation of Olaf.

The northern people were always greedy for land. If they couldn't find it in their own country, then they were brave enough to seek it elsewhere. Iceland had been colonised by the northerners, as had the Danelaw of England. It appeared that the Raiders were keen to take yet more of England.

Leofwine couldn't help but think that the heavier coinage issued last year might have contributed to the problem. If the king could afford to increase the weight of his coinage, what else could he afford? Leofwine imagined the Raiders shared his logic.

Leofwine had argued against the increase in weight. He agreed with the re-coinage but adding to the value of the silver pennies sent out all the wrong messages. He was amazed that none of the Raiders had taken advantage of the occasion to raid the moneyers in their scattered workshops up and down the land. After all, they'd done so before, and many were aware of the workings of the king's intricate coinage system.

The weather was bitter, although there was a hint of better to come in the slightly warmer mornings and longer-lasting evenings, each day seeming to stretch out further than the one before.

For now, Leofwine had travelled through rain and fog to reach his king. It was a journey of only a few days, but it was still time away from his heavily pregnant wife and child, apart from the comfort and ease of his own home, where nothing was ever moved without his permission and where everyone was mindful of his part blindness.

His loss of sight was something Leofwine had compensated for and accepted as a part of himself. He didn't need others who were distinctly uncomfortable with his ragged face to skirt around the issue or make allowances for him. It was doubly difficult when it was his king doing so.

With his fellow councillors, Leofwine was better able to react. He could tell them to leave him alone and make equally derisive comments about their lack of hair, height or sexual prowess. He couldn't do the same to his king.

Æthelred was a fickle character, and it was always best to tread carefully around him. The king preferred people who agreed with him and supported his plans and endeavours. To disagree with the king could be a costly experience, with a loss of position and land, but Leofwine knew that this time, he'd have to try and make the king see his reasoning as sound, even if he was unpopular doing so.

Leofwine had researched the conclusions he'd drawn about how England could be made safer, consulting the copy of the Anglo-Saxon Chronicle closest to his home.

And in that mighty Chronicle, he'd found what he'd hoped. Details of the old kings who'd faced the menace of Raiders and who'd attacked them. Taken the battle to them, instead of waiting for it to come to them, and he was hoping that with the support of the great scholar ealdorman, Æthelweard, they'd be able to convince the king that not only should they attack the Raiders, they should do so with the king leading the army.

The threat England faced was not unprecedented, and Leofwine felt sure that it was possible to counter it if they all worked together. England's king certainly had the money to rebuild his fleet. They just needed the right man to lead both the land and the sea army. Leofwine was going to argue that the right person was the king himself.

Not that he didn't understand the former reticence of the witan to ask the king to lead an army. With no other designated heir, it had been imperative to keep the king safe when he was younger and the only surviving male member of the House of Wessex. It had been preferable to endure the Raiders than to endure internal strife if there had been a succession crisis. Equally, it would have done the country no good if the Raiders had besieged them,while the few powerful ealdormen vied for the throne if the king had fallen in battle.

All in all, Leofwine didn't feel prepared enough to meet the onslaught of vested interests that would infect the witan, and yet knew that he must act decisively. He'd told Æthelflæd to stay behind in Deerhurst. There was no need for her to be at the mercy of the men who'd once seen to her virtual imprisonment in the nunnery when they'd thought him dead. She'd happily agreed, her advanced pregnancy another reason for her not to travel, but only on the provision that he take Wulfstan with him.

Horic, she was happy to have with her as she found his sharp humour easier going than Wulfstan, and she also got on very well with his blunt-speaking wife.

The journey from his home was only a relaxed two days in the late days of March. His usually calm horse was infected with the joys of the coming summer, evidenced in the blossom that was just beginning to form on hedgerows and trees. Leofwine constantly reined in the horse as he attempted to sidestep every little disturbance that skittered across the trackway they followed.

The track ran parallel with the Thames for much of the journey. Wulfstan and a small contingent of his men accompanied him. He's taken only five men, leaving the rest behind to guard his land. With the beginning of summer, Raiding activity was likely to take place, and he didn't relish the thought of his wife falling victim to such an attack.

They entered Oxford through the west gate, and Leofwine started as his horse's hooves caused faint sparks to rise as they clattered over the metaled road. He laughed at himself as Wulfstan rolled his eyes. It didn't matter how often they came here. He always forgot about the better roads running straight through the settlement from east to west and north to south. At the west gate stood one of the many churches that found their home in Oxford. St Mary's the Virgin stood at the east gate.

Leofwine was pleased to note that the rampart protecting the central part of the settlement was in good repair and in the process of having its ditch cleared from winter debris. The men and women who removed the muck and filth were coated from head to toe in mud and stagnant water and yet laughed and joked with each other as they worked industriously away.

Leofwine didn't envy them for their task. They called greetings to him as he rode past them, and he raised his arm in reply. He was a regular visitor to Oxford and was now even more recognisable with his ruined face.

Leofwine had sent ahead and arranged to stay with a far distant relative, but more importantly, a friend, while within the town. The king would take up residence near one of the churches, and there wouldn't be room for all to stay within the same religious house as him. Oxford was an entirely different venue to one of the king's palaces. The officials had more say over where they went and when they went. Something the king did not always desire but which apparently, this time, had decided was acceptable.

The settlement was filled with neatly placed wattle and daub buildings crowned with turfed roofs and, every so often, a timber building that had a second story. It was towards one of these structures that he and his men made their way on the second night of their journey.

The king would convene his witan on the next day, and Leofwine could tell that the settlement was filled to near capacity with those attached to the court or who'd come to pay their dues to the king. The roads were filled with horses and carts and the cries of sellers announcing their stock.

Smoke was billowing from the chimney of the home Leofwine stopped outside, a neat and tidy property close to one of the metalled roads but with lean-to stables evident to the rear. Leofwine gratefully slid from his still restless horse's back and was greeted by a man slightly older than him, wearing a long green tunic and trousers to match. A huge smile came to Leofwine's lips, which still tugged at his long-since healed wound, and he took the offered hand and clasped it warmly.

Oswald was an old friend from his time at court as a young man. They'd behaved passably well whenever their respective fathers were in attendance, but they'd misbehaved at the slightest opportunity. Oswald was now a much-respected reeve of Oxford, but Leofwine could see the younger man shining out of the older blue eyes. He didn't doubt that it would take little for them to get into such scrapes again.

Oswald clapped him warmly on the shoulder without even grimacing at the visible scar. They'd met many times since Leofwine had received his injury, and Oswald seemingly no longer even noticed it was there. Leofwine felt himself relax a little. It was always good to be amongst friends who made him feel comfortable without worrying about his lack of sight.

'Welcome, my friend. You are well?'

'Indeed, more than well. And you. You look as though you thrive a little too well.' Leofwine pointed at Oswald's slightly expanding stomach. Oswald laughed away the comment good-naturedly.

'There's far too much good eating to be had here. Come in, come in. I'll show you the feast we've laid out for you tonight.'

Leofwine handed the reins of his horse over to Oscetel with a slap to the horse's backside and followed his friend through the open wooden door and into a vast and airy room, adequately ventilated so that the smoke rose out of the vent holes at its centre.

There were candles and lamps all around the hall, and Leofwine made out a good number of people already within and sat at their board. Hunter stayed faithfully at his side, deflecting him around three obstacles - a chair, an abandoned set of shoes, and a freestanding table.

'You're a little later than I thought, and so I'm afraid the feast has already started. But not to worry. There's much to go around. Come sit and eat.'

Oswald pressed a drinking horn into Leofwine's unsuspecting hands and almost skipped back to his seat at the table. Leofwine walked a little more sedately behind him until he heard a great growl from his stomach as the tantalising smells of a freshly cooked meal assaulted his nose.

The food was delicious. A whole pig roasted over the fire, accompanied by bread and seasoned with delicate herbs and honey. A meagre selection of root vegetables accompanied the meal, the year still being too young for much to be ready for harvest. Still, it was a grand feast for a reeve to serve just before Easter, and Leofwine absently noted that even here, in a simple meal, the wealth of his country was in abundance.

The next morning Leofwine woke early from his well-earned sleep and prepared for the day ahead. He sighed deeply as he shrugged into his tunic and trousers, mindful of the troubles that the day could bring. His was not a lone cautioning voice on the council, but it felt that way.

Leofwine was keen to take action when it was needed but was only too aware that men did lie and steal and cheat, and sometimes a man's word should be considered in light of all the available evidence. His king was not so broad-minded and never would be.

In many ways, Æthelred was his own worst enemy, keen to listen to the voices of dissent around him rather than those who supported him.

It had rained long and hard during the night, and Leofwine could clearly hear the slosh of water as people ventured through rain-drenched streets.

Breakfast was a muted and rushed affair, his friend only too aware of his guest's trepidations of what the day would bring. While Oswald would himself be attending, it would be in a far more minor role than Leofwine's own.

Outside, the sky was a pale washed blue as if the torrential rains had taken much of the colour with it. But there was no sign of further rain, and Leofwine splashed through the puddles, smiling as he remembered his toddling son being berated by an irate Æthelflæd only a few days ago for doing the very same thing.

As Leofwine neared the site of the witan, held in one of the great churches that dominated the thriving settlement, the amount of footfall increased, and he found himself calling out greetings to those he recognised or those who remembered him.

He and the other dignitaries knew how vital it was to show a face of unity to those not summoned to the witan. It wasn't necessary for the general population to be aware of the wrangling and name-calling that resulted during the often-heated debates.

Leofwine specifically looked for the aged Æthelweard but didn't see him and hoped that today he'd not hear bad news. He should perhaps have sought him out earlier to discuss his views on the Raiders, but he'd not fancied a cold and long ride in the dark days of winter to reach the ealdorman of the Western Provinces.

Leofwine berated himself slightly for his indolence while acknowledging that he'd needed the seclusion of the winter months to recover from the attack early last year. He'd not fully appreciated how much it had stolen his confidence in his abilities.

Leofwine now felt stronger than before, more adept at his swordplay and ready to face anything that the hostile Raiders presented him with.

Perhaps his king needed a similar awakening. Maybe then Æthelred would be fuelled by the same desire to seek not revenge but a grudging respect from the men who called themselves Raiders and looked with disdain on the armies of the ealdormen and their king. Perhaps.

Inside, the church was crowded with men who sat not quietly but respectfully. He noticed Lord Æthelmær first and then quickly scanned for his father. Thankfully, Ealdorman Æthelweard was present. Leofwine offered a small prayer to his God and then set out to greet him, Wulfstan at his heels and Hunter before him to warn him of any uneven flooring.

The church was a magnificent structure, half in stone and half in wood, with a roof that seemed to stretch enormously high on its intricate crossed stone arches. There were a large number of windows, most filled with coloured glass, although, in the far reaches of the church, where the congregation couldn't necessarily see, the windows were covered in more mundane skins held taut to prevent them from flapping in the wind.

It was reasonably cool within the great room following the rain of last night, and Leofwine was pleased that he'd worn his ceremonial cloak as opposed to just his most elegant clothing.

There was a fire burning in a small brazier near the entrance to prevent the smoke from filling the room, but much of its heat was being pushed out of the open door. Leofwine shivered slightly in anticipation of the long hours he'd spend inside. Wulfstan turned a wry glance his way. He must have been having similar thoughts.

Æthelweard was already seated near the front of the church, ready for the opening sermon that would be given by Wulfstan. Bishop Wulfstan was already within the church, fiddling with the candles to ensure maximum light fell over the magnificent copy of the bible chained to the podium.

The cover of the bible glittered with jewels and gold, and Leofwine again realised that even in the church, the wealth of the land was on copious display.

Æthelweard rose to clasp the forearm of Leofwine and spoke gruffly,

'It's good to see you hail and hearty. I feared for you after the attack, but I can see that some time away from the court has allowed you to recover fully.'

Leofwine smiled at the warmth in the older man's voice. He was another who'd tried to fill the void left by his own father's death.

'I'm well recovered now.'

'I see that you are, and no doubt, filled with plans to combat the scourge of the Norsemen.'

Leofwine looked at him in shock, and the old man chuckled good-naturedly,

'I'm no fool, Leofwine. Old I might be and happier with my quills and parchment than here, but I still know the way the mind of the young works.'

Leofwine made to interject, but Æthelweard forestalled him.

'I'm not saying that I disagree with you, either. Come, we must speak of this more but not now. We'll let the bishop say his fill, and then we'll share a meal together. For now, sit with me and present a united front.'

Leofwine did as he was bid, and only moments later, the king arrived in his bejewelled robes and with his ceremonial crown around his head. The king loved the initial pomp and ceremony of the convening of his witan, although, by the end of the day, he'd be cursing the weight of the crown and decrying to all who would listen that he'd not be wearing it again any time soon.

All the men quickly bowed their heads as the king passed and then hastily sought seats as bishop Wulfstan warmly greeted them all before starting the service. Unsurprisingly bishop Wulfstan had chosen as his sermon a long and complicated discourse on avarice and protecting the innocent. The king was transfixed throughout the long speech, and even Leofwine found himself being swept along by the force of the words. The man could certainly speak.

The sun crept around the clear sky as the service continued, and only as Leofwine felt a bone-numbing chill creeping up his body did the bishop stand aside and allow the rest of the day's events to get underway.

The podium was moved aside with great care, and a great wooden chair was placed where it had stood. The king swept to the seat, ordering the brazier be brought closer, and the witan was convened with kind words of welcome from the king himself. He looked as hale and hearty as ever and was noticeably in good cheer, his crown resting on his head.

The king laid some issues before his ealdormen and thegns and ecclesiastics that he'd like to discuss over the next few days, and then he sent them all on their way. They'd reconvene tomorrow in the king's hall in Oxford, and there they would discuss matters of state and then feast.

Leofwine struggled to rise when the king swept from the church, his legs stiff from a day of unusual inactivity. Besides him, Æthelweard's joints creaked as he rose, and Leofwine offered him a steadying arm. Clasping his arm tightly, Æthelweard stumbled to his feet and out into the fading light of the cool day.

Around them, the other men and women parted on good terms or cut away in small groups. Leofwine noticed with interest who went with whom. It was worth the inconvenience of hanging back to see who might have paired up during the long winter months when they'd been stirred to seek allies and alliances in the hope that they'd profit from them during the year.

Only the churchmen presented a genuinely cohesive front, trickling from the open doorway in a stream of soft rustlings from their ceremonial robes. Through the still air, Leofwine could hear them congratulating bishop Wulfstan on his sermon before they walked around to the rear of the church and entered the hospitable dwelling of the king's high reeve, crowned with bright lamps, the door half open, emitting an enticing glow from inside.

Æthelweard stood quietly at Leofwine's side, his son hovering uncertainly on the periphery until Leofwine offered him hearty greetings. They were of a similar age and had known each other since boyhood. Their relationship was not as easy as that between him and Æthelweard, but Leofwine persevered with the son for the sake of the father.

Leofwine found Æthelmær to be a little dull-headed, too set in his ways to see possibilities in the constantly changing atmosphere of the witan, and too slow to react to the machinations of the other ealdormen, churchmen, thegns and the royal family. That said, Æthelmær had a small group of men around him who were his constant supporters, and he included amongst them the king's uncle, Ordulf, and ealdorman Ælfhelm's sons, Wulfheah and Ufegat and his Uncle, Wulfric Spot and also Wulfgeat.

All of these men were loosely bound together thanks to Lady Elfrida. When cast out from the inner working of her son's court, she'd found her own way of infiltrating it. Even now, Leofwine was unsure if the king was even aware that they all had split loyalties.

Æthelmær was almost a double of his father, only less stooped with age and exuding an air of action. His eyes were a deep hazel brown to match his slightly darker complexion, and he wore his beard long but well-groomed.

Leofwine clasped his arm in greeting, and the younger man broke into a smile of welcome. That was another thing. Æthelmær was aware of his lack when compared to his father and was overly touchy if not acknowledged in his right. Leofwine wondered if he himself would have been such a complicated man to be around if his father had lived as a shining example of courtliness and military action, not that he had been a shining example, but all the same, the thought amused Leofwine.

Together the small group of them strolled down the street that was quiet as the day drew to an end, and back towards Leofwine's lodging for the night. They talked in muted tones as they walked, enjoying the activity after the long day of sitting but mindful of Æthelweard's older, shorter and more laboured steps.

'The Raiders you encountered, I take it they were the normal blood-thirsty lot,' Æthelweard asked Leofwine in an undertone.

'Regrettably, yes, but not a full contingent of them, no more than seventy, either only a small ship or some scouting party. Still, the low numbers didn't make them easy to drive back.'

'No, it never does. They move like ghosts across the land, and they're totally unpredictable. I assume you plan on petitioning the king about them?'

'Yes, I do. I'd hopes of your support in the matter. I've read the histories in the Chronicle and know that in the past...'

'The king led his army against them.' Æthelweard finished the sentence for him.

'I've read the Chronicle as well, translated it for my own Latin version.' Leofwine had been aware of the work but glanced at the ealdorman in surprise when he seemed embarrassed by his abilities and skill. But Æthelweard didn't notice his surprise, his eyes firmly on the floor beneath his walking stick as though daring it to trip him.

'I believe you're reasoning is sound. I'm not so sure the king will agree. Even his father had little cause to ride out against the Raiders, although he did once, if I recall correctly, to the north.'

'And when the south was attacked, when Æthelred was still a child, it was the ealdormen who fought in his place. Ealdorman Bryhtnoth knew his responsibilities and took them seriously, as did other men, they perished in the fight, and I'm afraid, I forget their names.'

'I know. I need to think about how best to approach Æthelred. But it's difficult. I can't imply that he's weak and without honour because he doesn't want to face the Raiders. They're a terrifying force to be reckoned with, regardless of whom they call their leader.' Leofwine spoke with feeling.

'The men I encountered in Shetland were truly horrifying in their systematic slaughter of all those who stood in their way. We were lucky to escape alive. And this other force last year, they were just as brutal if not more so because they were on hostile land.'

'I pity you your experiences with them. They've scarred you but given you something that too few of the rest of us have, the actual experience of fighting them and seeing them in full flow.' Leofwine feared the older ealdorman was humouring him, but there was something in Æthelweard's eyes that spoke of his own experiences.

Leofwine would have liked to ask the question but

realised that if none knew about it, it should stay that way. But it meant a great deal to him, all the same. Better to know that he was not alone.

Ealdorman Ælfric only ever ran from the Raiders. Ealdorman Ælfhelm was a man of the north and, therefore, most likely to be allies with them, whereas Ealdorman Leofsige appeared to have as much military experience as the king. Essentially none.

'Do you think I should approach the other ealdorman outright? Perhaps if we all advocate it, the king will agree without the witan having to force him.'

'Oh no, that's the worst possible tactic imaginable. The king doesn't like to feel that he's being forced or coerced. We'll need to ensure the king decides it's his idea. Leave it with me for now. I'll think about it further, but now, I must seek some rest. Good day to you, Leofwine.'

'Good day, my lord.' After another hearty arm clasp, the older man limped away, his son and the remaining entourage flanking him.

The conversation had gone well, and yet Leofwine felt deeply unsettled. The old man was, well, old. He'd not be here forever. Leofwine needed to learn how to handle the king better himself. He could have blundered even more magnificently than when he'd missed his step at last year's witan. He sighed deeply and heard a soft grunt from Wulfstan behind him.

'Surely you didn't expect it to be easy?'

Leofwine smiled ruefully at the man, resplendent in his court clothing that had been stitched personally by Æthelflæd as an apology for flaying him with her tongue when they first returned from their ill-fated trip. He, too, was an older man, and yet he carried his years far more lightly than Æthelweard. Leofwine knew he'd live well into his old age.

'I suppose I had *hoped* it might be a little easy,' Leofwine complained. 'But then, I should have known better.'

'Æthelweard knows what he's doing. Watch him and learn from his manoeuvrings.'

Leofwine chuckled, 'I was just thinking the same thing, and now I think I should look at you too and learn from your ways. I believe you know more than you're letting on.'

Now it was Wulfstan's turn to offer a brief smile.

'I'm, regrettably, a little older than you, and I've watched our king since he was a boy. He has many qualities to esteem him, but I fear his decision-making is not always as it should be. Æthelred always needs to be right and will never apologise for mistakes unless he can blame them on others. As he does now when he blames Ealdorman Æthelwine for his greed towards the church.'

'Much easier to blame someone when they're dead,' Leofwine mused.

'Indeed. And if they're not dead, then the king tends to forgive some too easily.'

Leofwine held his tongue. There was no need to mention the name of ealdorman Ælfric. He was far from the king's wisest choice of ally, and yet he could be forgiven anything, even treason. Leofwine tried not to become too frustrated by that fact.

The two men walked home in comfortable silence and were greeted with tantalising smells as soon as they neared Oswald's home. Leofwine's stomach rumbled once more, and he was pleased to be welcomed inside, where plentiful food was available, and it was warm, and not everyone was trying to exploit his weaknesses.

12

AD998

The new day saw the work of the witan begin in earnest.

The king arrived in the pomp and glory he enjoyed, escorted by Lady Elfrida and his sons. Leofwine met the inquisitive eyes of Lady Elfrida with an incline of his head. He was always aware of just how much he owed to her and just how influential she had the potential to be with the king.

Not that her priorities in recent years had been the king, but rather his sons. All the same, Leofwine could appreciate that the woman he watched was a rare thing in Æthelred's court, someone who had clung on to power for many, many years and, more importantly, had fought her way back to the king's good graces.

Leofwine allowed much of the day's business to pass over his head. He knew of complaints about Æthelred's new law code and of Æthelred's pleasure with how well the new coinage had been implemented next year. That was not what interested him.

Only as the day was drawing to an end inside the cold church did anyone dare to raise the issue of the Raiders, and Leofwine was most intrigued to see it being done by Ælfric, the ealdorman of Hampshire, who had such a stormy relationship with the king and yet remained his ally.

'My lord king, I must alert you to a series of raids within the lands I govern and would like to seek your approval to meet with the leader of the men and agree to terms with him.'

Ælfric was a stocky man of middle years, with a neat beard and receding hairline. He carried his best court clothes well, and Leofwine considered how well the clothes had been designed to mask the older man's protruding belly so well.

Ælfric stood alone before the king as he spoke, but his words were greeted with nods of agreement from all around him, even from Leofwine. The king, who until these words had been paying rapt attention to everything happening in the church, turned sharply to gaze at the man he was unable or unwilling to remove from power despite his contrariness and past treasons.

'I've heard of these Raiders. Are they the same ones Lord Leofwine defeated last year with the help of the household troop and who attacked the Western Provinces?'

Leofwine lowered his head to hide the sudden smirk that came to his face. The king was needling Ælfric, implying that if a half-blind man could defeat them, then surely he could.

Leofwine didn't watch Ælfric's reaction to the king's needling, preferring to work on clearing his expression. When he raised his head once more, Leofwine caught the glance of the king and bowed to acknowledge the endorsement in his words. Ælfric had by now recovered enough to continue speaking in an almost smooth voice. His face, no matter his inner thoughts, was a mask of agreeability.

'Regrettably no, my king. I understand that particular set of ships has left our shores now and have sought aid from the king in Dublin.'

Leofwine started at those words. He'd not known that the ships had sailed over the narrow stretch of sea to Ireland. He'd hoped that they'd turned tail and returned to the chill Northern lands.

'This is a new set of ships, only recently come, I fear, with the assistance of our neighbours in Normandy. They've attempted many small raids along the coast, but I worry that they may only be scouts and that a larger ship army is coming this way.'

Æthelred looked concerned as Ælfric continued to explain the situation, his forehead furrowed in thought.

'Have you already met with them?'

Æthelred's eyes narrowed as he tried to gauge a reaction from the semi-traitorous ealdorman.

'Not I, my lord king. They arrived as I was preparing to travel here for the witan, but I've left half of my household troop behind, and they're sending me updates daily.'

The king ceased to watch the man with narrow eyes and instead looked around at the faces of all before him.

'These Raiders will not leave my land alone. We've tried buying them off, and still, they come.' His voice was growing angry as he continued to speak.

'Do none of you have a good idea as to how to drive them from my shores?'

Æthelred's eyes glinted angrily at all who sat before him, and even Leofwine felt the heat of his wrath. Before he could stand and offer his suggestion, Wulfstan laid a steadying hand on his arm and nodded to where Æthelweard was slowly rising to his own feet.

The king turned to him respectfully and dimmed his anger a little in the face of the wise old man he'd known all of his life, although Leofwine understood that Æthelred had not always respected Æthelweard.

'My lord king, they've been a scourge on us for many a year now, and I agree that we must do something decisive to drive them all back. The geld we paid to Olaf Tryggvason certainly worked, and he's taken to our faith with a passion I find almost hard to accept, but the reports from the priests we sent with him are filled with tales of his good deeds and good works, and so we cannot totally discredit them.'

'There are rumours he's converted the Outer Islands of Shetland as well as the people of Trondheim and greater Norway. The problem is that there are simply too many of the Raiders for us to do the same to them all.'

'The men have not fallen for our rouse that we paid all our available gold to Olaf Tryggvason and come looking for treasure as great as his. They set fire to our settlements and monasteries.'

'They kill our holy men and abuse our women. There are little ship armies everywhere, and many are led by men who are either incredibly lucky or exceedingly well trained. Some of them are even scions of the royal houses in the Northern lands of Denmark, Norway and Sweden. I'm afraid that they see us as easy pickings, a quick way to get rich and then go home and live a life of luxury.'

'I know all this, Æthelweard. I know all this. Do you have anything new to add?'

Æthelweard fixed a mild eye on the king and continued to speak as if his liege lord hadn't interrupted him.

'I think it's time we thought about why these men act as they do, what compels them? Only I think the answer might be in 'who' compels them?'

'Who, I don't understand? Are you saying we need to look to their Gods for a reply?' Æthelred's voice showed his confusion.

'No, my lord king, no. I think we need to look at the men who lead these ship armies. I believe that they are the answer.' Æthelweard's voice was even-tempered as he tried to explain his thoughts.

Æthelred still looked puzzled by the older man's words, but it was clear that he was at least considering them as he sat in pensive silence. All around, the other men of the witan were equally looking at Æthelweard with either disbelief or with a begrudging approval.

Leofwine watched his king intently and then tracked the course of one of Lady Elfrida's young servants as he scuttled across the open area between the king and where she sat, and whispered a quick message to the king, all blond hair and brand-new clothing gleaming under the candles.

Æthelred looked up with a slight smile on his face as the servant ran back to his mistress. He eyed Æthelweard with an excited smile.

'Do you mean that I should examine their leaders and learn from their actions?'

'I do, my lord king, I do. Some of these men are dull beyond words, and yet something lends an almost magical air to their endeavours, and I think it's their leaders.' Leofwine was amazed that Æthelweard managed to keep his voice so smooth. Surely he must have wanted to speak with condescension for his king's inability to see the truth of what was happening.

'I confess I'd not considered that in the past. I believed that it wouldn't matter who led my men, provided they were acting on the king's word, but now I think you might be correct. Perhaps if I led them myself, I'd not endure such bitter disappointment in my ealdormen again.'

Leofwine was overjoyed to see the beaming smile tugging at his king's lips. And even more amused by the bitter smile on Ælfric's own. Hopefully, Ælfric was remembering his failures, which ultimately had led to the Raiders being so successful that ealdorman Bryhtnoth had been forced to face them at Maldon, the battle his father had met his death in, alongside Bryhtnoth.

The king was studying the faces of all the assembled ealdormen to determine their reaction. Only Ælfric did he studiously ignore. The assembled churchmen were whispering to each other, and even the king's mother, Lady Elfrida, was drawn into a debate with Ælfgifu, the king's wife, who sat in honoured attendance but had no role in the witan. She was the king's wife, not his counsellor.

As the hubbub quieted at the king's command, Æthelweard was bowed back to his seat, and in his wake, Leofsige bounded to his own feet. Leofsige looked smug when he spoke.

'But, my lord king, it's surely too dangerous to send you into a battle against the heathen mob? You might be injured, as dear Leofwine was only last year, although his obvious disfigurement may have contributed to that, or even worse, you might be killed.'

The king's face fell at the softly spoken words, and Leofwine groaned inwardly at the man's choice of words. Not for the first time, Leofwine labelled Leofsige a coward and thanked God that it had been him after all who'd faced the ravages of the Outer Isles attack.

Leofsige would not have fought for his life as he had. He'd not have gained the respect of the few northern men who currently called Leofwine their lord and who spoke with him at length about the inner determination of these Raiders to make themselves rich and retire to a secluded location with their shipmen to guard them in their advancing years.

And Leofsige had, of course, chosen just the right approach to make the king doubt the initiative.

In the sudden silence, no one moved, the other ealdormen waiting to see who would speak next. Surprisingly it was the bishop, Wulfstan. He stood quietly and spoke as sincerely as when he'd been preaching the day before, his hands clasped before him.

'My lord king, I humbly request that you consider these wisely spoken words. I know from my brief experiences as bishop that the congregation can be called upon to carry out significant tasks if they see that I, too, am willing. I've personally assisted with the dredging of the ditches around the walls of London. It's dirty, filthy work, not unlike I imagine battle to be, and yet they all worked willingly when I was amongst their midst.'

The king accredited the bishop with a brief smile, and then he sighed deeply and spoke to them all,

'I'll think on this. It's an idea not without merits, and I'm positive that if my lord Æthelweard is promoting the suggestion, then it must have worked in the past. In the meantime, we must make plans to attack these Raiders.'

'Ælfric, I call on you to raise your fyrd and patrol your coastline and rivers. They seem overly familiar with your land there, and Leofsige you must do the same. Leofwine, I assume you have already put plans into place.'

Æthelred turned a questioning face towards him.

'Yes, my lord king. Even now, many of my men are in training, and those who are too infirm to face them are out recruiting for the force. We plan on patrolling the exposed coastal areas, and along the vast estuary. I'm also planning on meeting with the Welsh on the other side of the border to ask them if they'll at the least do me the courtesy of informing me if they see the Raiders. I hope to gather a few extra supporters.'

'Excellent idea, Leofwine. And Æthelweard, I imagine you are taking precautions and Ælfhelm, what of you?'

'My lord king, as you know, with the vast numbers of Norsemen who already live on the lands north of the Humber, there's a significant amount of contact with these Raiders who seem strangely determined not to raid the lands of their compatriots. Still, I have a small, highly mobile force at the ready, and I have thought to recruit some mobile traders to my side. They've agreed to listen out for any mention of possible raids and inform me as soon as possible.'

Ælfhelm worked hard for his king and understood the curious nature of his divided lands and people. Rumour had it that while he was a converted and committed Christian, he did attend pagan rituals to keep the goodwill of his people.

Leofwine found him curiously hard to speak to. He was a great bull of a man, burly and hairy all over and with the energy of three men. He always had a massive ceremonial sword at his waist, bejewelled with a fortune in precious gems. Leofwine didn't doubt that many of his subjects were converted to his particular point of view due to his sheer size and dominating demeanour.

Æthelred nodded in agreement as he spoke.

'All good ideas, my lords, but still, I think we must work on a more cohesive strategy. I'd ask you all to think about this further and let me know your thoughts. But for now, I'd like to move to more pleasant thoughts. I think we should stop for the day and seek our feast. Come.'

The king strode from the front of the church as his pages and children ran to greet him, and even his mother, stooped with age, sought his attention. The assembled dignitaries moved no less quickly. It had been a long day, and all were hungry and thirsty.

The king had ordered the feast to be served within the largest building in the town, the hall of the town reeve, Brithstan. It was located behind the church and was an excellent building made of sturdy wood with a neatly thatched roof.

As Leofwine wearily left the church, he was greeted with the welcoming sight of light spilling from the open door of the hall, enticing smells which made his empty stomach rumble, and smoke from the indoor fires was drifting lazily in the slight breeze which blew the flowering trees with a quiet rustle.

Wulfstan was as ever at his side. He was no longer watching him as intently, but he had not relaxed his guard either. As they left the church, Oscetel peeled away from the tree he'd been standing under and walked nonchalantly over towards them. His face was perfectly smooth, betraying no sign of any worries or fears, and for a moment, Leofwine could not decide whether he was there to inform them of anything or just to check in on how the day's events had gone.

As Oscetel drew closer, he nodded in acknowledgement of his lord, and Leofwine realised he was just there for the news. Oscetel strode confidently through the highest men in the land, and Leofwine was gratified to see his confident warrior.

They exchanged a little news from the day's events, and then Oscetel returned to the rest of the men and his own, smaller feast at the home of Oswald. Leofwine left with Hunter and Wulfstan to attend the king's feast.

The feasting hall was more substantial than at Deerhurst, and it was crammed full of men, women and scampering children serving as pages to the highest dignitaries of the land. Smoke billowed from a huge hearth set in the middle of the hall and was filtered through an opening in the roof, which was constructed in such a way that the smoke escaped without letting the slightly damp air inside to torment the fire.

There was a delicious smell of roasting meat, and over the hearth, a large pig and the carcass of a cow were still being roasted. A string of well-behaved dogs stood to attention near the cook, who kept shooing them with a good-natured kick while, a moment later, offered them tiny offcuts.

At Leofwine's side, Hunter stood faithfully and patiently, ever ready to do her master's bidding. Again, Leofwine was astounded by just how well he'd trained the hound. He would be well and truly lost without her. Perhaps he needed to consider training another to do his bidding in case he lost her.

But the thought was too sullen for the feast and fled from

his mind as he was shown to a table and bench and helped himself to tasty morsel after tasty morsel. There were summer vegetables and roasted birds and beasts of every variety waiting for him to taste, and he dug in with an appetite that surprised him.

The welcome horn was passed along to Leofwine, and he raised it high to toast his king, catching his eye, before he drank deeply of the rich, strong ale contained within it. Its tang complemented the beef he ate, and he quickly grew a little drunk, feeling safe in the company of Wulfstan.

The king seemed to be enjoying himself as much as his men. Æthelred sat on a slightly raised platform at the front of the hall for all to see. With him sat his mother and wife, separated by the king, and his sons, Athelstan, Ecgberht, Edmund, Eadred and Eadwig, ranging in age from about fifteen to no more than five.

Bishop Wulfstan joined the king and his family on the dais, as did the more elderly Ælfheah of Winchester and Godwine of Rochester, a man currently high in the king's esteem and rumoured to be about to benefit from a significant restoration of land previously plundered from his bishopric. Ælfheah was all smiles and muted courtesy to the king he'd not always enjoyed a hospitable relationship with.

The king's sons were a real mixture of their mother and father. His oldest, Athelstan, carried himself with his father's erect bearing and shared his blond hair and high forehead, but his face was far more open than his father's. When things offended or annoyed him, the emotion always flashed across his face, just like it did on his mother's face.

Ecgberht had his father's closed face and his mother's build. He was smaller and more compact and shared her chestnut hair. He was a year younger than his oldest brother, and next to him sat Edmund, more a copy of his oldest brother. He was still a joyful young man, not yet fully grown into his more regal stance.

The two younger brothers were spitting images of Ecgberht. Eadred was not yet eight, and Eadwig had only four or five years to his name. Eadwig had only recently begun attending the king's witan, and Lady Elfrida was vigilant in ensuring he did nothing to embarrass himself.

The children were rarely seen without the king's mother. Even when they trained with the king's war band, she would frequently be watching and remembering who had the best stance and the best strokes.

Leofwine often wondered what sort of warrior Lady Elfrida would have made had she been born the man and not the woman. He was sure that England would not have fallen prey to the Raiders had she been the king.

Behind the heads of the royal family and those honoured by having the king's ear, there was a halo of light from a giant rack of fat candles and by it, all of the æthelings looked almost like Christ depicted in the magnificent church illustrations that Leofwine had seen. He doubted it was by chance.

Around him, Leofwine could see the other ealdormen with their chosen few from their household troops, all unarmed apart from a table dagger or seax. His son flanked Æthelweard, and the other men close to Æthelweard also stayed close. They were mindful of their lord's great age and drank sparingly while eyeing everyone in the hall, waiting to see if any had more to say about his earlier suggestion that the king should lead his men into battle.

Added to their number were Lord Ordulf, Lady Elfrida's

brother, and his own sons. Leofwine raised his drinking horn in acknowledgement of the older man's gaze.

Ealdorman Ælfric looked resplendent as ever in his expensive court clothes, but that didn't mask the almost permanent sneer on his face. He knew how everyone gossiped about him and his treachery, but there was little more anyone could do as he was so blatantly favoured by his king.

Leofsige's large figure was the next to catch Leofwine's eye. He seemed to be in excellent spirits, and Leofwine immediately wondered if his speaking up for the king meant that he was already being signalled out for more royal favour. Leofwine suppressed a sigh of annoyance and regret. He didn't hate Leofsige, but he certainly made his blood run cold with displeasure.

Ælfhelm of Northumbria had been in attendance at the witan earlier but was missing from the feast. Leofwine looked for him while trying to appear that he wasn't but finally had to mention it to Wulfstan.

'He's slightly out of favour with the king, my lord. He's spoken with Æthelred about his dissatisfaction. The king was unsurprisingly unhappy, and so Ælfhelm's absented himself from the feast.'

Leofwine was intrigued by the news. Frequently Ælfhelm and the king managed to maintain a charade of camaraderie. He wondered what had so offended Ælfhelm on this occasion. Leofwine would perhaps approach him and ask him. They were neighbours regarding land, if not ealdordoms, and Leofwine worked hard to keep on top of any developments that could concern him and his properties in Mercia.

Leofwine's landed interests were not exclusively concerned with the area of his ealdordom. He held land from the king within the Hwiccan kingdom, while his commended men held land throughout England.

It was, however, the land left to him by his father that formed the basis of his wealth. Leofwine held that land no matter what, provided he never set foot outside the law that might cause him to forfeit it. Similarly, Æthelflæd held the land that her father had bestowed on her at her marriage.

There were other types of landholding, too. The land the king had given to him to assist him to rule in his Hwiccan lands could be given and taken away just as quickly by the king. It was, in effect, the king's land, which he loaned to his ealdormen for the duration of their appointment.

While the king was not overly keen to replace his ealdormen, what had happened to his father-in-law, Thored of Northumbria, was a sobering thought. He'd lost all his loan-land as it had been transferred to Ælfhelm. Thored had still held his land in his native Mercia, but the majority of his wealth had been removed almost overnight when he'd lost his position as ealdorman. And, of course, not long after, he'd also lost his own life.

Now that Leofwine was ealdorman in his own right, he had duties to enforce in exchange for the land gifted by the king. On occasion, he also had to pay fines to other lords and act as sureties for his commended men.

Most of Leofwine's tenants held their land through dependent tenure. At some point in the past, they'd forfeited their land to him, or his father, or his grandfather, and had then received the land back as a sort of gift. They were bound to Leofwine for their work and livelihood, and it was not always a natural alliance.

Still further, Leofwine held some land due to clauses where he or his father had been loaned land for a set period, usually from religious foundations. Leofwine was aware that much of his grandfather's acquisitions in this way would need to be renegotiated soon, and he didn't relish the thought. The negotiations were often tedious and complicated, and the churches that loaned a vast majority of the land were often not keen to lend the property again, preferring to have it to hold themselves.

The complicated arrangement made for strange alliances and some that were just plain uncomfortable.

The night passed pleasantly in a whirl of food and drink, and the next morning Leofwine woke hazily, his head pounding and his mouth awash with the taste of sour ale. It fell to Wulfstan to chivvy him from his bed, force him to eat, and make it to the witan before it commenced.

The day was fresher than the one before, or Leofwine was simply feeling the effects of his overindulgence as he huddled deep in his cloak, making the short walk through the few streets miserable and wishing he could return to his bed.

The vendors were busily about their day's tasks, and it was clear that a market was being held. Everywhere Leofwine looked, he could see horses and ponies and oxen laid down with goods and carts pulling heavy loads towards the street where the other church stood.

Leofwine splashed through puddles and tried his best to avoid walking into anyone, or anything, especially the piles of dung left scattered here and there. A young lad was dashing to and fro, scooping up the manure with a happy smile on his face, and Leofwine shared a quiet laugh at the joy a giant pile of dung could bring to all people who needed to rely on their crops to survive the next winter.

The church was lit with many lights on the cold day, and

Leofwine took his seat moments before the king strode into the assembly, wearing a magnificent purple robe trimmed with fur at the collar. It suited the king's scowling face well, and Leofwine looked around to the others for any sign of what was causing the king upset.

His answer was not long in coming as Ælfhelm pointedly ignored the king's look of loathing and continued talking to his circle of close supporters. Perhaps today would be harder than he'd imagined, even with a terrible headache.

The morning passed slowly as points of law were debated for yet another new law code, with bishop Wulfstan being outspoken on many counts. Almost every word spoken was faithfully scratched onto fine vellum by the king's monks so that the laws could be passed and proclaimed all over England once they were ratified at a future witan.

Leofwine found himself, on occasion, struggling to stay awake, the events of the night before catching up with him. Wulfstan kept him alert until the king turned to the matter of him fighting at the head of an army.

The king had been almost as impatient as Leofwine for the law code to be finalised, which Leofwine had found strange, as he'd chivvied along bishop Wulfstan and the others who wished to argue and discuss. It was, after all, the king's idea to enshrine the laws. All became clear, though, as soon as the king began to speak.

'I've thought about your wise words, Ealdorman Æthelweard, and while I can see great merit in them, I must for now, and until my heirs are older, insist that my armies are led by my ealdormen. As Leofsige correctly stated yesterday, it wouldn't be in the best interests of the land if their king was wounded or something worse should befall him at the hand of these Raiders.'

Leofwine managed not to allow his emotions to show on his face as the king spoke calmly and deliberately from the front of the church.

'I have, however, decided that we must act against these other powers offering aid to the Raiders. I'll be pursuing more diplomatic means to stop those in Normandy and those in Dublin.'

'However,' and here Æthelred turned to Leofwine with a small bow of acknowledgement that surprised a smile to Leofwine's face, 'I'll not be sending my ealdormen this time. I think perhaps some of my clerics will be able to assist, and certainly some of my royal officials. Ealdormen, you are to have your fyrds on standby and your household warriors to hand so that you can lead them against the Raiders while the churchmen try and find a more peaceful solution.'

Leofwine couldn't deny that it was a well-thought-out policy, yet he was still disappointed that the king wouldn't face the Raiders himself. Leofwine knew that while it might not bring all the fighting to a stop, it would undoubtedly be a very firm affirmation of the king's desire to end the attacks.

As the assembled crowd murmured about the news, an old, tired Ealdorman Æthelweard rose to his feet and thanked the king for considering the idea. Leofwine was amazed yet again at the stamina of the man. Forty years of kings and still he could play the courtly dance so well.

Leofwine was pleased to have been singled out by the king, but his relief was short-lived. When it finally came time to sign the charter, which did indeed return the misappropriated land to the bishop of Rochester, he still found himself as the most junior of the ealdormen, with the cunning Leofsige jumping to third place behind Æthelweard and Ælfric.

Leofwine didn't need to see the look on ealdorman Ælfhelm's face as he swept from the church to know he was angry with the king. Third out of all the ealdormen, since he'd become ealdorman of Northumbria, he was plainly unhappy to find himself pushed to fourth and with Leofsige in the ascendant.

Surely the king was tempting fate by angering the powerful ealdorman of Northumbria. Leofwine felt uneasy at the discord between the two. Leofwine left the witan aware that little had truly been settled. The Raiders were still a huge problem, but so to was the lack of harmony between the king and the men who governed in his name.

The rest of Leofwine's time in Oxford passed quickly as he gathered supplies for Æthelflæd and initiated a few more contracts for the produce from his land to be taken in exchange for goods needed for his home.

Leofwine also took the time to visit with ealdorman Æthelweard one more time. The man was sunken and low in spirits after the king had refused his recommendation, and Leofwine walked away from the meeting thinking that he'd never see the wise scholar again and wondering what the future would hold without him.

THE ANGLO SAXON CHRONICLE ENTRY FOR AD998

This year coasted the army back eastward into the mouth of the Frome, and went up everywhere, as widely as they would, into Dorsetshire. Often was an army collected against them; but, as soon as they were about to come together, then were they ever through something or other put to flight, and their enemies always in the end had the victory. Another time they lay in the Isle of Wight, and fed themselves meanwhile from Hampshire and Sussex.

13
AD999

Rumours of Raiders and attacks dogged the rest of the year 998, and Leofwine grew despondent and wary as he spent equal time between his home and that of his other properties, dispensing justice and the king's writ at every location.

Leofwine's second son arrived safely almost the moment he returned home from the witan as if he'd been waiting for his father to be present. Leofric was a larger baby than his now toddling older brother had been.

Æthelflæd assured him that his birth had been quick and easy compared to that of Northman's. Leofwine had almost hidden away from the women when labour had begun, finding any reason to keep out of the way.

Horic told him it would all become so much easier with more practice. Æthelflæd had not shared Horic's exuberance at the thought of a host of children when Leofwine had shared the information with her. She'd offered an ashen smile as she'd clutched her newborn to her breast and threatened to speak to Horic's wife herself to ascertain the truth.

Horic had paled somewhat when Leofwine had shared those comments and had laughed heartily at Horic's obvious discomfort at the thought of having his words gainsaid.

Northman had become an engaging child with a fierce personality. He followed his father where ever he went and whenever he thought he could get away with it. If not following his father, it was his mother or Wulfstan or Horic or one of the servants.

Northman had a curiosity about everything, and after being caught trying to lift Horic's giant war axe in the hall, he'd been gifted with a small wooden copy by the large man and with a short wooden sword and shield from his father.

Leofwine worried that it was too much too soon for the little lad, but as he was so interested in all the weapons, it was only wise to let him have his own, less lethal ones. Æthelflæd laughed to see him with his little weapons, but Leofwine had also heard her sobbing brokenheartedly to see her firstborn so outfitted. It had made him consider just what his mother would have thought of him learning to fight and defend himself when so young.

Still, it seemed that no matter where he turned, there were reports of attacks on the lands and churches and monasteries. And then, most worryingly, reports reached him that the Raiders had attacked Hampshire and Sussex and that Ælfric had retreated under the onslaught of their attack, agreeing on a self-serving peace with them.

Still, the king did not act, and as the year slowly turned to 999, the worst possible news arrived on a wintry day; muted with thick snow and a bone, numbing chill of

Ealdorman Æthelweard's death, having succumbed to a winter illness.

The news arrived too late for Leofwine to attend the man's funeral, so instead, he took to his knees in the church at Deerhurst and prayed for the man's soul.

It left the king without his wisest and most able counsellor at what Leofwine thought was his time of greatest need. Apart from his mother, Uncle, and a handful of churchmen, Æthelred's court was now bereft of all counsel from an older generation. Foreboding shot through Leofwine's mind at the news.

As the summer months slowly began, the first real disputes broke out amongst his tenants and landholders. The winter had been harsh, food was scarce, and worry was rife that the Raiders would come and take what little anyone had. It caused small niggles of years gone by to flare up and minor disagreements to become full-blown feuds.

Leofwine had his work cut out trying to fight his way clear of the multiple personalities he had to face, and finally, exasperation overcame him, and he called all his commended men, landholders and those who owed him sake or soke together for a magnificent feast at Deerhurst.

With the help of large amounts of mead and wine, Leofwine managed to reassert his authority and garner agreements from the men and women who held the grudges. Leofwine was pleased that his idea averted any murders or accidental deaths. He was not sure that next year if the Raiders continued, he'd be met with the same success from such a simple expedient.

When the king called him to the witan at Wantage, he was almost pleased to go for one. It was time for action, and he carried with him the hope that the king realised the same.

Reports had reached Leofwine of an alliance being concluded with the new Duke of Normandy, Richard II, which would prevent the Raiders from using his lands as a base to launch their attacks on England. It was time the ealdormen, the thegns, and the king all worked together to drive the Raiders from their land and not rely on other people to do the job for them.

The witan that convened was noticeably absent its wisest ealdorman, Æthelweard, and Leofwine caught his son Æthelmær staring long and hard at the king throughout the day-long mass held in honour of Easter.

Leofwine didn't think the young man had much chance of succeeding his father; the king was not often minded to work quickly when it came time to replace an ealdorman. Leofwine's rise to the ealdordom had been a case in point, motivated by twin desires. The first was to see the area governed by someone close to the king. While secondly, it had been important for the new ealdorman to be someone replaceable enough to be risked on a diplomatic journey to the North.

Leofwine knew he owed his rise in status to Lady Elfrida but was unsure why she'd have wanted him to journey north and risk his life. But he'd never asked her and no doubt never would. Wulfstan's reticence on the matter alerted Leofwine that he was unhappy with Lady Elfrida for the choice or that he knew something Leofwine did not. Perhaps, or so he hoped, it had been her wish to see Leofsige travel north and not him.

Mass said, with praise for the dead Ealdorman Æthelweard, their king, in a less than congenial atmosphere, feasted the many thegns and churchmen. There were rumours and scare-mongering aplenty. And most of it proved well founded the next day when the business of the witan began.

The king's deliberations with his witan were interrupted by a dishevelled messenger from Ælfric's household, sent to inform the king of Raiders sighted in the Kentish lands.

Leofwine hoped the news would spur the king to action, and it did, but only for him to call out the Kentish fyrd immediately. The king didn't even consider the words of ealdorman Æthelweard the year before, who'd suggested he lead an army himself.

Æthelred dispatched Ælfric and his men without pausing for thought and returned to his agenda with barely a breath between actions. The other ealdormen and their thegns and the churchmen were not even given time to discuss their needs with their men before discussions resumed on the king's agenda.

Æthelred seemed oblivious to the hastily stifled conversations and didn't notice when each and every ealdorman and churchmen still present in the room had one of their men depart in haste.

Leofwine had barely to look at Wulfstan before he abruptly left. They'd discussed at length the actions they'd take in the event of another raid. Horic stayed close to Leofwine, but his legs didn't stop tapping throughout the remainder of the meeting, and Leofwine knew he was desperate to be on his way to protect the lands of the Hwicce, which now incorporated his own.

When the witan finally concluded business for the day, Horic leapt from his seat, almost forgetting Leofwine in his haste to be gone. Leofwine watched him go with a concerned smile tugging at his tight facial muscles. He, too, wished to rush out and find out all the details but knew he must bow and make small talk with the rest of the attendees, and so he called Hunter to his side.

As Leofwine stretched out his stiff legs and a numb arse, Hunter came and stood next to him, her head under where his hand would naturally fall. He was about to let her lead him away when a distinct voice spoke quietly to him. It was intentionally pitched low, but there was no doubting that the authoritative voice was that of the king.

'My lord Leofwine, I'd very much like to talk with you if you have the time?'

It was phrased as a question, but Leofwine knew better than to try and walk away. Instead, he turned his head toward Æthelred and took in his agitated face and rapidly shifting eyes.

'My lord king, it would be my pleasure. Shall we sit again, or would you prefer to walk back to the palace?'

'Here will do as well as any.'

As the church cleared of the rest of the attendees, many curious stares flicked over the sight of the king sitting stroking the half-blind ealdorman's dog. Leofwine noted all who looked displeased and those who only looked curiously.

It was the king's eldest son who stared most openly. Leofsige also had his own man check what was going on. The man purposefully dawdled until it was evident that he'd done all he could to offer his respects to the church and the holy relics, and if he lingered any longer, it could be to eavesdrop.

When they were finally alone in the large church with no one for company apart from the flickering candle flames, the king began to talk in his more normal voice.

'Leofwine, I have need of your advice.'

'Of course, my lord king. Ask what you will.'

'It's the Raiders, as I'm sure you can appreciate. I know you didn't speak out last year, but I also know that you agreed with ealdorman Æthelweard's words because he sought me out himself when I didn't follow up on his idea to let me know who else he'd discussed the situation with. Do you honestly believe that the answer is for me to lead the men to battle?'

Æthelred's tone was merely curious, betraying no hint of his feelings towards the idea of riding into a battle against the Raiders. Leofwine was surprised to be asked for his advice. Ever since his injury, Leofwine had felt as though the king often just tolerated him. Leofwine thought carefully before answering.

'My lord king. I do believe that if the Raiders saw you at the head of an attack, they would reconsider their actions. I know we've tried hard to convince the Danes and Norwegians that England is weak and without resources, but they simply don't believe it.'

'Every church and every monastery simply gleams with gold and jewels. We always seem to have food to spare and coinage aplenty. The Raiders aren't stupid. They've realised that we say one thing and act the opposite. I also fear that they say, and I'm sorry to say this, my lord king, that we have a weak king who lets the attacks happen unopposed.'

Leofwine didn't flinch as he spoke, although he didn't enjoy sharing his thoughts with Æthelred. However, Æthelred didn't look at all disturbed by his words.

'You say nothing I've not thought myself. Still, it's rare for someone to speak openly and honestly with me when the words are not ones I want to hear. I thank you for that, Leofwine. I don't know if you've indeed considered the import of what you ask of me. Whom should I fight against?

Where should I fight against them? How am I to make my power felt without displaying even more of my wealth?'

The king's expression was pensive as he spoke. There was a genuine concern on his face, and Leofwine did him the honour of considering his words fully.

'It's obvious that you can't be in two places at once, even if these Raiders can. I'd suggest that you strike somewhere unexpected, and it needs to be with the weight of the English warriors behind you. Are the reports of an alliance with the Duke of Normandy correct?'

'Yes, yes,' the king's voice was slightly contemptuous and rushed. 'My emissaries have worked well and managed to obtain an agreement from the new duke. The only slight problem is that they wish to cement the alliance with marriage. I'm not sure if it's me they want to marry the girl or my son. I'm awaiting further details. It's a painstakingly slow process negotiating for peace.'

Æthelred's voice trailed away to wistfulness as he finished speaking, and Leofwine waited for a beat before answering. As his mind considered what he should say, he considered what the king hadn't said when he discussed the terms of the treaty. The king was already married, his wife once more pregnant if the rumours were to be believed. Would the king put her aside to marry another for the sake of an alliance with Normandy? Leofwine wasn't at all sure.

'If that's the case, then we should see a lessening of attacks from that quarter. It would perhaps be sensible to strike towards the borders or even against the Irish raiders. I'm assuming that you've not been as successful with them as I've heard no reports to the contrary?'

'Certainly not. They're not keen to even meet, let alone discuss any alliance. I find I can't get on with them. They're not much different from the Raiders, for all that they call themselves kings. But how would we attack them? We can't launch a raid over the sea. We've few enough ships and not enough trained men who can travel by ship and fight on land.'

'They've allies in the lands to the north or the west of here, don't they?'

'You mean the kingdoms of Gwynedd, Powys and Strathclyde?'

'I do, yes. They all seem to stand together against your rule, for all that they fight often and frequently amongst themselves.'

'I find Gwynedd, Dyfed and Powys to be of little concern. Strathclyde, however, continues to attempt to take land that's not theirs in the north. I'd like Ælfhelm to stand against the attacks, but he insists that he has too few resources because he's already trying to maintain peace amongst the English and the settled Raiders in Northumbria. I've attempted to send envoys, but their king, Malcolm, won't discuss the situation with my representatives.'

Æthelred's voice trailed away as he spoke as if he was thinking out loud as opposed to having a conversation with Leofwine.

'Perhaps an attack on Strathclyde would be of benefit?' Leofwine prompted him after long moments had lapsed.

'I've been wondering the same. Perhaps if I follow in my ancestor's footsteps of nearly fifty years ago, we may deter them from taking my land and offering assistance to the Raiders. It may also prove to the Irish kings that I'm not a weak king.'

'We'd need to call out the fyrds but also ensure that our coastline was secure at the same time.' Now it was

Leofwine's turn to talk out loud as if his king was not listening to his thoughts.

'We would, indeed. It would be a huge undertaking, but not without merit. I'll think about it further, and the reason I wanted to speak specifically to you was because of your man from the North. Will you ask his advice on the enterprise? He may be able to assure me that it's a worthy endeavour.' Leofwine hid his surprise at the king's words. He'd not thought he'd even realised that Horic had previously been a Raider with Olaf Tryggvason.

'Of course, my lord king. I'll speak to him as soon as possible. Would you prefer him to seek you out, or do you just want me to speak for him?'

'If he thinks it's an idea with merit, then just speak to me yourself. If he has any reservations, then I'd ask that you both seek me out so that we can discuss ideas further.'

With that, Æthelred rose smoothly and walked reverently down the aisle of the church. He bowed his head as he went and even turned at the door and bowed down low again. Leofwine was always a little surprised by the deeply felt genuine belief his king carried within him. For a man who'd been accused of despoiling church lands in his youth, Æthelred was now going out of his way to right those wrongs and to show his adherence to the true faith.

Leofwine stood more slowly, his legs cramped and ungainly. Hunter was instantly at his side, and the pair of them strolled towards the exit, the dog matching his speed to that of his tired master.

Leofwine felt a little older but not necessarily any wiser as he exited into the cool evening. He was honoured that the king had finally sought him out and pleased that the king was finally waking up to the realisation that he needed to be seen as a leader to deter the attacks. Still, there was a huge difference between advocating a course of action and the reality of carrying that action out.

If Leofwine was honest with himself, he didn't think he'd like to go to battle again, but he'd have no choice. If his king went, he'd need to go, too. The action was necessary, and he'd need to be a part of it if he was to keep his position and the respect of his king.

The feast that night was more muted than the evening before. The king was pensive as he ate and paid almost no attention to the gossip ricocheting around the room. There was a noticeable gap where Ælfric should have been, but Leofsige was quick to exploit the weakness, engaging the king repeatedly in conversation, apparently unaware that Æthelred was paying less than full attention to him.

Ælfhelm was quietly conversing with many of the king's thegns, and Leofwine wondered what they discussed. He was sure it was probably not the recent attack in the South as it would be of little concern to him. The laughter from his followers made Leofwine think that they were discussing very little of importance.

Amongst his men, there was quiet conversation. They were concerned enough about the attack to be discussing their preferred tactics if they had to face the attackers again but also distant enough that they didn't feel immediately threatened.

Wulfstan was absent, as were Leofgar, Ælfnoth, Eadred and Wighard, who'd been chosen to travel back to Æthelflæd at Deerhurst and protect their lord's land. Even Horic was thoughtful as he ate his way through a considerable portion of the finest beef stew Leofwine felt he'd ever tasted. Horic was spooning the mixture mechanically into his mouth, and Leofwine doubted that he even tasted it.

As the evening wore on, Leofwine became aware of many stray and some pointed looks his way from within the crowded hall, but only Leofsige was forthcoming enough to come and speak to him. Leofsige walked with almost a swagger to accommodate his vast girth, and Leofwine wondered how the man could ever hope to fight when he carried so much extra weight.

'Leofwine, I wonder if I might trouble you for a moment or two?'

Leofsige asked the question civilly enough, but there was steel behind the request that perversely made Leofwine want to be as obtuse as possible.

'Of course, Leofsige. You're well?'

'As always. As always. And you look in good spirits as well. All things considering.'

Leofwine chose to let that comment go. Leofsige could have been referring to his most recent battle or even the raid when he'd been blinded, down to just his part blindness. Leofsige's comments were notoriously hard to pinpoint, and Leofwine had long since given up trying to determine just what the other ealdorman was trying to bait him about.

'I was wondering if you would share your earlier discussion with the king.'

As to the point as ever, Leofwine wondered how Leofsige ever accomplished anything by guile. For Leofwine, Leofsige always seemed to be far too easy to read. Perhaps that was why the King looked to him above himself. With Leofsige there was no chance of him lying or attempting a lie without being able to see right through it.

Leofwine briefly considered how to answer the man. It

was evident that if the king had wanted to have his discussion open knowledge, he'd have spoken before the witan and not just to himself.

'It was just a brief conversation about the details of the attackers in the Kentish land. He wanted my opinion as to whether I thought it might be the same Raiders as before.'

Leofsige briefly narrowed his suspicious eyes as he gazed at Leofwine. It was evident he didn't believe him, but it was also apparently the only explanation he was going to get.

Idly, Leofwine wondered if he'd tried to ask the king the same question. Somehow he doubted it. The man was notorious for having an ear to every developing situation. Clearly, the king had not thought to inform him or any of his contacts directly, and Leofsige had been forced to approach the only other person who was aware of the King's possible plans.

For the first time since his injury had been sustained, the king seemed willing to look upon Leofwine as a full ealdorman and not an invalid to be pampered. Hopefully, his ungainly fall had been forgotten about or at least forgiven.

Leofsige spoke to Leofwine for a few moments longer, attempting to draw him out in other ways, but Leofwine offered only vague responses, and the man quickly grew tired of the lack of information on offer and returned to his men.

For the rest of the evening, Leofwine was well aware of the scrutiny he was under from the man, and a brief surge of satisfaction made him more expressive and jolly for the rest of the evening. It felt good to be in the inner circle of the king's congress for once.

When the feast was done, and he and his men had retired for the night, he sought out Horic's advice as the king had requested. Leofwine called Horic to his room, and they carried out a subdued conversation in which Horic advocated the king's action while wishing it could be more directly linked to the Raiders.

Horic spoke of how good it would be to offer more counterstrikes like the one against the Normandy duke, but they both knew in their hearts that it would be almost miraculous if Æthelred decided to attack Strathclyde, let alone agree to an attack somewhere in Denmark or Norway.

14
AD999

The next day, at the end of another long session of deliberating and arguing, the king sought him out to see if he'd been able to speak to Horic. For the sake of the king's ears, he explained that Horic thought the reasoning was sound, and the king thanked him and left the hall, deep in thought but not forgetting his duties to his God.

Leofsige had blatantly watched the exchange between the king and Leofwine with a tight expression on his face, unable to determine about what they spoke, as both kept such bland expressions on their faces. It was clear that Leofsige thought the matter was of great importance, for all that his and the king's body language worked to offer the opposite impression.

Leofwine found the whole thing entertaining. He'd not yet really been a participant in Court politics and thought that he would perhaps like to be.

On the final day of the witan, with no clear message from the king about whether his proposed attack would go ahead, a messenger arrived from Ealdorman Ælfric to apprise the king of the developing situation.

It wasn't good news. The Raiders appeared to have overwhelmed much of the southeast, attacking the Thames and the Medway and advancing on Rochester. Ælfric had ordered his fyrd to attack the Raiders, but they'd not been able to stop the horde, which had slipped passed him, and taken his own men's horses.

The king was understandably deeply unhappy at the news. He called on the men of the surrounding lands to add their strength to Ælfric's. But the king did surprise Leofwine with his final announcement.

'Send a messenger to the king's fleet. Have them plan and carry out a raid on Normandy. The bloodier, the better. My cousin, Lord Wulfgar, will have the command.' Leofwine watched the king as he made the announcement, a flicker of hope starting to kindle inside him. Perhaps the king could be enticed to ride to war himself. After all, he seemed keen to send his cousin.

Leofwine watched as surprise covered Lady Elfrida's face as she gazed out into the room, no doubt to gauge her brother's reaction.

The witan broke up in a rush after that, with the remaining ealdormen anxious to get back to their lands. Leofwine needed to call out his fyrd, and Æthelmær, while not promoted to the role of the ealdorman of the Western Provinces, was instructed to coordinate the fyrd in the Western Provinces.

Ælfhelm was simply to maintain the peace in his northern lands, and Leofsige was to call out his fyrd, too. It was not quite a war footing for the entire country, but it wasn't far off.

The king announced that he'd expect regular updates but that he'd stay mobile and away from the areas that the Raiders were infiltrating. It was clear Æthelred wished to take no chances with his person. The king transcribed a letter to the people of his land, calling out the fyrds he wanted and arranging for copies of his letter to be distributed to the great men of the council who would then need to see to its disbursement amongst the more local clergy.

The journey home was accomplished more quickly than usual. Although Leofwine knew his household troop were there protecting Æthelflæd, he was still happier when he rode through his gated enclosure and found her hard at work organising supplies and provisions.

Æthelflæd had called in the aid of the abbot who was waiting for the announcement that Leofwine carried. It was a simple message, calling out the fyrd and informing them of the actions of the Raiders. The abbot offered Leofwine his good wishes and assurances that he'd pray for them all before returning to his church to allow Leofwine's men to work.

Around his home, there was a tense feeling of activity. The two young squires were busy running between the members of his household troops, polishing swords and cleaning byrnies. The smith was hard at work re-shoeing the horses, and his forces were practising with an intensity that surprised Leofwine.

The servants were working busily at Æthelflæd's bequest, walking from hall to work shed or hall to a storage area, collecting food items and storing winter equipment that was no longer needed.

Æthelflæd came towards him with a forced smile on her

face, worry plain in her slightly hectic eyes that darted from side to side as she took in the whirl of activity around her.

'I assume you've heard the news then?' he asked.

'Yes, a trader passed through here last night, all a twitter with the latest court gossip. The abbot also sent word that he'd be calling today, and I realised that the trader more than likely spoke the truth.'

'Indeed, the king has decided to act against the Raiders, and he's called out the fyrds from everywhere apart from Northumbria. They're already maintaining the border.'

'Are you to journey to the south, or are you to protect your people?'

'Our people here. The south is to be protected by Ælfric, and the fyrd in the Western Provinces is to be under the control of Æthelweard's son. He's not been made an ealdorman, but he's been given the responsibility. I only hope he can live up to the expectations he has of himself.'

'Then I need not fear that you'll be gone for a long time?' Æthelflæd's tone was merely curious, but her eyes betrayed her barely stifled fear.

'No, no. Not unless something goes badly wrong will we leave our land. After all, that's not the point of the fyrd. It exists to protect the people of each of the ancient kingdoms. I think the king would struggle to get people to act in lands they don't know.'

'Of course, of course,' Æthelflæd said, although she'd plainly not remembered that in her worry for him.

'Still, it's a good idea. I'm not sure the king has even considered calling all his fyrds together. I wonder how magnificent the sight would be.' Leofwine's voice trailed off as he thought about the possibilities, and only a stifled sob from Æthelflæd returned him to the here and now.

'Ah, my love. I know I've not done the best in the past, but hopefully, I can now match those who come against us.' Leofwine didn't dare mention the name of Swein. Æthelflæd was already far too distressed.

He gathered her into his arms and held her tightly as she composed herself. It wasn't like her to show so much emotion in public, and he wondered if it was just worry about what was to happen or whether something else had upset her.

Taking her hand, Leofwine guided her back inside his hall, bright with daylight, and seated her before the fire. Her eyes were a little glazed, and he reached for a small mug of ale and pressed it into her hands. Beneath him, she shook slightly.

Wulfstan entered the hall and looked his way. He shrugged a little hopelessly, and the man quickly turned around and went back the way he'd come. Whatever his question was, he'd plainly decided to solve it alone.

Leofwine looked around the hall and found the nurse who was minding a fretful Leofric and rebellious-looking Northman. She was a fresh-faced young woman and was also a confidant of Æthelflæd's. He looked at her with what he hoped was a question on his face, and she sent Northman stumbling towards him.

The boy was sure and steady on his feet and came and planted himself before his father, clutching his wooden sword with pride. Leofwine bent down on his knee so that his face was level with his son, and the boy flung his arms around his neck in welcome. Leofwine grinned at his son.

'How are you, young man?'

'Good, father, good. I've learnt a whole new set of moves with my sword. Shall I show you?'

'Yes, please. Has Horic been teaching you?'

Northman's face twisted for a moment, aware that he probably shouldn't be telling his father the truth. He'd been told that only Horic or one of the troops could teach him, and Leofwine was sure that they'd all been far too busy to teach the boy. Instead, the little lad leant forward and whispered,

'It was Horic's son. He taught me.'

Leofwine made his face look cross, and his son cowered behind his small shield.

'There was no one else, and he promised that I wouldn't get in trouble,' Northman finally announced defiantly, and Leofwine grinned to hear the pride in his son's voice.

'Well, very well then. You must show me, and then I'll tell you if he can continue to teach you or if he needs disciplining.'

Northman's face clouded with concentration as he thought over the bargain, and then he nodded.

'Can I show you now?'

'Of course. Do we need to go outside?'

'Yes. I need more room here because young Horic says I have a big swing.'

'Lead the way then.'

His son walked smartly out of the room, and Leofwine had a moment to look at the nurse. She was looking with concern at Æthelflæd as she held Leofric in her arms.

'I'm not sure what ails her, my lord. But go, see to Northman, and I'll sit with her.'

Leofwine shot her a grateful look and checked his wife one more time. She was no longer shaking but now sat rigidly still. He could not determine what was wrong with her either.

Outside, there was a bustle of activity, and he watched Northman march smartly between the legs of the scurrying servants until he reached the area where the household troops trained. Wulfstan and Horic stopped their discussion to watch Northman walk with purpose, and they called to Leofgar and Ælfhun to finish their training. The two men turned in surprise but then moved quickly aside as Northman took their place.

The little boy checked to ensure his father was watching him and immediately launched into a quick routine of strikes and parries, which had all the men cheering before he'd finished. Leofwine was amazed by his son's prowess. The boy turned to him, his eyes shining,

'Has he taught me correctly? Can he carry on teaching me? He's much easier to understand than Wulfstan, and he's here *all* the time.' Northman's little voice stressed the 'all', and Leofwine pretended to seriously consider the question while his son jiggled up and down in impatience.

'I suppose he can. If Horic agrees and provided he has some more lessons in how to teach you.'

Northman beamed in triumph and walked up to Horic, who was watching the display and conversation in surprise.

'Horic, could you please tell your son that he can continue to train me but that he needs some more training from *you*.'

Horic was speechless as he looked between his lord and his lord's son. With a none-too-gentle nudge from Wulfstan, Horic eventually remembered where he was and who was talking to him.

'Of course, Northman. I'll speak to him when I find him.' His voice held some menace for his son, but Northman didn't notice. He merely turned about and strutted back into the hall, calling for his dog as he went. As soon as he'd re-entered the hall, everyone burst out laughing, and even Wulfstan had an amused smile on his face.

'He's very like you, Leofwine,' Wulfstan called, and his words intensified the laughter, leaving Leofwine feeling proud and also a little envious of his son's self-confidence. Shrugging in helplessness, Leofwine turned to walk back towards the hall, only Wulfstan called his name. He turned towards the man and saw all traces of mirth had left his face.

'Yes, Wulfstan, what is it?'

'It's just a little question concerning the groups you want the troops to operate within. Do you want us always to be in the same groupings, or should we shift around a bit?'

It was a good question, and Leofwine thought it over. The men all worked well as a team. Each had his strengths and weaknesses, but there were also groupings that rubbed along together better than others. It would perhaps be best if the men patrolled to a rota, that way, they'd never grow tired of each other or too comfortable in each other's company.

'I think a rota. Do you agree? '

'I do, yes. I'll draw one up as soon as I can. Will you be a part of it?'

'Yes, but not all the time. I'll leave it to your instincts as to when I should patrol.'

Wulfstan bowed to acknowledge his words, and he and Horic were instantly deep in conversation again. Leofwine turned to walk back towards his hall as his troops resumed their training.

Æthelflæd was sitting quietly by the fire, and the nurse beckoned him over.

'I think it's simply worry, my lord, for you. She's not

spoken, but she calmed as soon as you walked into the room and became agitated when you left.'

Leofwine thanked her, and she returned to minding the children. Northman, now his task was done, had happily returned to a game with wooden pieces, and he was totally absorbed. Leofwine turned to Æthelflæd and found her staring without seeing. He'd never expected to see her so distressed and worry gnawed at him. How could he calm her and win back her trust in his abilities when he still doubted his own?

Her suddenly fragile beauty stirred him, and he gently picked her up in his arms and carried her away to their room. The nurse watched him as he walked past, a ghost of a smile on her face. Hunter walked before him, her nose to the floor as she reacquainted herself with her home.

Once through the doorway, he laid his wife on their bed and quickly removed his sword, seax and byrnie. Not once did she stir or even look his way. He climbed laboriously onto the bed next to her and gathered her into his arms. She felt as light as a feather, and he couldn't understand how he'd allowed her to become so weak and never noticed before.

Lying slightly above her, he gently began to stroke her chestnut hair, all the time speaking of comforting thoughts, of his hopes for his sons, and his dreams for his home and presents he still wanted to buy his wife. He didn't once mention the Raiders or the raising of the fyrd, and slowly he felt her relax into his embrace, and finally, she drifted to sleep and soon afterwards, so did he.

When he woke, she was gone from his side, and Hunter was nudging his exposed hand where it fell over the bed. Leofwine groaned in discomfort, having fallen asleep with his boots still on, and shuffled towards the end of the bed. Night had apparently fallen as he'd slept, and he could hear his men and servants walking around in the hall as they ate.

A bowl of tepid water on the wooden table allowed him to clean his face, and then he stepped out of his temporary sanctuary to check on Æthelflæd. The men in his hall didn't look his way as he entered, even though they must all have heard his tread on the floorboards. Instead, they continued eating and drinking as he sought out Æthelflæd.

Æthelflæd was sat with the nurse and a few of her women servants, and Horic was regaling them with loud tales of his daring deeds as a much younger man. Leofwine was pleased to see the smile on Æthelflæd's face. He walked over towards her and placed a kiss on top of her head. She reached up and rubbed his cheek in response and then turned her attention back to Horic.

Leofwine settled in his chair and was served food and ale, which he hastily consumed. He watched Æthelflæd as he ate until Wulfstan joined him to resume their conversation of earlier regarding patrols. Wulfstan had decided that Leofwine should lead the men at least every four days, and Leofwine gave his consent to the idea and then suggested that to prevent his routine from becoming known to any who wished them harm, perhaps they should fluctuate it each time.

Wulfstan agreed, first berating himself for not thinking of that sooner, and left to redraw his careful plans. Leofwine watched him walk away, deep in thought. This call to arms was giving his second in command a purpose that had been missing for some time. Leofwine suddenly realised that playing nursemaid to his best friend's son was perhaps not the way Wulfstan had seen his later life playing out.

That night Æthelflæd again slept in his arms, but this time he was awake long into the night. He felt as though some monumental moment in his life had been reached and there would be no turning back from it. He was not entirely sure that he liked the feeling.

In the weeks that followed, the raising of the fyrd was proclaimed by the churchmen and those men who owed service to their ealdorman convened at Worcester on the designated day. Leofwine was struck by the number of the men and the vast differences in how well-armed they all were.

Some were the king's thegns, equipped with a horse, byrnie, shield and sword, while others were simple farmers who carried only common tools with them. Leofwine was pleased that he was better able to provision those without sword or seax or axe or shield from the tithes gathered in by the king's reeves.

In total, there were about five hundred men, and these he divided into smaller, more mobile forces with either his men or some of the king's thegns in command. For their two months of service, they were dispatched to strategic locations where Leofwine thought any invaders might attack.

One party went south to the coastline, while another was sent towards Winchcombe, and another was stationed in Gloucester itself. He also had a mobile force on continuous duty around the borders with the Western Provinces. His ship had been pressed into service for the king, and it was waiting patiently in the seas around Kent in the case of further attack.

For two months, there was near constant activity, with messengers flying between Leofwine and his commanders and his king. Æthelflæd stayed resolutely calm, becoming used to the constant interruptions at all times of the day. Nothing happened, and in no time at all, it was time for the fyrd to return to their fields and for their counterparts to take their two months of service. Again, Leofwine dispatched his men as he had the first time around, and again, they saw no action.

The same could not be said for Ealdorman Ælfric and the fyrd of Hampshire. They were embroiled in some skirmishes that concluded with a battle at Rochester. Ælfric did not bathe his king in glory but again sought to make peace with the Raiders. As the rest of Leofwine's fyrd was stood down to allow the harvest to be collected, the Raiders made themselves comfortable with the horses of the Kentish people and settled down to enjoy another winter at the cost of the English.

The king didn't call his witan together again that year, but reports and messages reached Leofwine of his great anger towards Ealdorman Ælfric and his growing frustration with the Raiders. Leofwine hoped that now, at last, the king would see it truly was time to act. The cold winter months gave them time to regroup and retask without fear of possible raids. He hoped his king would take the time to devise a suitable retaliatory strike.

THE ANGLO SAXON CHRONICLE ENTRY FOR AD999

This year came the army about again into the Thames, and
went up thence along the Medway to Rochester; where the
Kentish army came against them, and encountered them in a
close engagement; but, alas! They too soon yielded and fled;
because they had not the aid that they should have had. The
Danes therefore occupied the field of battle, and, taking
horse, they rode as wide as they would, spoiling and over-
running nearly all West-Kent. Then the king with his council
determined to proceed against them with sea and land
forces; but as soon as the ships were ready, then arose delay
from day to day, which harassed the miserable crew that lay
on board; so that, always, the forwarder it should have been,
the later it was, from one time to another; — they still
suffered the army of their enemies to increase; the Danes
continually retreated from the sea-coast; and they continually pursued them in vain. Thus in the end these expeditions
both by sea and land served no other purpose but to vex the

people, to waste their treasure, and to strengthen their enemies.

15
AD 1000

The turning of the millennia brought no let-up in the ongoing diplomatic bargaining between the Dublin kings, the Duke of Normandy, and the kings in the north, in Strathclyde and Alba. The king of Strathclyde was reluctant to hear the words of Æthelred.

The attack on Normandy the previous year, led by Lord Wulfgar, the king's cousin, had been a success, and Leofwine still hoped that this would encourage the king to ride to war.

At the Easter witan, again held at Wantage, Leofwine, Ælfric, and Ælfhelm presented a united front to the king, joined by bishop Wulfstan and even archbishop Sigeric of Canterbury, who had recently returned from a journey to the holy capital of Rome. The success of the expedition against Normandy showed once and for all that England had the strength to fight its enemies if it only had the will.

The oldest athelings were also now of an age much greater than Æthelred had been at his coronation. The senior members of the witan pledged their support to stand behind whichever son the king chose as his successor, should the worst happen. The king could no longer deny the logic of their advice. Again, his ealdormen and reeves had let him down when faced with the Raiders.

Sigeric had quietly whispered that there was much discussion of the weakness of the island of England from all who travelled the long and weary path to Rome, and his quiet assertion to the king of this fact stirred him further to action. The only problem was that with the end of the winter, the Raiders who had overwintered in England had disappeared almost as quietly as they'd come. They waited patiently for news of attacks, but none came.

In light of the absence of the Raiders, there were endless debates and discussions about whom they should attack. Vast quantities of candles burnt as the witan talked or argued the day away for over a week. Eventually, a decision was reached that the king would instead make a stand against the Raider's allies, the kingdom of Strathclyde. They had refused to entertain any form of communication from the king as he tried to make peace with his neighbours and so they were chosen to be made an example of.

A date was set for all to meet at Chester in the early summer. The ealdormen, king's thegns and reeves journeyed home to their respective properties to gather together their men owed to the king's service with the provision that nowhere should be left wholly unprotected while the majority of the fighting force headed to the north. The Raiders might have seemingly disappeared, but it was not worth risking stripping the people of their military protection while they sought out their enemy slightly further from home.

When Leofwine rode through the gates of his home, Æthelflæd was busily supervising her servants. Her hair tied back under her headscarf and her clothing covered in a coarse apron, she stood surrounded by servants running to carry out her demands. She glanced up first in shock at hearing the horsemen approach and then on recognising Leofwine, quickly turned back to the task at hand, the set of her stiff back an indication of her festering anger at him. Northman was at her side, watching and learning how to run a busy household, and she answered his inquisitive questions concisely and to the point so that the little boy did not comprehend her rage.

It was clear that news of the intended battle had preceded him once again. He hoped she would not allow her panic to show as she had last year. He'd wanted to tell her himself that he would be riding out to battle and knew that he'd now be berated for not sending a messenger before him. She flashed her eyes to glare at him, and he met her gaze fully. It would be better to deal with her understandable anger immediately.

He swung down from his horse, Hunter at his side immediately, and walked towards her. She met his gaze the entire way, and he didn't flinch either, not to look at his eldest son, or to wonder where his youngest was, or to see what commotion had erupted behind him, although he surmised it was probably something to do with his tetchy mount and his squire.

The servants melted away as he walked closer to Æthelflæd. He did not doubt that she'd been venting her anger and frustration towards them since she'd heard. Internally he smirked a little. The servant's reactions were a clear indication of just how angry their Lady was.

Before she could even open her mouth to lash him with her tongue, he gathered her into his arms and planted a kiss on her unresisting lips. She was apparently so surprised by his actions that she was responding before she could even think about what was happening.

He held her close to him, able to smell her fresh summer fragrance. He clutched the back of her head delicately, allowing her to move away from him if she wanted to. But she did not. Instead, she responded passionately and wrapped her arms around him, pulling him close, even though he still wore his helm and byrnie.

A hush seemed to descend on the area of previous activity, and Leofwine was not sure if it was because everyone had walked away to busy himself or herself elsewhere or whether he was simply too focused on what he was now doing to hear what was going on around him.

Playfully, he flicked his tongue inside her mouth, searching for her own, and he heard a gentle gasp of pleasure. He pulled her headscarf clear and ran his hands through her bound hair, causing the bindings to come loose and hair to splay over his hands. And still, the kiss deepened, and his desire grew for her. He'd been away for longer than usual, and he'd missed her.

Behind him and in front, twin distractions co-occurred. A polite cough behind him and an outraged question from Northman. Neither caused him to jump away from his wife, but he did slowly release her as she giggled in embarrassment.

'As I said, my lord, it's the way you surprise us all with your actions that make you so effective as a leader.'

Wulfstan's tone was matter-of-fact, and there was almost an amused twinkle in his eye.

'Now, I think you should hand young Northman to one of

the servants, and you two should go and discuss all this in a little more detail.'

Wulfstan bowed slightly and turned to walk away.

'Oh, and perhaps you should take your armour off, my lord, the squire needs to clean it,' Wulfstan called over his shoulder.

Leofwine laughed out loud at the comment, the tension of the moment suddenly released.

'Tell him I will leave it outside my sleeping quarters when he wants it.'

'Indeed, my lord, I shall.' Wulfstan reached for his horse's bridle, and Leofwine stifled a sigh. There was no way that Wulfstan would leave his horse while he indulged in a warm welcome home. Æthelflæd seemed to read his mind.

'Go on, see to him and then you can come and find me. I'm feeling quite exhausted, and I'm going for a lie-down.'

With a swish of her unbound hair, she walked enticingly inside. His heart thudded deeply in his chest, and he felt genuinely torn. He wanted to do his duty to his horse, but he wanted to spend a little more time with his wife first.

Catching a faint aroma of sweat and horse, he realised he needed to bathe. Resigned, he turned and led his unruly horse to the stables as his men had not managed to get the beast to move. He hastily saw to the grouchy animal's needs before sliding out of his armour and leaving it with his squire and then dunking himself in the cold water of the river running close. The young lads who were checking the fishnets let out a small cackle of laughter at seeing him bathe in such a way, and he favoured them with a lopsided smile. One day they would understand his urgency.

He walked inside his house, naked to the waist, and found the hall curiously quiet. The fire was tended by one of the young boys who seemed to inhabit his home with ever-increasing frequency, and there was also the tantalising aroma of pork roasting over the open fire pit.

He ignored both boy and meal and those of his household troops who were being feted along the farthest bank of benches within the large hall, lit only by the light from the open doorway and the small smoke hole in the ceiling. Hunter preceded him eagerly into his private room, where he found Æthelflæd, true to her word, curled in sleep on their bed. Neither of his sons was to be found, and with only a slightly guilty conscience, he climbed into bed beside his wife and held her close. She stirred from her sleep, and he realised that he was about to enjoy himself waking her up.

16

AD1000

Like the year before, preparations for the coming hostilities proceeded smoothly. The king had again written to all his subjects, explaining his intentions and urging the members of the fyrd to follow their ealdormen or reeves into battle even though it would be outside their lands. There was grumbling from all the men who could fight, but there were also those who were pleased with the king's decision.

The king and his witan had calculated how many men were due from each ealdordom. They'd then decided that roughly half of each fyrd should engage in battle while the other half would defend their land, especially the fortified towns which would serve as shelter to the local inhabitants within a day's fast walk of their homes if the Raiders should suddenly reappear.

It was an uncomfortable decision for Leofwine to decide who would stay and who would go, but in the end, he realised that there was little point in taking all his most skilled king's thegns and soldiers. If he left behind only farmers and occasional troops, his lands would fall if Raiders attacked.

He also arranged for a very unwilling Æthelflæd to stay with her parents in the protection of their household troops. Her father had decided to send another to serve in his place and was keen to ensure that he was as well protected at home as his king would be on the campaign. As Leofwine was taking his men with him, it seemed only sensible to leave his wife where she was better protected. She argued and protested for almost as long as it took the fyrd to gather, and in the end, only the realisation that she was again pregnant made her obey his words, albeit with ill grace.

As the summer began to take hold over the land, with green shoots and frolicking lambs, he took his leave of his almost tearful wife with a promise to return. Northman was able to ride his small pony while the younger Leofric looked on with longing.

Leofwine felt a mixture of pride and remorse as he rode out, Hunter as ever at his side. He had accomplished much since becoming ealdorman, but now he needed to prove to his king that he could fight well in a battle he had been advocating for privately since his return and publicly for the last two years. He must not let himself or his king down, and he felt the pressure of the enterprise weighing him down more than his shield and helm.

The journey to Chester took less time than he could have thought possible in the early summer weather and he arrived after only three days of gentle gallop to find that none of the other ealdormen had yet reported. Æthelred had arrived with his household troops numbering into the hundreds and had plainly been fretting that his ealdormen and king's thegns would not produce the fighting force he'd hoped. They'd set up camp on the outskirts of the prosperous small town, almost doubling the size of it, and they were only a tiny proportion of the intended force.

The king greeted Leofwine far more warmly than ever before, taking the time to inspect the men and comment on their excellent provisioning. That night, the king invited Leofwine to feast with him in the hall of the local reeve, and the two men spoke almost as equals.

Æthelred allowed his nerves to show, and Leofwine did his best to assure his king that he would be a force to be reckoned with on the battlefield. The king's uncle, Ordulf, had escorted the king on his expedition north. Ordulf was far from a stranger to the Raiders.

There had been no word from the kingdom of Strathclyde, only worsening reports from Ælfhelm about incursions in the northern lands. He and his king had decided that the fyrd of Northumbria could best be employed along the border areas of Cumbria and Strathclyde, and so he'd not be meeting them at Chester. They were communicating via messengers, although they had a pre-determined action plan.

The king spent that night within the hall, but Leofwine returned to his men, sleeping in tents that had been constructed while he feasted with the king. They'd been instructed by the king to make camp in the far corner of a large field that had been left fallow by the local reeve. It was on a gentle curve but was cushioned with soft grasses, which made up for everything refusing to lie flat on the floor.

The structures were only just better than sleeping out in the open but meant that they stayed dry when the early morning rain struck unexpectedly. Leofwine was pleased that Wulfstan had insisted so firmly on the tent's fabric being smeared with pig fat even though it had made his home and his servants stink for the past few weeks.

The noise of the rain on the unbleached linen woke Leofwine long before he wanted to stir, and meant that he endured the rainstorm surrounded by snores and grunts from his men, alongside the battering of the rain above his head. He was just pleased that he was dry.

The king had arranged for a training session on the following day, pitching his men against Leofwine's. Leofwine thought that his men would benefit from any practice they could get. It was one thing to train against men you knew and trusted, quite another to face an unknown enemy, even if they were, ultimately, on the same side.

The king had chosen an area of gently undulating land not far from the campsite, and all the members of Leofwine's force noisily made their way into position, clutching their weapons, helms and shields or arrows if they were one of the few archers. The king and Leofwine, and a few other members of the king's household, were the only men on horseback.

Leofwine himself didn't take part in the training, and neither did the king. Instead, the king allowed his Uncle to direct the two hundred and fifty household troops that had command of for the duration of the expedition, while Leofwine split his own selected two hundred and fifty between Horic and Wulfstan. The remainder of the Mercian force stood and watched, jeering menacingly at the 'enemy'.

Wulfstan arranged for his men to form a tight shield wall to the left of the massed troops under Lord Ordulf and Horic copied his actions to the right. The best-provisioned men tightly formed up at the front, their shields overlapping and their weapons of choice in their free hands. Behind them came men who carried long spears suitable for jabbing through any gaps that formed in the shield wall and with shields that they would carry above their heads to protect those who stood directly before them.

Behind them were a further three ranks of men, all well supplied but with shields on their backs and not in their hands. If the worst happened and the initial line of defence failed, these men would be able to grab their shields quickly and use them defensively.

In the centre of the two shield walls, but positioned behind them, were the small group of archers. They'd target the massive shield wall the opposition was forming and would hopefully pick off a few of the enemies. For the purpose of the training, they'd bound their arrows with cloth to prevent them from actually spearing their allies.

Ordulf had not split his forces, preferring instead to form one long shield wall, stretching almost the same length as Leofwine's split force, only not as deep with only three men in total behind the shield. Ordulf was in the shield wall alongside his men, as were Wulfstan and Horic amongst Leofwine's own men. Behind Ordulf, an equally small number of archers had lined up.

As the two parties announced each other as enemies and began chanting and taunting each other, they began to slowly shuffle forwards toward each other, arrows flying in the air and causing many of the men to look upwards as opposed to at the force coming towards them, the fear of a whistling missile the greater of the two threats. Leofwine noted it with a wry twist of his lips.

His warriors needed to trust that those who protected their heads would actually do so.

Horic roared his exuberant battle cry, which caused a few

of Ordulf's troops to pop their heads up from behind their shields to see what form of a beast was attacking them. Quickly they ducked back down as the whistle of arrows sounded close to their exposed helmets.

Leofwine smirked a little to himself. Horic's war cry was legendary amongst his household troops. On the other side, Wulfstan was encouraging his men with a more muted roar but one that still infected all around him to give voice to their hatred of the 'Raiders'.

Ordulf's side moved forward almost quietly in comparison, and Leofwine saw that Æthelred was smiling with joy. Leofwine considered that stealth was Æthelred's preferred method of attack.

And then, without any warning at all, Horic and his men sprinted forward, clashing head-on with the stunned first rank of Ordulf's men. No sooner had the air stopped ringing with the cries of the surprised men, who'd bunched together to deflect the force of the advance, than Wulfstan rushed forward with his men. Ordulf's household troops were quick to react but then delayed because they'd already unconsciously started to counter the initial attack.

Æthelred turned towards Leofwine and offered him a waxen smile at seeing his uncle's side so stunned.

'A new attack technique?'

'Horic suggested that as the Raiders use the element of surprise themselves then so should we, even against a shield wall. He says it's customary for the name-calling to continue for hours until one side plucks up the courage to attack, having drunk themselves just about blind. He thinks we should do away with that custom.'

Æthelred smiled at the idea, his face, for once, looking younger than his years as he realised the possibilities.

'Horic, he's an exceptional warrior?'

'Provided he's on our side.' Leofwine offered slyly.

Æthelred grinned ever more broadly at those words.

'Indeed, indeed.'

Before them, Ordulf and his commanders were doing their best to rally the troops against the slightly unexpected attacks, but it appeared as though the damage had been done.

The force facing Horic were fighting to the best of their ability, but those facing Wulfstan were trying to recover their position, having initially gone to the aid of their comrades who faced Horic.

There was a mass of confusion that Ordulf was trying but failing to re-organise as he stepped back and observed what was happening. Then Wulfstan was through the front line of the shield wall and able to come around behind those men who were more exposed on the left side.

A few more clashes rang out across the site of the mock battlefield, but effectively the fight was over, and Wulfstan and Horic were victorious.

The king harrumphed in pleasure at the tactics on display, and Leofwine was ecstatic at the excellent show his force had demonstrated. When he, Wulfstan and Horic had discussed strategies, they'd taken great pains to dissect the battles they'd fought in before. Horic's experiences against the English had been invaluable, as had his tactical mind.

Ordulf walked sedately over to where his nephew sat on his horse. He'd pulled his helmet free from his flushed face, and Leofwine could see he wore a perplexed expression.

Wulfstan and Horic quickly joined Ordulf to walk towards those on the rise, and a lively debate gathered in intensity as they neared, the three men plainly exhilarated by their recent activity. It was clear that far from being perturbed by his apparent failure to hold his shield wall, Ordulf was more intrigued by the methods his opponents had used.

Leofwine knew it was the mark of an able tactician to yearn to learn from past mistakes.

The king heaped praise on his commanders and made a speech of congratulations to all who'd taken part, which had the men cheering. The rest of Leofwine's force was now desperate to show their prowess before the king, but Æthelred called an end to the mock battle for that day and asked his uncle, his commanders, Leofwine and his men to join him for an impromptu dinner. The rest of the warriors he dispersed to their activities, a proud flush on his face after the applause and cheers from his fighting force.

Instructions had clearly been left with the king's servants as when they all noisily clattered back towards the tents, pulling helmets and byrnies from around their bodies, a meal was nearly ready for them, cooked over a large camp-fire, and benches had been pulled up for all to sit on. There was a table heaped high with apples and pears and freshly baked bread that the local thegn had more than likely provided, as there were no ovens on the campsite.

The king had his squire remove his helm and byrnie that he'd proudly worn throughout the mock battle. Leofwine had been amazed by the sheen that both had been cleaned to and thought that he must perhaps mention to the king that making himself so distinctive in a battle was not the best course of action. Wherever the sun shone, Æthelred was brightly illuminated.

Ordulf strode towards his nephew once he too had been divested of his armour, and Leofwine allowed his squire, who'd run to him on his return, to take away his equipment for cleaning, even though it had seen no action.

The men were in good spirits, even Ordulf, who was advancing steadily in years but seemed keen to show his military prowess. Leofwine idly wondered how many battles the man had seen in his time. He was aware that Tavistock, his home, had been attacked on at least three or four occasions in recent years. Leofwine was sure that Ordulf must have been involved in trying to defeat the Raiders on those occasions.

As the food was served and a drinking horn passed around filled with fine mead, the good mood of the company increased, and Æthelred made a point of coming and sitting next to Leofwine.

'My lord Leofwine, I must speak honestly with you and inform you that, as you probably already know, I've long thought your injury was debilitating and wouldn't allow you to carry out your functions as I thought an ealdorman should. However, I owe you an apology, and I'm pleased to give one.'

'You've always been loyal and worked for the good of my kingship, and your command of the fighting men of Mercia is excellent. The men are all keen and loyal, and your commanders are outstanding. I must admit myself a little envious. If only I'd been blessed with you as my representative in Kent, I think that the Raiders would have been run out of the country long ago.'

Leofwine choked quietly on his food at the king's unexpected praise, and the man thumped him comfortably on the back as if they were equals, not king and liegeman.

'I must also confess that I think I've treated you a little

unfairly, unable to see past your part blindness and see your advice and advocacy as well-intentioned.'

Leofwine still didn't speak as he choked back mead passed to him in the drinking horn by Wulfstan and attempted to still his breathing.

'I expect huge things from your men when we engage with Strathclyde.'

Leofwine had still not responded, both from shock and from his choking, when the noise of horses was heard in the distance. The king stood abruptly, as did many of the men, with an immediate sense of urgency in case it was a Raider attack.

Leofwine himself half rose and then recognised the flag being flown by the standard bearer as it flapped yellow and white in the wind. It was Leofsige and the fighting men of Essex and southern Mercia.

Leofwine and the others stood by and watched as the horde of men rode or marched into camp. It was an impressive sight with the late summer sun glinting on the brightly scoured byrnies and helms of the men near the ealdorman. Leofsige's force was of a similar number to Leofwine's own, and he hoped that they'd looked as impressive when they'd arrived.

The king had his horse brought to him, and as the animal stamped in agitation, the king mounted and, with Ordulf as his companion, rode out to meet more of his army. Leofwine was left feeling slightly disappointed that the king's candid words to him had been cut so abruptly short and by his personal nemesis at that.

Wulfstan and Horic quickly surrounded him, the serenity of the feast disrupted by Leofsige's arrival.

'Ah, I see he's come and is looking as fat as always,' were

Horic's loudly spoken words which occasioned snickering from most of the men around them. Horic knew only too well how much Leofsige grated on Leofwine's nerves.

'I pity the poor little squire who had to clean that monstrous byrnie.'

Leofwine shot him a glance with his eyebrows raised in amusement, and Horic stifled his laughter. Wulfstan appeared oblivious to their exchange. He was counting softly under his breath, and Leofwine realised he was checking that the man had brought the fighting force he should have done.

They watched as the long line of men thankfully came to a stop, some collapsing on the ground beneath their feet in exhaustion while others turned immediately to the task of erecting tents for the night. In the far distance, Leofwine could see further glints of iron as a few carrying the ealdorman's provisions came into view. He squinted into the bright sunlight, only to have Wulfstan confirm what he'd just realised.

'He's not protecting the baggage train, and he's surely a thousand men down on what the king expects. I can't say that they're the best provisioned, either.' His words were soft but audible above the din of horses, men, and accompanying shouts and cries as Leofsige's commanders took charge of their contingent of men.

Horic offered his assessment.

'I agree. The numbers are small, and the warriors look like they're all farmers first. Only the front twenty or so lines of men appear to be correctly provisioned.'

'I suppose he's seen more of the Raiders than we have. Perhaps he's lost many men in the skirmishes.'

'Perhaps, my lord, or maybe, he just prefers to keep his

better men guarding his home and land while he shows tepid support for the king. You shouldn't give him the benefit of the doubt.'

Leofwine mulled the words thoughtfully. Was it possible that Leofsige didn't want this endeavour to work? He'd certainly not offered it much support in the meetings of the witan and had spoken to convince the king not to ride to war in the past.

A cold lump of fear settled in Leofwine's stomach. After the triumphs of the morning, the idea of their attack ending in failure because of a less than enthusiastic ealdorman was sobering.

Clearly, the king had considered the possibility of treason and betrayal from his ealdorman, and that was why he'd been so relieved when Leofwine had ridden in. Leofwine wondered what the king would think now that Leofsige had come under-provisioned and undermanned.

Leofwine watched the king and his uncle ride to meet Leofsige with a feeling of apprehension that quickly solidified into outrage as the king abruptly turned and raced back, his black stallion flying over the grassy terrain. Æthelred's fury was easy to read, even from such a distance. His anger was etched into every curve and line of his body. Behind the king, Ordulf looked just as angry as he rode back toward Leofwine, and it was evident that Ordulf was trying to speak with Æthelred; only the king kept urging his horse to outpace that of his uncle's.

Leofwine waited for his king to return to the scene of the earlier feast, his unease growing with each passing moment. Leofwine was sprayed by tufts of ground thrown up by the king's horse as Æthelred abruptly brought the animal to a standstill from a hard gallop.

The king jumped from his horse and, without meeting the eyes of any of the assembled men, thrust the reins at Leofwine as his squire was absent and marched into his tent without so much as a word. Abruptly, the squire ran from the tent, dipping his head in thanks, and took the reins from Leofwine. Leofwine waited for a beat just to check the king didn't require him and then decided it was time to get back to his men.

As Ordulf dismounted from his horse more sedately than his nephew, Leofwine turned to walk away.

'My Lord Leofwine, could I speak to you, please?'

'Of course, Lord Ordulf.'

Leofwine stopped while Horic and Wulfstan peeled away from him, interest clear on their faces but too well mannered to linger. At his side, Ordulf carried a long, broad sword decorated with elaborate jewels and an intricate pattern visible on the tiny part of the blade that poked out of its sheath.

'Leofwine, thank you for speaking with me.'

'Of course, my lord,' Leofwine dipped his head.

'I imagine you've counted the men that Leofsige's brought. I'm sure that you can tell that they're poorly provisioned. The king is incoherent with rage. I wondered if, perhaps, you could speak to Leofsige and determine his intent.'

Internally Leofwine groaned at the thought. The last thing he wanted to do was talk to the man who'd so enraged the king, but he supposed it made sense. Perhaps lord Ordulf was hoping that he'd be able to get the ealdorman to apologise to the king or make good on his deficiencies.

'Of course, my lord. It wouldn't give me pleasure, but I'll do my duty.'

'Thank you Lord Leofwine, thank you. I knew I could rely on you, just as my sister does. She's not at all convinced of Ealdorman Leofsige's loyalty, and I've yet to be shown either way. I don't wish to undermine my nephew's harsh words to the man, but we can't have a rift in this action.' Ordulf's wisdom was sound, and Leofwine allowed his annoyance at being compromised once more to drain away.

After all, the king had just made a public show of apologising to him. Surely that would leave him in good stead with the king, even before he tried to convince Leofsige to be more conciliatory towards the king.

'It's taken far too long to act as it is, and we need every man we can get, even if they are poorly outfitted. God only knows what the man has done with all the money he's gathered through the tithes.'

Ordulf walked despondently away, clearly as disappointed as his nephew and agitated to boot. Leofwine wondered what Æthelred could have said to his erring ealdorman in such a brief amount of time that had his uncle trying to resolve the problem behind his back. Certainly, it was unlike Æthelred to make any hasty actions. It was a sign of just how furious the king was.

Leofwine walked back to his part of the camp with a heavy heart. Luckily the men he commanded had not noticed the king's anger or the brief exchange between him and ealdorman Leofsige, as they called greetings to him, complimenting him and themselves on their successes earlier.

Leofwine forced a smile to his face and responded as gleefully as the men, even though it was a great effort. Only when he was inside his tent, with Wulfstan and Horic at his side, did he quietly vent his frustration at Leofsige, the king, and Ordulf.

Horic winced at the unwelcome task given to him, and Wulfstan shook his head in annoyance, even being prompted to speak his anger.

'My lord, again, you're given a most unwelcome task. It seems that your king and his uncle see you as a flexible tool and nothing more, even after all you've done.'

Wulfstan's tone was outraged, causing Leofwine to flinch and offer a report of the king's words before Leofsige's untimely appearance. Wulfstan was slightly mollified but still continued to pace around the small tent in annoyance.

Leofwine was aware that Wulfstan's relationship with the king's mother extended much further back in time than his own. While it had always served them well in the past, Wulfstan was quick to anger when he thought Leofwine's trust and his own was being unfairly abused.

With nothing to be gained from continued discussion with his men, Leofwine drank deeply from his water bottle and wound his way back through the camp to where Leofsige's commanders were directing the troops to set up their tents. More men called to Leofwine as he weaved his way through the orderly camp with Wulfstan and Hunter at his side.

He'd left Horic behind to deal with a disagreement that had erupted amongst some of the men who'd bathed themselves in glory during the morning and those who'd not yet had a chance. Horic had been roaring, as was his usual behaviour when faced with any form of a conflict he didn't quite understand. Leofwine assumed he'd have a good number of the men digging latrine ditches by the time he got back, and they'd have seen the errors of their ways.

The camp was as neatly laid out as one of the planned burghs dotted around much of England, built by Alfred and his children during the first Viking Age.

At a crossroads, in the middle of the camp, where in almost any town there'd have been market stalls and probably a church, a small collection of traders from nearby Chester had gathered and were busily shouting to all and sundry of their wares.

There was also a small contingent of churchmen, dispatched northwards at the command of the bishop of Lichfield, who were making up a tent from which they'd be able to offer blessings and services for the king and his army.

Leofwine noticed the hive of activity without paying close attention as he considered what approach he should take with Leofsige. He couldn't admit that the king's uncle had sent him on his errand. Most importantly, he couldn't offend the ealdorman. His ragtag force was better than no army at all, and the king would need them and realise so once his anger cooled sufficiently to allow reasoned thoughts.

Beyond the crossroads, Leofwine was aware of activity amongst Leofsige's men. There was a motley collection of tents, not quite in the neat and tidy arrangement of Leofwine's own force, and he could also hear the angry cries of men who were tired after a day's marching and could find no one in authority to see to their needs.

Leofwine couldn't see a single cook's fire amongst the sea of men, although he could practically hear men's stomachs rumbling. It appeared as though Leofsige had not provisioned his men at all.

A few richly decorated tents were the temporary home of the Essex thegns and were attended to by squires. But for the farmers with their homemade weapons, there seemed to be nothing to shelter them from the elements.

Leofwine finally stopped his determined stride towards Leofsige's complicated arrangement of tents and stopped at a fire he had found and where flames spluttered ineffectually on damp wood. There were eight men sitting around it, trying to coax the flames to take hold. They were all dirty and dishevelled, and most of them watched him with suspicious eyes, taking in his clean, luxurious clothes, thick fur cloak and boots made for surviving a muddy campsite.

'Evening, men,' he began, his voice echoing his authority. 'Has your journey here been good?'

Leofwine's words were greeted with silence as sixteen incredulous eyes turned his way.

'My lord,' one began, 'or at least I assume it's my lord?' The speaker was a large man, well built, with deep russet hair and striking blue eyes, wearing a threadbare byrnie over dirty trousers. His boots were worn thin, and Leofwine fancied he could see where his toes would first push through the flimsy bottoms as they reclined on the soft ground.

'Yes, I'm the ealdorman of the Hwicce, Leofwine.'

'Ealdorman is it, my lord? I thought it must be with your rich attire and well-fed look.' The tone wasn't quite disrespectful enough to warrant a comment, but Leofwine vowed to keep his temper anyway. These men had been badly used.

'I can tell you that our journey here has been miserable. Ealdorman Leofsige has had us running all day, with no time to stop for food, water or a piss, not that he's made any food or water available to us.'

'We've nothing ourselves but some measly pieces of wood, gathered as we ran, and the odd berry that was snatched from a passing hedgerow. We've had no supplies since the second evening when we moved beyond our homelands. Only then did the ealdorman announce that we should have brought our own food and that we'd been told as much.'

'Only we hadn't been, and he knows it. We're only here under pain of a fine which he insists he'll levy on all who return home, a fine none of us could pay and still feed our families come the winter.'

Leofwine was stunned at the man's words and embarrassed for Leofsige. How could Leofsige expect to rule these men fairly if he treated them in such a way?

'I'm distraught to hear this. I hope there's been a simple misunderstanding and that a quick resolution can be found. I must speak with Lord Leofsige. I see you at least have a tent?'

'Oh yes, my lord. The holiest of all. It's hardly worth being inside when it rains.'

The other men were all grunting in agreement, and Leofwine turned to Wulfstan, who nodded his understanding. Wulfstan marched off smartly, back the way they'd just come, and Leofwine knew that he'd be seeking food and fuel for the men from their supply train and that of the king's.

Leofwine didn't tell the men of this, fearing that it would cause a ripple of excitement that might make the men rush for the food. Instead, he assured them again that he'd speak to ealdorman Leofsige and set off at a faster pace to find the man.

When Leofwine finally found Leofsige, he almost wished he hadn't. The man was being feasted by a small collection of scantily dressed women who rubbed suggestively against his ample form as they fed him. Seeing Leofwine, Leofsige hastily pushed the girls inside his canvas and righted his clothing, but it was too much for Leofwine.

'My Lord Leofsige, I see you've finally come to the king's call,' Leofwine was barely containing his fury and had to bite back his angry response when Leofsige smiled slowly at him, the grin spreading into his cheeks only to disappear amongst the folds of extra fat there.

'I hardly think 'finally' is a fitting word. I understand that Ealdorman Ælfric is still notable in his absence and that you only arrived yesterday.' Leofsige's tone was smug and condescending as he plucked a piece of meat from the table before him.

'I'm sure Ealdorman Ælfric is on his way and has probably travelled a little slower to allow for the baggage carts. I don't think I've seen all of yours. Where are they, my lord? I've just walked amongst your men, and they're hungry and half dead with running.' Somehow the words came out without a threatened edge of violence. Leofwine was proud of himself.

'Ah, the farmers. They're always happy to moan and don't like being far from their lands. I told them they needed to provision themselves, but they have, regrettably, forgotten. I'm unsure what you would have me do here and now, lord Leofwine. Yes, I fully understand that Chester is near, but the coin for the fyrd has been spent on military expenses already. Purchasing food is not an option now. The men will have to make do.'

Leofsige's voice was level and calm as he spoke, and Leofwine realised that the man genuinely thought his explanations and excuses were adequate.

'Leofsige, the coin is not to buy you women and food and the odd helm. It's to provision the men for the honour of the king. They pay their tithes, and now they expect to see how the money is spent. I hardly think the king will be pleased with your words and even less with your actions.'

'Oh, sod the king. He's got us all traversing around the countryside when we should be manning our burghs and coastlines. This idea of his will fail, and I don't expect to use all of the resources at my disposal to see that happen.' The man was happy to speak his mind and paid no heed to the men who were passing as he was talking, most of whom turned to look at him in shock as his overloud voice permeated through the temporary canvas tents.

'Lord Leofsige, I must protest. We're here on the king's commands to ensure that this battle is a victory for us. You must send for more provisions and for your full quota of men.'

'Lord Leofwine, my good man,' Leofsige's tone dripped with contempt, 'you always try too hard to impress ever since your little injury and your small skirmish with the Raiders. The king will accept what he gets, and he'll be grateful for it. Speak of it no more. Come and join me and eat.'

Leofwine was disgusted with the man and barely contained his fury.

'No, thank you, my lord. I need to speak of this with the king, and you need to give me your word that you'll feed your men.'

'My word? What will you do if I don't? I can as easily march away as take your criticism of my organisation of this pathetic offensive. What would the king think of you if he found out your petty ways had driven a quarter of his army away?'

Leofwine leant forwards, right into the face of Leofsige, who stank of stale sweat and day-old sex.

'The king is no fool, Lord Leofsige, no matter what you might think. He'll not allow this to stand. He'll take action against you, and I'll advocate it. Your men won't move from the spots where they've dropped. They're weak and exhausted, and you're a fool if you think that threatening them with a fine will make them act to the contrary when they have the support of the king.'

Leofwine's anger was simmering dangerously as he strode away from the fat fool and marched back through the tents. He was pleased to see that Wulfstan had somehow discovered the identity of Leofsige's commanders and had gathered them to him to discuss food and better provisioning. Leofwine nodded his thanks as he marched straight towards the king's tent, which had grown a mellow yellow with the setting of the sun. His anger buzzed in his ears like a nest of angry wasps.

Ordulf saw him coming and intercepted his trajectory smoothly.

'I take it that speaking with Leofsige didn't go well?' Ordulf looked concerned once more, his face lined against the glare of Leofwine's simmering anger.

'The man's a fool and an arse. His men are starving and exhausted and without wood to warm themselves. I confronted him, and he accepted it all but offered useless arguments about how he'd told his men to provision them- selves. That's not the way, my lord. Not at all.' Leofwine's words tripped out, gaining momentum as he vented his anger.

'I feared as much. I don't understand why my nephew rates the man.'

'I think he'll not after this debacle.'

'I only wish that were true, Lord Leofwine. My nephew forgives too easily and doesn't impose his will as he should. It won't help that we'll have to make up for Leofsige's lack. I've already sent my men to Chester and the surrounding villages to barter for any excess foodstuffs.'

'And I've sent Wulfstan to see what we can spare from our provisions and from the king's own.'

'Excellent. I suggest that the two of us make ourselves visible to the men so that they can see how a lord should act. Hopefully, it'll restore faith in the king, and we'll be able to use the men, after all, having earned their respect.'

'My lord, it's not our duty,' Leofwine complained, still determined to speak with the king.

'I know it's not, but we must. Our obligation is to our king, and he wishes this battle to go ahead. We can't let him look a laughing stock in front of the people of Strathclyde or his own warriors.'

Leofwine sighed in resignation. He couldn't deny the truth in Ordulf's words.

'You've served the king for many years,' Leofwine muttered, turning away from where the king's tent lay. 'You know him extremely well.' There was resignation in his words.

'My sister's son has long been a difficult man to please. But he is our king, and for that, he must be shown our respect, even if others refuse to do the same.'

'Now, please go about your duties, and I'll go about mine. Tomorrow king Æthelred will have forgotten his initial anger, and Leofsige is too stupid to realise how far he's erred to mention the problem again. Hopefully, the men will be better fed and keener to continue our journey north then.'

Leofwine took the older man's words as a dismissal and seethed on his way back to his camp. Horic had restored order, and Wulfstan had arranged for Leofsige's men to be fed a warm meal from the many hundreds of campfires dotted around the neatly organised tents of the Mercian and Wessex force.

Leofwine thanked his commanders and entered his tent before he said things that would more than likely reach the prying ears of Leofsige. His anger didn't fully abate until early the next morning when he finally managed to sleep as the cocks crowed in distant Chester.

Leofwine was woken mere moments later by Wulfstan, who conveyed a message from the king that today the rest of their force would take on the full might of Leofsige's men. Leofwine groaned deeply at the news and hastily called Horic to his side. They briefly discussed how they could make the men of Essex and Southern Mercia look good before their king without highlighting the genuine lack of training that the men hadn't received.

Wulfstan and Horic arranged the men as they had the day before, only there was a whispered instruction to fight well but less well than the day before and not to employ Horic's tactic of a surprise attack.

The men were understandably unhappy that they wouldn't gain an easy victory as the others had the day before, but as the morning exercise lengthened into the afternoon, Leofwine thought the practice was still a good one. Perhaps they'd face an army from Strathclyde who were as ramshackle as the one Lord Leofsige had brought with him and was arrayed before them.

Leofwine spent most of the time deflecting his king's comments as to why his men fought poorly that day, while

Leofsige bluffed and fidgeted his massive bulk throughout the king's equally probing questions.

Ordulf remained beside Leofwine during the long, tedious day, nudging and occasionally breaking into the conversation when it became too much for Leofwine to answer pleasantly. Ordulf had arranged for Leofsige's force to be provided with foodstuffs and fuel from as far afield as Lichfield, and as the men fought, distracting the king, wagonload after wagonload joined the back of the already tented community.

As the sun began to set on a tense day, a cry was heard, and the king was mollified to see the force from Hampshire and Kent arrive at the mustering point. He rode away to face Ealdorman Ælfric, and Leofwine prayed that Ælfric had at least provisioned and trained his men. Leofwine thanked Ordulf for his support and departed to seek the sanctuary of his canvas.

Leofwine's men were disgruntled that night, and both Horic and Wulfstan became involved in disciplinary issues that grated on them all. The men were right to be angry. They'd fought poorly that day, and the king had not feted them as he had yesterday. It galled because they all knew they could fight just as well, if not better than their compatriots. They didn't understand the commands that had been given to them in hushed whispers.

Leofwine slept deeply, exhausted from his lack of sleep the night before. When he woke, it was to another message from the king. There'd be no mock battles that day, as the following day, they'd pack up and move on toward enemy lands. Leofwine was pleased and exhilarated. He didn't want to have to see the smug face of Leofsige again and knew that his duties would prevent him from leaving his men.

There was an increased hum of activity amongst the Mercian force. They were keen to get on and give battle so that they could show their king how well they could fight, and the sooner they fought, the sooner they'd return home. Leofwine echoed the same sentiments.

Leofsige, however, seemed intent on causing discord. As rainclouds blotted the horizon and fat drops of water began to bounce on the ground, worn smooth by the passage of too many feet, he came and announced himself at Leofwine's tent when Leofwine happened to be there.

Leofsige was all puffed up and angry and made no attempt to hide his outrage from the men busily at work around him. He looked even fatter and redder in the face than the day before, and Leofwine knew that he glared at the man with contempt written on his face, but he couldn't help it.

'My lord Leofwine,' Leofsige spat angrily, 'I've heard rumours that you've been speaking with my men and seeing to their childish bleats about the lack of food. I thought I'd told you that they were to provision themselves. You've no authority within my force.'

'My Lord Leofsige,' just using the title angered Leofwine, but he persevered, 'I don't know of what you speak, and I'd thank you for leaving my tent. I've not invited you within.'

The other ealdorman was spluttering with rage.

'But the men, the men. They told me you sent your perfect Wulfstan to organise supplies.'

'Why would I do that? And why would you believe the words of men you've already informed me tell lies?'

'But they said… they said…'

'So you say, but you said that I shouldn't believe their words, and so how can I have done anything?'

Leofwine knew he was acting contrarily and argumentatively, but the man was a useless slug, and he wanted him away from him as soon as possible.

'Now, good day to you. I've my men to coordinate.'

Leofwine swiftly turned his back on the man and returned to his task. Behind him, he heard Leofsige take a deep breath, and Leofwine feared what he'd now say, but Leofsige released the breath without speaking and marched from the tent, or rather, waddled, muttering all the time. Leofwine suppressed a shudder. The man was genuinely odious.

Wulfstan entered as soon as Leofsige had departed, a question on his face.

'He came to accuse me of feeding his men. The audacity of the man. First, he doesn't feed them himself, and then he threatens me when I do feed them. I fear for his part in our enterprise. Is there any news from Ælfric?'

'Nothing of concern. He's here, with his full contingent of men, and he and the king have been seen smiling and talking.'

'Excellent. That means that other than bloody Leofsige, everyone is keen to make this attack work. If the rumours are true, and the Raiders have left England's shore for good, this victory will have them thinking twice about coming back.'

'I couldn't agree more. Now come. The men are keen to march tomorrow, and we must set about determining who's to go where in the marching orders.'

17
AD1000

Moving such a vast horde of men took time, energy and skill. Æthelred proved himself to be an exceptional planner when all his army marched out on the same day and covered a similar number of miles. Ordulf and his household troops were tasked with riding ahead and reporting back on possible disturbances, but all was quiet as the men heaved and groaned their way through the next four days of constant marching.

Leofwine found that morale amongst his men was still high, although he worried as he looked behind him and saw stragglers from Leofsige's force. Leofsige could be heard shouting and bullying his men as he rode his massive warhorse, almost as wide as Leofsige himself. Leofwine flushed with anger every time he heard even the faintest whisper carried on the breeze of Leofsige and his acidic tongue.

As they drew nearer and nearer to the site Æthelred had stipulated battle should take place, Leofwine was sure Leofsige's army grew smaller and smaller. Happily, the king didn't appear to notice, but Leofwine didn't doubt that everyone else was aware of Leofsige's total disregard for his king's wishes.

The weather changed drastically from the hot summer sun, with the odd downfall, to clinging mists and rains as they journeyed higher into the mountains, and the men grumbled a bit more about the physical discomforts they were under. Provided they were fed a hot meal morning and night, they seemed to cope quite well, but still, it was with pleasure that they burst out from the cloud banks on the fifth day to be greeted by the sight of Ealdorman Ælfhelm and his force of Northumbrians.

There were perhaps not as many men as Leofwine would have liked to see, but he could tell that they were all exceptionally well provisioned; spare horses, squires, byrnies, spears, swords, war axes, archers, arrows and shields, all newly decorated or polished. They were a welcome sight to the foot-sore sick army.

Leofwine left his men and rode towards where Æthelred and Ealdorman Ælfhelm were greeting each other. Æthelred was thriving on the activity and the physical show of power he commandeered, while Ælfhelm congratulated him heartily on arriving on time and in the correct location.

Behind them all, the men set about making camp as the ealdormen and lord Ordulf joined the king for a final meeting. Ordulf had reported earlier that day that he'd seen both Ælfhelm and his troops and also the enemy amassing before them. Æthelred, desperate to choose the battleground, had pushed his men onwards into the long summer night and was now happy that they'd camped where they should to be in the best position to meet their opponents while still being within the deserted borderlands of England.

The king wanted to ensure that his people wouldn't suffer unnecessary hardship when the battle began.

The discussion between the king's men was brief. Their plans had been made months before at the witan, and now all that remained to be done was to either attack the people of Strathclyde or reach an accord with them.

Leofwine hoped that an agreement would be achieved, even if that meant his king wouldn't go to battle with the enemy but knew that based on experience, it was more likely to end in a bloody battle such as Brunanburh just over sixty years ago. He sincerely prayed it would be as victorious as that battle and would stop the encroachments of the Raiders and the natives of Strathclyde.

The use of the king's ship army, as small as it was, should act as a further deterrent, provided it saw active service. Even now, his ship and that of the other ealdormen, if they had ships, and the king's force was following their journey by sea.

It was decided that the men would spend another night as a combined force. and then Ordulf would push on quickly, taunting the king of Strathclyde. Æthelred hoped that the opponent's forces would have already mustered and would see the small mobile force as easy to conquer.

They'd then fall into a trap as the king and Ealdorman Ælfhelm stationed their forces as Leofwine and Leofsige both took their men to the left and the right of where they wanted to fight. Ealdorman Ælfric's strength was to be used as a backup, hidden away behind the attacking force, staying in their camp unless needed.

It was a position that suited Ealdorman Ælfric, although Leofwine couldn't help feeling uneasy. It would be far too easy for Ælfric to desert the king if he wasn't expected at the battle site.

The following morning Ordulf rode off with a determined scowl on his lined face and the best wishes of his nephew. A great mass had been performed before the king and his amassed army, and then the great force had split, each to their specified destination.

Æthelred and Ealdorman Ælfhelm rode off as fast as could be expected, with over three thousand men between them. Ealdorman Leofsige made his way slightly inland with his grumbling men while Leofwine hugged the rugged coastline.

Only Ealdorman Ælfric didn't move from his camp. He was tasked with holding the line there and not allowing the Strathclydians to venture any further into the heart of the English kingdom. With a final look of misgiving, Leofwine tried to dismiss ealdorman Ælfric from his mind. He had to rely on ealdorman Leofsige, and he wasn't to be trusted either. Leofwine hoped his own men would prove their loyalty and more keep themselves safe from harm.

ONE OF THE KING'S HOUSEHOLD TROOPS RACED TOWARDS THEM, HIS horse blowing hot. Leofwine had heard from his scout as the barely visible sun had reached its zenith in the cloud-filled sky, and he and his men were ready and waiting as the king's messenger informed him that they should advance quickly. The battle had begun.

Ordulf had tempted the enemy force forward and had then raced back to his force. Even now, long shield walls snaked across the land while the Strathclydians, more on horseback than on foot, attempted to penetrate its collective with their long spears. The messenger assured Leofwine while casualties were mounting, the king was still winning the day.

With a grim nod of acceptance, Leofwine directed the messenger to continue back to Ealdorman Ælfric and called Wulfstan and Horic to him to relay his orders for the men.

The battle was taking place a good run from where they stood. Still, the men cheered as they ran forward in battle-ready formation. Leofwine kicked his horse to attention and called Hunter to his side.

He had little choice but to take the dog with him as the two animals would keep him safe while Wulfstan and Horic ran with their contingents of men. Leofwine hoped, not for the first time, that Hunter would stay with the horse when he joined the force and had brought along his squire to take charge of the two animals.

After all these years of forcing the animal never to leave his side, he was concerned Hunter would simply not obey his instructions to stay behind when Leofwine ran off.

The sky was turning a menacing grey as they sprinted, threatening rain, although the ground they crossed was currently dry. The wind blew gently, and as they crested a small hill, they heard the cries of the ensuing battle and could see it arranged before them in miniature. The king's forces were fighting slightly downhill while the Strathclydians attempted to push them upwards. From where he sat atop his horse, he couldn't judge who was winning.

Jumping down from his horse, he sent his hound and horse back with his young squire. The young lad looked intrigued and scared all at once. Leofwine hoped his face didn't so plainly reflect his thoughts.

Hunter growled at him, unhappy with the command, and in the end, Leofwine was forced to harness the animal to ensure she went with the squire. The young lad struggled with the powerful animal, but as Leofwine glanced back one final time, he could see that the hound had been won over, no doubt with some tempting morsel.

The opposition below had not seen Leofwine and his troops arrive. But Leofwine couldn't attack yet, for Leofsige had yet to appear on the opposite rise with his men.

It took so long, Leofwine sent some of his fastest runners to ensure that they were coming. Every moment that they waited, Leofwine could barely watch the scene before him, as the Strathclydians seemed to be gaining ground at the expense of the king, ealdorman Ælfhelm and lord Ordulf.

When Ealdorman Leofsige finally appeared, as the rain began to fall in a steady stream, Leofwine's anger was intense. How dare the fool fail to act as quickly as had been discussed? Pushing his frustration aside, Leofwine gave the agreed signal to Leofsige's commanders, and as one, both splinters of the force started to advance at a quick run to meet the king's forces below.

As they'd practised before, Horic and his men moved to one side, with Wulfstan and his men at the other. This time, though, Leofwine and his cohort formed up in the middle, with the few archers behind them, safe from immediate attack and able to make good use of their arrows.

In the surge of running and elongated war cries, Leofwine couldn't tell at what point the opposition became aware that the small force they'd been arranged against and were succeeding in pushing slowly backwards had suddenly doubled in size.

As Leofwine reached the scene of the confrontation, his men quickly formed their shield wall and advanced forward slowly. As soon as they came into contact with the original shield wall, the men who comprised it, well, those who still stood and were capable of doing so, melted away and formed up behind them, making use of the gaps between Horic, Wulfstan and his group of men.

Once all were through, Leofwine and his men proceeded forward with the full force of the king's men still standing at their backs.

There was a press of bodies and heat and sweat as Leofwine held his shield firmly, overlapping with the men from his household troops who flanked him at all times, Oscetel and Wighard. As the shield wall stretched further outwards, he knew less and less of the men by name, although he tried to remember their faces, as he believed all good leaders should.

No one should risk their life knowing that they'd be forgotten about if they died.

The warriors they met screamed and raged as their easy victory drained away. They didn't turn and run, though; instead, they stood and fought with their strange square shields and long spears, their faces invisible behind the shield and below their helms.

The spears were effective at wounding those in the shield wall behind Leofwine's row of men, but went straight past him as he crouched behind his rounded shield, completely protected, apart from where the shield didn't extend down the length of his legs.

Abruptly, Leofwine realised that being able to see was of

little importance in a shield wall, working as it should do. All he needed to do was crouch low, hold his place, and pray that those to either side of him and behind him concentrated on the task at hand as single-mindedly as he was.

The shield wall advanced with agonising slowness, crushing those who'd already fallen dead underfoot. The cracks and snaps of human bone being trampled underfoot were horrifying to hear, and Leofwine again appreciated that his partial vision was helping him, not hindering him.

Behind him, he could hear the war cries of his men and the shouted instructions of the king and his commanders as they attempted to direct the battle, but he couldn't always make out their words, so he shouted words of encouragement to his men to hold their line and continue as they were.

Above his head, he could hear the thunk of spears and arrows as they hit the shield held in place by Brithelm, and behind him, Ælfhun, who shielded his own and Brithelm's head. Still, the opposition screamed and stabbed at his shield with their weapons, and the weight of the shield slowly increased with each agonisingly slow step forward.

Leofwine could feel the burn across his back where his muscles screamed in agony, and still, he held his place, yelling to his men to do the same, slowly pushing the enemy backwards.

Suddenly, he felt fresh air on the back of his neck and realised the shield held by Brithelm had fallen away. Hastily, Leofwine glanced behind him, to where Brithelm lay with a war axe clean through his unhelmed head, eyes staring forwards vacantly, and then Ælfhun was stepping over his friend and replacing him, his eyes focused on what must be done and not the ruin of his friend.

Behind, another raised their shield and lifted it above

Ælfhun's head. Leofwine was sickened and confused. How had the axe penetrated the shieldwall so easily?

'My lord, hold the shield wall. Brithelm wouldn't want it to fail now.'

Ælfhun's words penetrated Leofwine's shocked thoughts, and hastily he turned back. He hoped he'd have time later to mourn his friend. Leofwine stepped ahead quickly to close a small gap that had formed in the shield wall due to his inattentiveness and redoubled his efforts as his arm began to tremble from the exertion.

Leofwine could hear Ælfhun breathing heavily behind him, and his head remained dry as the rain sheeted around his shield.

And then, unexpectedly, it was all over. The shield wall surged forward and met no resistance. No weapons banged against the wooden shields, and no war cries from the enemy could be heard.

Hesitantly, Leofwine raised his head above his shield and looked before him. There was no one. As if on cue, the men who'd been attacking them had run up their side of the hill, desperately trying to get away. Leofwine dropped his shield to his side and grabbed his sword, replacing his war axe on his weapons belt, shouting for the men to do the same.

Whether they heard him or not, up and down the disintegrating shield wall, the sound of swords being drawn echoed loudly, and then the men ran screaming towards the few enemies who were trying to escape with their lives.

Leofwine ran over crushed skulls and dead staring eyes, yelling at the top of his voice. He caught the foot of a man above him up the hill with his hand as he was straining to escape, pulling him level with his seax before slicing him across his exposed neck. Blood spurted, covering the parts of

Leofwine's face that were exposed, and on he ran, not even registering any details of the man he'd killed, just content to know that he could claim a kill.

Again, Leofwine caught another foot and dispatched the warrior in the same way as the first. Then he was at the top of the hill, panting heavily and looking all around him. Leofwine could see only a few stragglers running to mount any available sturdy horses before riding off back across their border.

Leofwine stopped to catch his breath, and Ælfhun rushed behind him to guard his suddenly exposed back, but there was no need. There was no enemy to be seen. Instead, the men of the shield wall all stood around, tasting the rain on their lips and grinning wildly because they still lived and had vanquished the enemy. Magnificently.

Looking back down the hill he'd just clambered up, he saw a deep trench of churned, dirty mud littered with men's bodies exhibiting terrible injuries. He could make out Æthelred, his byrnie blood splattered, surrounded by his best household warriors, grinning broadly at the slaughter they'd created. Leofwine felt a slight smile tug at his tightened face.

At last. At last, his king had seen battle and been rewarded for his efforts with a great victory.

18

AD1000

AFTERMATH

The rain, so insistent throughout the long, dreary day of fighting, was finally starting to lift and lighten the sky to the east, while in the west, the skyline was littered with bloody reds and purples, mirroring the harrowing image arrayed before him.

Leofwine felt sickened by the carnage while overjoyed at the same time. It was over, and more importantly, it had been a victory for Æthelred. For an action he'd been vehemently advocating since his return home from the Outer Isles, Leofwine was elated that it had ended so well.

He'd often stood as a solitary voice in the witan amongst a host of others who didn't understand the need to attack first, to be on the offensive instead of on the defensive. It felt good to know that he'd been right.

Æthelred rode up to him on his magnificent black warhorse, brought forward from the temporary camp, calm now after the furore of battle. The king looked flushed with triumph and yet a little haunted too, and Leofwine noticed that his trusted priest was in close attendance. Blood covered Æthelred, and it was clear that the king had seen a fair share of the battle or that, like Leofwine, he'd claimed a kill when the enemy had retreated.

Leofwine slid from his horse, which his squire had returned to him, along with an overly eager Hunter and knelt before his king.

'My lord king, congratulations on your decisive victory.'

'My thanks, ealdorman Leofwine. Let us hope it works as intended.'

'Indeed, my lord king. This will be a decisive deterrent for the people of Strathclyde and their leaders.'

'It will, although I can't help feeling that my conscience is clearer when coin is involved. All these men died at our hands or their own.' Æthelred stretched his hands towards the scene of the battle where his housetroops were busy clearing away the dead and dumping them in a huge ditch that the Wessex force was busy digging. Æthelred's voice was strong and wistful at the same time.

'It's a heavy price to pay for my soul.'

Leofwine gave him a measuring look. The king's thoughts so clearly mirrored his own that it was a little disconcerting. Quickly he decided candour was the best approach.

'I find myself in total agreement, my lord king. Many have fallen here who would, perhaps in time, have been our friends. And yet, we must defend ourselves. We must discourage them from taking our land and sheltering our enemies.' Determination flooded Leofwine's voice as he spoke.

'Quite so, Leofwine, quite so. Come to camp, join me in a

prayer for those who've lost their lives and then perhaps we can begin to forgive ourselves.'

Leofwine bowed low again and stumbled up from his bone-weary knees as the king kneed his horse and cantered tiredly away from the battlefield, his priest near and his uncle at his right hand. Ordulf had supported his nephew throughout the fighting and had fought exceptionally well if the rumours already circling were to be believed.

The older man looked exhausted but pleased at the outcome of the battle. Leofwine assumed that back at their camp, the churchmen would be raising masses to the glory of the king.

Behind him, Wulfstan coughed hard, and Leofwine turned to look at him in concern. His old friend looked old and haggard, the first time he'd ever truly carried his many years so openly on his face.

'Are you injured? What are you not telling me?'

Wulfstan winced at his hard tone, and as Leofwine moved towards him, he held up a hand to forestall him.

'It's not nothing. I can't say that, but I think perhaps only bruising. Although it hurts like hell. I'll be fine until we can seek a healer.' Wulfstan wheezed out his words, and Leofwine shot an accusing look at him.

'Really, Wulfstan, you expect me to believe that?'

'I do, my lord, as I know you would if our situation were reversed.' Wulfstan sounded exhausted but determined. Leofwine gave him an appraising look and quirked a smile.

'Fine, you stubborn old goat, but when we make it back to camp, we'll seek a healer for you, and you'll do as you're bidden by them. Whatever it is.'

Wulfstan bowed his head to acknowledge the words, and

Leofwine turned to mount his horse again. Just like his king, he didn't wish to linger with the dead and the dying.

As Leofwine turned away from the scene of carnage, he caught sight of a horseman flying over the land. Leofwine looked around in shock, trying to determine if some catastrophe had befallen the king,or if some further sneaky attack was underway.

He could see nothing to concern him. No smoking fires filled the horizon around him, and when he turned to Wulfstan, a question in his eyes, he confirmed in a quiet, stoical voice that he could see nothing either.

Intrigued, despite his fatigue, Leofwine encouraged his horse to a steady canter, ready to intercept the horseman. Leofwine's horse stumbled once or twice on the churned-up surface of the ground but made it to the horseman in good time, Horic and Wulfstan at his side, Hunter pleased to be away from the stench of the battle.

As Leofwine neared the lone rider, he could see no distinguishing marks on the horse or on the clothes the man wore, who seemed to carry neither weapon nor shield as his stumbling horse brought him ever nearer.

Again, Leofwine turned to Wulfstan with a question in his eyes. Wulfstan's face was screwed tight with pain, but he glanced at the man and then looked again more thoroughly.

'I think I recognise him, but I can't place from where.'

And then Horic spoke, his voice thick with emotion,

'I know him, my lord, as did you, briefly. It's Finn, Lord Olaf's scribe.'

Leofwine glanced at Horic in shock, wondering why Finn would be seeking him out, and here of all places? The look on Horic's face, which had bleached of all colour, answered his unspoken question almost before he could think it. God, no, surely it couldn't be true?

As Leofwine drew closer to the man, recognition flashed, and his unsettling feeling of moments before returned in fall force. Surely they'd have longer to luxuriate in their victory? Surely this hadn't all been for nothing?

Finn drew level with him and, recognising Horic with a start, bowed his head low before Leofwine and then raised it immediately. Finn looked miserable, underfed and dishevelled, and dirty from head to toe. His horse was almost dead on its feet, and Leofwine wondered if it'd make it back to their camp only a short distance away.

'The men I passed told me that I'd find you here, my Lord Leofwine. I'm afraid I carry a heavy burden.' Finn's voice was strong and formed the words well as he spoke, although his accent slewed some of them. Before Finn could speak further, Horic burst forth, his voice raw with grief

'Can it be true? Is he ...?'

'Yes, Horic, it's true. Lord Olaf died in battle at the hands of his old enemy Swein of Denmark, who grows ever wilier with his advancing age. I'm here as part of Olaf's last request, to inform my Lord Leofwine and to gift him with this.' Finn turned to rummage amongst the bags he carried on his horse. He pulled forth a luxurious wolf pelt from a saddlebag, and Leofwine felt himself grow small at being remembered from such a distance by someone who'd never truly been a friend.

'Olaf had written that this wolf pelt was to be yours in the event of his death before yours. He said it would be significant to you. He also requested that you take me into your service if you so desire. He'd heard great things about you and thought your actions should be chronicled by one such as I.'

'When, when did this happen?'

'Last summer, my lord. There was a great battle, and king Swein personally slew king Olaf. It was a good death, even at the hands of an enemy such as Swein. I carry a warning to you as well from Swein himself. He now styles himself king of Norway and Denmark.'

Leofwine felt that he knew what the warning would be and so steeled himself for the words that would undo all his work of the last few years when he'd managed to convince himself that Swein would have more pressing concerns than tracking him down to kill him.

'And what's that message?'

'I'll be coming for England soon.'

Leofwine swallowed at the unwelcome voicing of his fears, and then Wulfstan let out a strangled cry of pain, diverting him from his all-consuming fears.

'Come, we'll seek shelter for the night and think on this more. It's terrible news.' Leofwine was pleased he sounded in command as he spoke. It wouldn't do if any of his men appreciated the bottomless pit of fear now opening up within him.

Leofwine turned tail and began the slow trot back towards their camp, his heart heavy with loss and grief for lord Olaf and the knowledge that soon all who'd not carried his conviction that the king must launch an offensive attack, especially Ealdorman Leofsige, would harangue him for his false assertions.

Perhaps the king had been correct after all. There was no way to rid his land of the Raiders. If Swein had personally killed Olaf, what hope did he have? Surely, it would only be a matter of time before Swein arranged Leofwine's murder as well, and then what would he want? England was a too tempting target, especially for a man who'd already attacked England once and failed to achieve anything.

Fear descended on Leofwine. He had no hope that England was safe. None at all.

Swein would be coming. It was only a matter of time.

THE ANGLO SAXON CHRONICLE ENTRY FOR AD1000

This year the king went into Cumberland, and nearly laid waste the whole of it with his army, whilst his navy sailed about Chester with the design of co-operating with his land-forces; but, finding it impracticable, they ravaged Anglesey. The hostile fleet was this summer turned towards the kingdom of Richard (Normandy).

CAST OF CHARACTERS

King

Æthelred II b.965, king from 978 (son of King Edgar and his third wife, Elfrida, England's first crowned queen)

The Court

Lady Ælfgifu (Æthelred's wife – never queen)

Lady Elfrida (the king's mother)

Athelstan (the king's son, oldest son, b.c 986)

Ecgberht (the king's son, b.c 987)

Edmund (the king's son b.c 988)

Eadred (the king's son)

Eadwig (the king's son)

Edgar (the king's son)

Ordulf (the king's uncle and brother of Lady Elfrida)

Brihtwold

Wulfheah

Wulfric Spot

Ufegat

Churchmen

Ælfric, Archbishop of Canterbury

Ealdulf of Worcester

Ælfheah, Bishop of Winchester

Wulfstan, Bishop of London

Wulfsige of Sherborne

Athulf of Hereford

Ælfheah of Lichfield

Ealdormen

Æthelweard (of the Western Provinces)

Æthelmær (Æthelweard's son)

Ælfric (of Hampshire – Kent, Sussex, Surrey, Berkshire and Wiltshire)

Ælfhelm (of Northumbria)

Previously Thored (of Northumbria)

Leofsige (of the East Saxons – East Anglia and Essex)

Leofwine (of the Hwicce)

Leofwine's Household

Æthelflæd (wife)

Northman (first born son)

Leofric (second born son)

Wulfstan (commended man and war leader)

Horic (commended man and second in command)

Leofgar (part of the warband/household troop)

Ælfnoth (part of the warband/household troop)

Eadred (part of the warband/household troop)

Wighard (part of the warband/household troop)

Oscetel (part of the warband/household troop)

Brithelm (part of the warband/household troop)

Wulfsige (part of the warband/household troop)

Lyfing (part of the warband/household troop)
Ælfhun (part of the warband/household troop)
Ælfric (ship's helmsman)
Godric (shipman)
Hunter (Leofwine's hound)

Raiders and Kings
Olaf Tryggvason (King of Norway)
Bjorn (his ship's helmsman)
Gunnar, Thorkell (his ship's captains)
Swein (King of Denmark, Olaf's accomplice and enemy)
Axe (Olaf's warrior)
Finn (Olaf's scribe)
Malcolm (King of Strathclyde)
Duke Richard of Normandy
Duke Richard II of Normandy
Sigurd, Jarl of Orkney and Shetlands

HISTORICAL NOTES

The ealdorman of the Hwicce appears little in the sources for this period 994-1000. The Anglo-Saxon Chronicle does not mention him at all, which could be for the best, as the ealdormen it does mention are not always treated too kindly.

What can be said is that in 994, two documents name his as Dux (ealdorman). In 995 he attests 1 charter for the king, in 996, 3 charters, in 997, 2 charters, in 998, 2 charters, in 999 1 and in 1000 another possible 1. In 998 he is granted 'bookland' in Warwickshire by the king.

It is not known who his father and mother were with any certainty, although it is often said that his father died at the Battle of Maldon and was named in the poem of the battle as Ælfwine. If this is correct, then Leofwine and his father were related in some way to ealdorman Bryhtnoth, who died at Maldon.

NOTE FROM THE AUTHOR

The Earl of Mercia's Father, previously published under two different names, was my first work of historical fiction, first written from about 2012-2013, and with some major revisions since then. It's the first book in my planned series to tell the final century of Saxon England before the Norman Conquest. It is, I confess, perhaps not the most exciting of my novels set during this period, but it does introduce my reader to the wonderful Ealdorman Leofwine. Without him, I would not have continued writing, and so, if not for him, we would not have Coelwulf, Icel, Penda, and so many more wonderful historical characters I've written about in the last decade. I'm grateful to him and hope that if this is your first experience of my writing, you'll forgive its imperfections, of which I'm more than aware. If you've been reading my books for a while and have just stumbled upon the Earls of Mercia series, then I apologise for starting almost at the end of Saxon England and only then working backwards, but would thank you for sticking with me. I'm delighted to finally be able to share the amended and revised version of The Earl of Mercia's Father in ebook format once more.

MJ

September 2022

WHAT TO READ NEXT?

The Danish King's Enemy is the second book in The Earls of Mercia series.

I hope you've enjoyed meeting Ealdorman Leofwine. If you'd like to keep reading about Saxon England, and Mercia in particular, then please consider this series of interconnected titles, which I term 'The Tales of Mercia.'

The Dark Age Chronicles (the Sixth century)
    Men of Iron
    Warriors of Iron
    Lords of Iron

Gods and Kings (Seventh century)
    Pagan Warrior
    Pagan King

Warrior King

<u>The Eagle of Mercia Chronicles (Earlier ninth century)</u>
Son of Mercia
Wolf of Mercia
Warrior of Mercia
Eagle of Mercia
Protector of Mercia
Enemies of Mercia
Betrayal of Mercia
Shields of Mercia

The Lady of Mercia's Daughter (Tenth century)
A Conspiracy of Kings

<u>The Earl of Mercia Series (End of the tenth century)</u>
The Earl of Mercia's Father and subsequent titles (please note, perversely, I began this series first).

Enjoy

MEET THE AUTHOR

I'm an author of historical fiction and non-fiction (Early English, Vikings and the British Isles as a whole before the Norman Conquest), born in the old Mercian kingdom at some point since AD1066. I like to write. You've been warned! My first non-fiction title is also now available.

Find me at mjporterauthor.com. mjporterauthor.blog. I have a monthly newsletter, which can be joined here. All subscribers will receive a free ebook copy of one of my titles.

BOOKS BY M J PORTER (IN CHRONOLOGICAL ORDER)

<u>The Dark Age Chronicles</u>

Men of Iron

Warriors of Iron

Lords of Iron

<u>Gods and Kings Series (seventh century Britain)</u>

Pagan Warrior

Pagan King

Warrior King

<u>The Eagle of Mercia Chronicles</u>

Son of Mercia

Wolf of Mercia

Warrior of Mercia

Eagle of Mercia

Protector of Mercia

Enemies of Mercia

Betrayal of Mercia

Shield of Mercia

<u>The Mercian Ninth Century</u>

Coelwulf's Company, stories from before The Last King

The Last King

The Last Warrior

The Last Horse

The Last Enemy

The Last Sword

The Last Shield

The Last Seven

The Last Viking

The Last Alliance

The Last Deceit

<u>The Tenth Century</u>

The Lady of Mercia's Daughter

A Conspiracy of Kings (the sequel to The Lady of Mercia's Daughter)

Kingmaker

The King's Daughter

<u>Non-fiction title</u>

The Royal Women Who Made England: The Tenth Century in Saxon England

<u>The Brunanaburh Series</u>

King of Kings

Kings of War

Clash of Kings

Kings of Conflict

<u>The Mercian Brexit (can be read as a prequel to The First Queen of England)</u>

<u>The First Queen of England (The story of Lady Elfrida) (tenth century England)</u>

The First Queen of England Part 2

The First Queen of England Part 3

<u>The King's Mother (The continuing story of Lady Elfrida)</u>

The Queen Dowager

Once A Queen

<u>The Earls of Mercia</u>

The Earl of Mercia's Father

The Danish King's Enemy

Swein: The Danish King (side story)

Northman Part 1

Northman Part 2

Cnut: The Conqueror (full-length side story)

Wulfstan: An Anglo-Saxon Thegn (side story)

The King's Earl

The Earl of Mercia

The English Earl

The Earl's King

Viking King

The English King

The King's Brother

Lady Estrid (a novel of eleventh-century Denmark)

<u>20th Century Mystery</u>

<u>The Erdington Mysteries</u>

The Custard Corpses – a delicious 1940s mystery

The Automobile Assassination (sequel to The Custard Corpses)

The Secret Sauce - the third book in the Erdington Mysteries

Cragside – a 1930s murder mystery (standalone)

www.ingramcontent.com/pod-product-compliance
Lightning Source LLC
Chambersburg PA
CBHW030602170726

48283CB00002B/431